Angelina's Revenge

by

Carl & Jeanette Lees

authorHOUSE™

1663 LIBERTY DRIVE, SUITE 200
BLOOMINGTON, INDIANA 47403
(800) 839-8640
WWW.AUTHORHOUSE.COM

AuthorHouse™
1663 Liberty Drive, Suite 200
Bloomington, IN 47403
www.authorhouse.com
Phone: 1-800-839-8640

AuthorHouse™ UK Ltd.
500 Avebury Boulevard
Central Milton Keynes, MK9 2BE
www.authorhouse.co.uk
Phone: 08001974150

First published by AuthorHouse 4/13/2006

ISBN: 1-4208-9524-9 (sc)

Printed in the United States of America
Bloomington, Indiana

This book is printed on acid-free paper.

The Year of Our Lord 1726

The sloop *Angelina* had made her way north along the coast of the Americas. She was now forty miles north of the Yucatan peninsula and heading towards the Bay of Campeche. Captain Franco Amas had learned from his years as a pirate to keep away from the open sea. Franco's ship was only 60 feet long, single mast with full sails. She had only fourteen six-inch guns, 7 port and 7 starboard. *Angelina* was a quick ship with a shallow draft, allowing the pirates to go where larger ships couldn't follow. Franco was a man of few words, well liked and respected by his crew. He and his band had perfected hit and run tactics, which were particularly effective at night.

Franco was born in Cuba and had killed a man in a fight over a girl when he was only 17. Fleeing the law, he left his home and friends behind and joined the Portuguese Navy. While fighting in the English-French War he had become disillusioned with navy discipline. He jumped ship in Jamaica and became involved with the slave trade. Franco quickly advanced because of his ruthless nature. He became Captain at the age of 25 and soon set his sights on larger quarry. He put together a crew drawn mostly from liberated slaves. These were men he trusted with his life, as he knew how much they hated the countries that had so cruelly taken them from their families. Franco's officers were like himself, sailors who could not or would not take any more harsh discipline, bad food and low money.

Franco and his officers were content to let the British, French and all others fight between themselves. They just wanted the easy prey. The crew of the *Angelina* had learned that with stealth and cunning they could take a ship in the dark at anchor, or men on the beach gathering food and water.

After a fight the pirates would run and hug the coastline, enabling them to retreat to a shallow river or estuary where larger ships couldn't follow.

Angelina's latest voyage had been profitable: her hold, although not full, held a valuable cargo. They had plundered a ship that yielded much more treasure than they had expected. It was a Portuguese merchantman that they had boarded at night under the cloak of darkness. They swiftly and silently killed the watch then cut the throats of the crew in their hammocks. This was their way, cruel but expedient. The Portuguese schooner had two masts, 80 feet long, and a crew of 70 including officers and men. The ship was returning from Costa Rica and had anchored in a small, shallow cove just south of Panama. Captain Franco and the crew of *Angelina* had come upon the ship by chance and seized the opportunity to attack as soon as it was dark. After killing the Captain and the crew they disposed of the bodies overboard, giving the sharks a treat.

Rummaging through the hold and the manifest they discovered the cargo was nothing more than cloth, wine and Indian trinkets. The pirates decided to take all money, food and guns, ammunition and anything else that could be of use to them. The first mate of the *Angelina* was a swarthy man in his mid 30s named Aggan. Moroccan by birth, he was a mean man but good to have around when things got tough. Captain Franco heard Aggan's excited voice calling him from the hold. The crew had found a wooden chest sealed with metal bands and a heavy brass lock. Franco without hesitation took his flintlock pistol and blasted off the lock. Inside, to their total amazement, were bags full of gold coins. Every crewman on board was now full of excitement.

At that moment Franco noticed that below the first two bags lay a metal object, which he immediately pulled clear. The metal ring that Franco held in his hand was made of gold. It took the shape of a circle with a double crescent moon back to back in the center. Franco didn't recognize it but it seemed familiar to members of his crew who had been slaves and had come from tribal backgrounds. They appeared very unnerved and when asked they said, "It has some kind of magic." Ju ju, or voodoo, they called it, maybe some kind of religious talisman.

Franco and Aggan would have none of this; to them it was just a piece of gold, a meaningless relic. The crew members who had been slaves and came from superstitious backgrounds, however, wanted to get rid of it. "It will put a curse on the ship," they insisted.

Franco didn't believe in such superstition and although he didn't say it, he would have put the crew overboard before the gold. He ordered the Portuguese ship sunk; he couldn't set fire to it for fear she would be seen. Without hesitation his men cut holes in the hull and sunk her.

"Set sail north, Aggan," Franco ordered. "We'll hug the coast to the Yucatan, then sail east to the Keys."

Franco estimated it would take between 7 to 10 days with fair weather if they sailed day and night. The temperature was hot and humid but they made good speed. *Angelina* sailed North along the coast of South America without incident. Until on the fourth day, just east of Honduras, he noticed a difference in the mood of the black crew members.

"Aggan!" Franco called. "I need to speak with you!"

Aggan joined the Captain in his cabin.

"Captain, you called?"

"Yes, Aggan. I sense a different mood in the black crew members."

"It's that damn gold amulet, Captain. It's got them spooked."

"They want to throw it overboard. They think we're all cursed as long as it stays on board."

"And what do you make of this? You've been first mate for years. I never took you to be a superstitious man."

"Well, Captain, I tell you, there's twenty of them black devils and fifteen of us. That's my superstition."

"Listen, Aggan, they are good men, every one. In a fight, none better. Here's what I propose…"

Two hours later the Captain called the men on deck. "Ship mates, we've been together a long time, some good some bad. I have a proposition to make. The amulet frightens you, so we need to get rid of it. I, on the other hand, don't intend to lose it because of its value. What I intend to do at the next safe cove or anchorage, I'll put a boat ashore, take three men, the gold ring, and bury it. Since you hands are afraid of it, you don't need to know where it's buried. That'll get rid of the curse."

The crew didn't much like the idea but they were afraid of the talisman. They also knew that Captain Franco, although a liked man, was not to be doubted or crossed. He could be ruthless. The next day Franco chose three men and took a long boat into a cove that they had found on a little island called Puerto Cortez. They returned several hours later and resumed their voyage.

"Aggan!"

"Yes, Captain!"

"How do the men seem now?"

"Better, Captain, but still a little uneasy."

"That's to be expected, just keep an eye on them. Let me know if there's more unrest."

The *Angelina* made good time over the next two days with no incidents. They made it to the Yucatan then turned east. This was the part of the voyage Franco most feared, open water, but he had no choice if he was to make it to the Florida Keys and safety.

To these men, the Keys were home, a place where they could hide with ease. Amongst these islands a shallow ship could go from the Atlantic on the east side to the Gulf on the west. One hundred miles of shallow water, islands and places no large ship could follow. Pirates' paradise. Within easy reach of most trading places, the Caribbean, or the Carolinas.

Angelina continued to make good time. Franco was well pleased with himself. His crew was made up of fools; he had no intention of burying the gold ring. He took three men he could trust and made it look that way. These superstitious fools were right out of the jungle, but if it made them happy and kept the ship running smoothly, so be it. Two hundred and forty-five miles east of the Yucatan and approximately 80 miles west of Key West, his worst fears were realized.

It was a full moon and on the horizon his high watch saw a British warship. HMS *Plymouth* was a 160-foot ship of the line, all 1,400 tons of her. Eighty guns on three decks and 500 well-trained officers and crew. It was around midnight when they first sighted *Plymouth*. She was a behemoth looming on the crest of a dark primeval ocean under a beautiful moon, bigger than anything they had ever seen before. They knew of these ships but had never seen one up close. Franco did the only thing he could, he ran. He knew that the British and French, although always at war, both wanted the end of the pirates. Franco knew this time he was in real trouble. A cold mist walked over his heart. He felt the devil squeeze the life from his soul.

"My God, that's bigger than anything I ever saw before."

Franco was no fool. He knew these waters, and he headed for the Dry Tortugas. If he was lucky, he could make high water and gain time, as the monster that was chasing him drew a 25 foot draft.

They made it to the Dry Tortugas by four thirty in the morning. His luck held; it was high water. This gained them one hour. *Angelina* now set a straight course for the Florida Keys. Franco made it to the Keys, but the English monster was close on his tail.

Captain Niles Remington was a career Navy man. The sea was in his blood; it ran through his veins. He came from a wealthy family, with a long history of the sea, his father, his grandfather, all Navy men. He wasn't a brave man but he did his job. He had been in the Navy for thirty-five years, twenty as a captain. Niles had fought in the British and French wars, never had much of a name but did his job, a book man, a man of privilege who did the best he could. The crew of the *Plymouth* didn't think too highly of him. He wasn't a bad Captain, just average, a man who did a job as best as he knew how, always by the numbers. No room for gambles. Niles knew he would never make better than captain. He had been passed over too many times.

Actually, he was surprised to be given this commission, but it did make sense. He was due to retire shortly, and the deal was that the *Plymouth* pick up a Spanish lady in Wilmington, North Carolina. He was then to deliver her to northern Cuba. The Captain didn't know who she was, but she must have been very important to send a full Ship of the Line. Ships the size of *Plymouth* were usually kept close to harbor for blockade duty or to patrol local waters for security. Once *Plymouth* had delivered the lady, he was to go to Jamaica. There he was to deliver his ship to a new captain and then retire. He had already picked out a spot in North Carolina, just a few miles from Cape Hatteras. He was going to build a home there for his family. Niles thought he had earned his retirement and it was time to spend some of that family fortune. He truly believed that his class should be the one to colonize the Americas, and that the riff raff that were coming from all over the world should be there to work for them. It was on his return from Cuba that his crew spotted *Angelina*. He had carried out his mission, but all British Admiralty were ordered to seek and destroy pirates.

This ship posed no problem for the *Plymouth*, they were out manned and out gunned. *Plymouth* sighted *Angelina* in the early morning mist and gave chase. The first shot was fired at 6.30 a.m. and hit the water 40 yards to port, sending a plume of water ten feet into the air. Five minutes later, the *Plymouth* fired the second shot, this one crashing into the ocean 20 yards to port.

The crewman's voice rang in Franco's ears. "Captain, he's ranging us!"

"Yes, when she gets our range she'll turn broadside, then we're dead. Hard turn to starboard, now!"

They steered their way into the mouth of a river. As *Angelina* made the turn to starboard, another shot rang out. The ball hit the quarterdeck and sent splinter's flying. One hit a black sailor named August and almost disemboweled him, leaving most of his stomach splattered on the deck. He screamed and writhed in agony until someone fired a ball into his head.

The *Angelina* sailed into the inlet. Franco didn't know if this was a good move or a bad one but he knew that he had to get clear of the British guns or they would destroy his outmatched ship with the next volley. The river was about 200 feet wide and, fortunately, made a 45degree turn towards the north, giving them some shelter from the cannon fire. The depth of the water was 12 to 15 feet, fine for *Angelina* but inaccessible for the British.

On entering the river's mouth, Franco ordered all sails dropped except the mizzen, which he kept up for direction and stability. *Angelina* made it approximately 1,000 feet up the river, then Franco ordered all sails down and dropped anchor. As the bow anchor dropped he made a hard turn to port. On completing a half turn he ordered the two stern anchors dropped, bringing the *Angelina* 95 degrees to the river's mouth so that his 7 port cannons could bear down on anyone who would follow.

Everyone on board the *Angelina* could now catch their breath, and take in their predicament more fully. Though safe for the moment, still there was no escape. Franco ordered all cannons loaded and ready, and muskets, swords and pistols were issued to the crew. If it was a fight they wanted, a fight they would get.

"Captain, what's next?"

"Let's get ready, Aggan. The next move they'll make will be to send long boats and Marines, so we have to be prepared. Send five armed men in a long boat to the point to keep watch and to signal the British approach. Then I want you to dispatch another five men in a boat up river to examine how far we can run if need be"

One hour later shots rang out. All eyes on deck looked to the land to see three of the five men sent to the point running for their lives. One man, LaBelle, a big black man who was not very bright but could empty a room with just one hand, had blood oozing from a gaping hole in his left arm.

Franco knew right away that the British longboats had arrived. The first boat came into view at the river's mouth, 15 feet long with 15 Marines. Franco ordered "FIRE!" He had already given orders for the cannons to be fired in two volleys, 4, then 3, which would give time to load while keeping up pressure. The noise in such a small area was deafening but it had the desired effect - the British were taken completely by surprise. The first two cannon balls missed completely. The third hit the bow of the long boat, splintering wood but not doing much damage. The fourth, however, was a direct hit amid ship, almost destroying the boat completely and killing men on board. Blood and body parts flew everywhere. No one could have survived such a massacre. It didn't seem that anybody could have lived through this hell. The water turned red with blood.

The second boat never made the point; she immediately turned and ran beating a hasty retreat, leaving the dead to the fish and anything else that lived in that water. The short but devastating action was over in seconds, although it had seemed to go in slow motion and last for hours. "That British Captain was quick to launch those boats but won't make that mistake again," Franco said to Aggan, his fist mate.

LaBelle and his two shipmates were back on board in minutes, half running half swimming, and just a little, it seemed, flying. The ship's "doctor," as he liked to be called, was a fat little bald man in his mid 50s with a ruddy completion who drank way too much rum. He was really no more than a barber but did have his uses, digging out musket balls or cutting off limbs, and he was quite good with a needle and thread. His real name was Petra, he was a Frenchman born in Martinique. He served in the French Navy and like many others in the wars of the late seventeen and eighteenth century, Petra got out when he could and joined the slave trade. He learned basic medicine while working the slave boats from Africa to the New World. Many died because of his actions, but many lived too. He had also delivered his share of babies at sea. It was fair to say he tried his best.

Petra attended LaBelle's shoulder wound, which was not as bad as it looked. The ball had gone through the fleshy part of his arm missing any bones, so he just cleaned the wound with alcohol and stitched it. The man was then sent back to action.

Captain Franco questioned the three sailors who had reached the point at the same time as the first long boat. The Marines were more prepared and had fired the first volley, hitting and killing the other two immediately. One man's head disappeared in a mist of blood and gore that covered the other man's body. The second was hit three times in the chest and died instantly where he fell. After this they ran and never looked back.

"Captain, we can't get out that way they got it blocked."

"Relax and don't panic. Wait for the scouts to come back from up river."

"Captain, I tell you it was that dammed amulet."

"Don't be stupid, everybody has bad luck and this is our turn."

"Captain, the ship is cursed." This time the voice came from a little man in the center of the throng.

Franco had heard enough. "If I hear any other man crying about that relic I'll shoot him myself!" he thundered. "Now get back to duty."

Things went quiet for the next two hours giving everyone time to think and reassess. By 9:30 the scouts who had checked out the river returned. Franco took time to reflect. Could he really have been wrong? He remembered the old ways from his childhood in Cuba. He had always thought of them as nothing but silly superstition. Were they? "That damned gold talisman, could it really have a power?" he asked himself aloud.

"Snap out of it, Franco," he told himself. He couldn't let this nonsense cloud his thoughts and decisions.

Dungat came into his cabin. "Tell me," Franco said.

"We went two miles up river, Captain. We found a depth of between six and ten feet but it's pretty low now. It should reach more now the tide has turned."

"We have no time to wait. Move now we'll have to take a chance. The British won't wait, drop all boats at once."

Four six-foot boats were launched with eight armed men in each. Two ropes were tied in between *Angelina* and the boats.

The British longboat crew saw the terrible destruction and carnage of their fellow Marines and immediately put in to land out of sight of the pirate ship. Sergeant Wilson put eight men on land with signal rockets and flags for code. "Let us know the moment she makes a move." Wilson and what was left of his crew returned to the *Plymouth* to report what had happened.

Franco knew they would have left lookouts, and that he really only had one choice and he had already taken it. He could, of course, send a force to kill the lookouts, but the British ship would just send more. His decision was made; there was no time to look back. The river was the only way out. He estimated the time now to be between ten and eleven a.m. Franco knew that from high water at the Dry Tortugars his time had to be now. It was at this moment that the true depth of their situation struck him. It was mid July and the humidity was around a hundred percent, they were in a river surrounded by mangrove swamps, the temperature was in the 90s and the smell was unbearable.

Niles Remington was standing by the helm when the news of the attack came. He wrote it off to expendable losses and sent 30 Marines to shore to watch and snipe at the *Angelina*. But it was too late, Franco had already moved, and both Captains were aware of the situation. Franco's men used boats to tow, and also had men on the shore to pull with ropes.

Niles returned to his cabin. It was hot he didn't need this mischief so close to his retirement. He knew he had to move. Time was on his side but he had to sail north now. Tired and weary he pulled the pot from below his bed and urinated. His next action was to pour it out of his window. How could this possibly happen to me at this time in my life, he thought.

Remington returned to the deck. He called his first Lieutenant Bass off to the side. "Bass, there has to be a way out and it's got to be north."

Plymouth pulled anchor and set sail, making two miles while the *Angelina* made very slow progress. "Captain, we have ten men on each shore and two long boats pulling. We have only four hours of water."

The entrance was two miles north and it was very hard going. Sweltering hot and stifling humid but desperation can find unlimited resources. They reached the mouth of the river. Cries went up from the men. "You did it, Captain!" "We made it!"

Franco ordered the men and boats back to the ship and then set sail. He didn't have much wind but enough, he hoped, to make open water. His goal was that once they made it out of the river they would find more wind and escape the British ship. But deep inside he had a cold foreboding clutching at his stomach like a dead man walking through the graveyard after his funeral.

With all men back on board and the boats secured, they made full way to the mouth of the river. It was their salvation, and they gave praise to all the Gods they knew and thanked the earth to once again be free.

Captain Franco had the helm as they raced the devil. Fifty yards from open water Anise caught sight of what appeared to be the white paint of a long boat's stern. He knew at that moment it was all over; his luck and that of his crew had ended. He looked to the sky and smiled, as somewhere deep inside he felt at peace. *Is this the end?* he thought. He already knew they didn't have enough speed to outrun the British, his only hope was they would make a mistake. Deep inside he knew that wouldn't happen.

As the *Angelina* neared the mouth of the river, hell became reality as smoke and fire erupted from both the north and south shore. *Angelina* didn't have enough way to escape but Captain Franco already knew that. Muskets from among the Cypress Hammocks broke free. The decks of the *Angelina* ran red with blood. The carnage was horrific, dead and wounded men lay everywhere. Aggan lay dead at Franco's feet.

Franco took a ball to his right shoulder. It was over, but by all that was holy his every last breath would go to flight.

At that moment a four-inch hawser was lifted from across the mouth tied to the Cypress trees. *Angelina* lay dead in the water. Without wind the 4 inch rope had taken all momentum from the ship. Franco knew his time had come. He looked to the main deck. His crew was mostly dead, their bodies blown to pieces. There was blood everywhere.

Captain Franco's only hope now was that it would be over quickly. There was no pain as his life ended with a 750 ball from a Brown Bess musket ripping his head from his body. What was left of the *Angelina* and her crew was towed to Kingston, Jamaica, and the gibbet at the end of the dock.

The Arrival

They arrived in Charleston, South Carolina, around lunch-time on a hot day in the middle of summer. Nathaniel had insisted he wanted an old property with the grass running down to the ocean. Colonial, preferably haunted. Beth, on the other hand, just wanted it to work this time. Nathaniel was a good man, and she didn't want to make another mistake.

He was just 33, she was 40, a three time loser with husbands. Nat's wife had died in a car crash three years earlier, and he and Beth never talked about her.

The first time they met was in a bar. Well, it wasn't really a bar. The West Inn was rented by UCLA for the prime purpose of late learners (that was the polite euphemism they used). Nathaniel was Beth's teacher at 33 and I was his pupil at 40. "Life sucks!"

Nathaniel seemed sad so she loved him from the start. They had a drink, talked, and fell in love...with one problem. His name was Nathaniel. His friends called him Nate, but the new love of his life preferred Nat, which he said sounded like a bug. "Beth, please don't do that! Don't call me Nat." They laughed and the name stuck.

So one year and eight months later they found themselves in a solid relationship, moving into an old Colonial in South Carolina perched high above the ocean. Haunted, of course.

Nat was six foot one, lean, and he had a strong face with a rather large bridged nose. Beth always poked fun at him, saying that he looked like an old settler. Beth, at 40, was in terrific shape, thanks to taking good care of herself in the gym three times a week. *God it hurts; well, that's what you get for getting old*, she told herself. *This time I think I really have a chance. Anyway, I'm going for my life giving everything I've got.*

At 2:00 in the afternoon they had finally arrived. It was all I could have nightmare d about. Ten-foot gates met them at the entrance. They were not locked, but who would steal from this place? This house wasn't Gothic but it should have been. For Beth, it was just plain scary. They did the unthinkable and drove up the gravel drive that crunched under our tires. This house was so much not of this century. It had been a long time since she'd seen Boris Karloff but this brought it all back.

"Honey, what wine did you get?" he asked.

"I got a bottle of Chardonay. It's cooling on ice right now. Let's go inside and see if this Keep has a kitchen, I'll give you odds it's got a cauldron over an open fire."

"Come on, you know I have to do this, I didn't drag you along but I really appreciate you being here. Beth, I love you and I need you. Thank you for being here. Please give this project a chance to work."

"Oh, come on," she replied, "you know I'm only joking, this place just oozes charm and warmth."

The front of the house was kind of square, the front door was set back inside a porch supported by two cement pillars. The oversized door itself seemed out of all proportion to the rest of the house. "How many owners has this Mausoleum had?" Beth asked.

"Come on, Beth, this is no Mausoleum. It was built as a family home over 250 years ago."

"Yeah, for the Munsters."

The house was a two-story building built sometime in the 18th or 19th century. It had eighteen rooms, many of which had obviously been added over the years. "Nat, are you going to carry me over the threshold?"

"No, but that does bring up something I think we should talk about in the time we spend here."

They entered the front door into a hallway that was brighter than Beth had imagined. She was pleasantly surprised by the way the designer had allowed the light to filter in. The sight seemed to bathe her eyes with light and color. Above the doorway to the right about 10 feet sat a round window with an array of colored glass that allowed in a prism of light that gave the whole hallway a feeling of life and vitality.

They walked along the corridor and into the light. From the hallway they went into the morning room, a place for coffee and biscuits.

"Nat, I have to say this is not what I expected! This is not Dracula's Castle."

"No, Beth, we're in South Carolina not Transylvania."

"You and I have a strange relationship and we really do have to talk."

"Now?"

"This is as good a time as any, Beth."

They walked down the hallway and went through a door to the left, which took them into the kitchen area. Light from the two large windows immediately met Beth's eyes and seemed to engulf the whole the kitchen with brightness and warmth.

"O.K., you have got me this time, this is not the evil dungeon that I expected."

"Beth, I think I love you; no, I know I love you. We just needed time to find each other. It's that simple. Will you marry me?"

That simple conversation changed everything. They both knew their lives would never again be the same.

They cooked spaghetti and tomato sauce and drank wine until they were drunk. Then they went to bed. Beth had a hang-up about being seen naked. Nat went to the bathroom first, cleaned his teeth, washed all that was important and then went back to the bedroom.

The light was very low! Beth was fully dressed. As he crossed the room she arose and walked to meet him. As they made eye contact he knew right away this time was different, she had that aura of someone totally in control. They didn't speak, it wasn't a time for words. Every fiber in his body told him that this was going to be so much more than he could have imagined! His hand slipped into that beautiful place between her legs, the valley of no return. As he touched that damp spot all the emotions in him erupted at once. He felt a part of his body change shape, a feeling so demanding, so overpowering, he knew right away that this night was their time.

He mused to himself, *is this what the gods do for their amusement?* Then why did they take Linda, why did they destroy his life so totally? Was that then the reason for making this night so totally sublime? Please, God, leave me alone, not tonight - she deserves better, don't spoil what we have.

He shook all the negative thoughts from his mind. In his arms he held a very beautiful and delicate woman whom he loved with all his heart. He kissed her deep and hard on the lips. "Nat, if only tonight could last forever, I have never been so happy in my whole my life."

Their bodies came together in a frenzy of emotion. The lights seemed to dim all at once. They climaxed together in a world full of color and light.

The morning came with a shower of light. The bedroom windows seemed to invite the power of illumination, the entire house was so full of power and light. Beth got up and went to the kitchen to prepare breakfast. Her mood was such that nothing could hurt her. She now had body armor, the love of a good man. She walked down the hall and entered the kitchen. To her immediate left was a copper shelf adorned with nautical instruments. In the center was a sextant, flanked by a slide rule, a depth sounder, Nasa radio fix, a protractor and two small, oil-fueled hurricane lamps. She also spotted a small wooden shelf, a fixture that seemed to have grown from the very wall. On it sat a clay wine carafe and goblets. As she moved on there was one more shelf, on which lay a copper fondue set. Two fans revolved at slow speed mixing the air into a cocktail of freshness. The range sat majestically in the comer, surrounded by white melamine cabinets. To the left of the sink hid a small microwave and to the right stood a tall fridge freezer, with two straw dolls that seemed to have lived there forever. There was also a small window that enhanced the light from the two windows over the sink, next to the door to the garden.

Beth felt like never before, so full of euphoria. She had everything she wanted, a man who loved her, and wanted to marry her. She felt like singing, like those people she had seen in old Hollywood films. It wasn't raining, but if it was she would sing without the umbrella. She felt like laughing, she had never in her entire life felt this way. As these emotions rose inside her chest, she began to laugh. Joyous thoughts flooded her mind. Maybe children. After all, she was only 40. She was sure that she could at that moment hear children laughing, very happy, or maybe slightly sad. She wasn't sure, then again, it didn't matter. She had all she ever wanted.

Beth called to Nat, "Breakfast is ready."

Nat thought, *what a beautiful life this is. I could get used to this.* He walked into the kitchen to the smell of bacon and eggs, a man's delight. They sat at the table, the coffee was hot and the pancakes were sweet.

"Nat you never did tell me the story of this house."

"Well, five years ago when Linda died it destroyed my life. I couldn't eat, drink or sleep, I just wanted to die."

Beth reached over to put her hand on his. He continued. "A friend and colleague of mine tried to help by advising me to go and see a psychic. My first thoughts were it's just a load of bullshit, but I did go because of my state of mind. Honey, one thing in this life I don't believe in is suicide, although I leaned very much that way at the time."

She looked at him as he spoke, her eyes full of compassion,

"I visited one psychic, then another and another. The story always seemed to be the same, Linda was happy and well on the other side. It was explained to me that she now had to move on to a different existence. That she loved me very much, but I must move on with my life. This answer didn't sit very well with me, so I started my own investigation into psychic fraud. I spent every spare moment for the next two years, digging and digging, until I guess I became burned out."

"Go on, Nat," Beth said, her attention now fully captured. "Tell me what happened next."

"It was this same friend whom was incidentally the Dean, and also Linda's uncle, who finally stopped the madness. I knew he was right, at first it saved my life and my sanity, but now it was starting to destroy me. By this stage I had spent two years of my life investigating everything from psychic phenomenon to things that go bump in the night. I had become quite an expert, while losing myself and my mind. I met a lot of crazy people along the way and some very intelligent, not to mention some who couldn't be ignored because they made a lot of sense. I did nevertheless decide to give it up and put my life back in shape. Some time later I met you, Beth, and the rest as they say is history."

A perplexed look crossed Beth's face. "But Nat, that doesn't explain this house."

"Will you be patient and pass me some more toast?" he replied. "I'm just coming to that now. Back at school, I should call it University really, the Dean thinks I show no respect when I call it a school...excuse me, I digress. As I was saying, it was decided that a paper be written about haunted houses, because of the popularity of recent films out of good old Hollywood. Who better to head up such an investigation, but yours truly? I was given this assignment on the merit of my experience, and of course my relationship to the Dean."

"Don't be cynical, Nat! You know you have the background knowledge and experience to put it altogether, however sad its beginnings."

Nat shrugged. "Well, to answer your questions about this house. I spent weeks in books, on the Internet, every bit of information I could glean. Then one day I saw in an underground mag, houses and properties that cannot be bought or rented, on a scale of 1-10. I decided to search out any of the above that had a history of strange behavior. I got lucky, one magazine had the story of a house in South Carolina that had many strange happenings, most of which had not been recorded to any degree in the near past. It seemed that this house had been overlooked, and something about it pinched my imagination. I took the number and called, I was told that this property was not for rent and that they were fed up of psychic investigators. When I told them that I was a UCLA Professor of Language, the rules changed. I guess that $2,000 a month didn't hurt! So I took the grant, booked the summer break, and here we are."

Beth smiled coyly. "You left one thing out, Nat. Tell me about the haunting."

"Beth, I saved the best for last. This house has a long history of strange happenings going back maybe 250 years. According to the papers this house was once a cotton plantation. History tells us this property belonged to a prominent slave trader, who traded at the slave market down on the dock."—

"Nat, did you move the straw dolls on the freezer?"

He looked at her a bit puzzled. "What dolls, Honey?"

"The two on the fridge are back to front."

"Don't let your imagination run away with you, Beth."

"Nat, I will marry you, but you know I don't know if I can give you children."

"Let's not worry about children right now," he said. "Anyway, this conversation is too strong for this time in the morning. You asked me to tell you what I know about the house. But first, let me show you, I haven't been here before, but I did receive a well-documented fax and CD. This explained the history of the place. Come on, let's walk."

They left the kitchen and moved into a hallway she was familiar with from the night before. They had walked this way to the bedroom, though, she thought. I must confess, I don't remember with all that wonderful food, and too much to drink and the overpowering drug of passion. Now with the light of day it seemed somehow different, so much light, so full of life and energy. How could this house possibly be haunted? Beth couldn't remember being in so much light. It massaged every inch of her body. Her eyes felt like two iron plates had been lifted! "I don't understand one thing about this House," she said. "Why if it is so haunted is there so much light?"

"That's why we are here! Don't you see one thing abounds? Light! In all the rooms, it's the same, too much light. It's as though they were afraid of the dark. That's the answer, most of the haunting comes in the daytime; at least that's what I think."

They walked the corridors, and every room was the same: too much light. "Nat, tell me, who haunted this place?"

"To understand totally, Beth, we must finish the tour."

They went back to the kitchen. Nat opened a door that Beth had noticed before, but she had not been through. They walked through it. In front of them lay a 10-yard space. The floor was covered with gray flagstones. Although Beth's eyes were used to the light of the house, they were now shocked by the brightness of the day. Together they walked through a doorway that took them into another building. This structure ran maybe 80 feet to the south of the main building. Beth felt an immediate change in temperature from warm to warmer. This building was full of flowers, the smell was quite overpowering. Beth thought it also had the pungent odor of mothballs and age. Now all of a sudden her senses didn't understand, and for the first time she became afraid. A chill ran down her spine like an electric shock that ran all through her body.

"Nat, what is this place?"

"It's only the conservatory, Beth, a place to grow flowers."

"No, Nat this is a bad place."

"Ok, Honey, so now you're a psychic!"

"Nat, please don't be condescending. I have never felt like this before. There's something about this place that's oppressive."

"Beth, I remember a time not so long ago that you wouldn't even talk about this subject. The time I asked you to come with me and stay here you thought it one big joke! 'Wow! Let's stay in a haunted house!'"

Beth had had enough. She said, "I know this sounds strange, Nat, but please take me out of this building."

They returned the way they had come in, across the flagstones, back through the kitchen door. They returned to the biscuit and coffee room, as Beth now called it. "Nat, you were going to tell me about the haunting."

"It's only breakfast time, Beth, let's take a look around town or maybe go down to the beach."

"No, I want you to tell me about the house."

Nat smiled. "Well, if you insist I'll tell you what I know. The house or at least the first house was built 1730/1740. It belongs to an English family, title, money, big time society. They moved here in the early days of South Carolina, in the days of slaves, plantations and an easy life, if you have money. They built the house, grew a plantation and settled. The house still belongs to the same family; they live in England now. I guess they just keep the house as equity, a number on a piece of paper. I was told they tried to sell it, several times, but it stuck like glue. Now they just leave it and pay caretakers and cleaners I guess."

"Nat, the upkeep of a place like this must be phenomenal."

Nodding, Nat said, "Well, that's big money for you. The family grew and so did the plantation, several generations of family and slaves. In around 1840 the plantation was at its peak. Life was good in the South just before the war, and this place was thriving. The owners had a full time job on their hands. I'm told this was the biggest, cotton land in the South. The family held parties and courted society from the USA and Europe. This was, excuse the word, a very gay place in the true sense of the word. The family had two young children, twins, a boy and a girl. They were groomed to be the next generation. Their future seemed made, they had everything, the best tutors from Europe, all that money could buy. But as so very often happens, fate had took a hand and dealt a bad blow."

Beth raised an eyebrow. "What happened?"

"The twins were both born with a rare congenital blood disorder, which in those days could prove fatal. These days such diseases are easily treated, but not so back then. Oh, they had the best doctors from around the world and 24-hour nurses, but all that was not enough. You see, if they cut themselves, they couldn't stop the bleeding."

"Nat, you mean they had hemophilia, the blood wouldn't clot?"

"That's right and the poor kids were frightened to go out and play, just one fall could prove fatal. They were wrapped up in cotton wool and lived, I guess, a miserable life. At the very least they had each other, as the story goes, they were inseparable."

At this stage Nat sighed very deeply, and looked into space.

"OK, Nat," Beth said, "enough for now. What about that tour of Charleston you promised me?"

Nathaniel slowly drifted back. "What was that, Honey? What would you like to do?"

"Well, let's start with the ocean, we are, after all on the East Coast. Remember, I'm used to the cold water of the Pacific and this, so they tell me, is the warm Atlantic."

The rest of the day they partied, swimming in the ocean at the beach ad joining the property. Later they dressed and had dinner at one of Charleston's most famous and more expensive restaurants. "Nat, can we afford this place?"

"Absolutely not. But who cares, put it on the card. After all, we may be shut up in that place for some time to come."

Beth was drumming her fingers on her wine glass a bit nervously. "Nat, about the house, I know you have a paper to write, and I'm just here for..."

"For what, Honey? You're here because I thought that's what we both wanted, to be together."

"Nat, I'm happy and if it's possible, I want to help. I know I'm not as educated as you but I really would like to try."

Nat reached across the table, held Beth's hands in his, and said, "There is no person living on this Earth that I would sooner be with tonight. Please believe that!"

She looked deeply into his eyes. "Nat, you know I do. Let's go home."

They arrived back around 12.30 a.m., a little worse for wear. The driveway crunched the same. The house was dark but not foreboding. The lights in the front porch were on, they gave a kind of surreal atmosphere to the front of the building, bathing the doorway in a mixture of light and harmony. Beth thought, *How could this be from a haunted house?*

The next day Beth woke to find Nat gone. She searched downstairs and into the kitchen, the coffee was hot so he couldn't be far away. At that moment the kitchen door opened and in walked Nat with a bunch of orchids. "I hope the gardener doesn't mind, Beth, these are for you."

"Thank you, Nat, they are lovely, what a wonderful start to a day."

Nat went to the study to write, so Beth took a shower. For the first time in her life she felt whole, she knew now that this was what she had been waiting for all her life. She showered and dried herself with a towel, then looked in the mirror to see the damage. "Hey girl, you look good," she said to herself, "this life has turned your way at last; I guess everybody deserves their turn."

She dressed in a white blouse and blue denim mini skirt, knowing Nat liked to see her legs. As Beth walked down the stairs she had the strongest feeling come over her. A compulsion to go into the attic, up instead of down. She turned and walked back up the stairs. Along the landing was a pull down hatch with a ladder. Beth pulled down the hatch and climbed the ladder into the attic. The room was quite large, and like every other room in the house had an immense amount of light. The light surged in from a large window built into and above the roof. Beth looked around, like every attic this was no different. The room was full of chests clothes and rocking horses, but also full of light. As attics go this was about average, with dust everywhere.

Beth took in the scene. She was drawn to the west side of the attic that seemed to be comprised of chests and boxes. As she walked over one particular trunk with its lid slightly ajar caught her attention. She opened the trunk and peered inside. Her eyes were met with an array of letters and postcards. Beth picket up a pack of six or more letters that were tied together with a yellow ribbon. The letters were dated 1917, she pulled the tail and opened the ribbon. DEAR WILLIAM: TODAY I WENT TO TOWN. I DO NOT THINK I WILL EVER GET USED TO THIS INFERNAL HORSELESS CARRIAGE. HOW ARE THINGS WITH

YOU? I HOPE THIS LETTER FINDS YOU WELL AND THAT THIS SILLY WAR IS OVER SOON. JOHNNY SAID THAT HE PLAYED WITH HIS NEW FRIENDS AGAIN TODAY. HE WORRIES ME. SOMETIMES HE HAS SUCH IMAGINATION.

Beth looked at the date. It was August 16. She put the letter back in the envelope and moved on to the next. DEAR WILLIAM: I STILL HAVE NOT YET RECEIVED A LETTER FROM YOU. I AM GOING OUT OF MY MIND WITH WORRY. ARE YOU WELL? THE NEWSPAPERS TELL STORIES THAT SIMPLY CANNOT BE TRUE. IT SEEMS HARDLY POSSIBLE THAT SO MANY MEN CAN DIE IN ONE BATTLE. I GOT A CALL FROM JOHNNY'S TUTOR TODAY, SHE SEEMS WORRIED ABOUT HIS IMAGINATION, THOSE FRIENDS OF HIS AGAIN. TELL ME, WILLIAM, WHAT CAN WE DO?

This letter was dated September 29. Beth replaced it and moved on to another. DEAR WILLIAM: IT SEEMS SO LONG SINCE YOU HAVE WRITTEN. I DO HOPE NOTHING HAS HAPPENED TO YOU. I HAVE READ SUCH BAD STORIES ABOUT SOLDIERS BEING CAPTURED BY THE BOCHE. MUST I THEN ASSUME THIS OR WORSE IS YOUR FATE? LIFE HERE GOES ON THE SAME. I STILL WORRY ABOUT JOHNNY AND HIS IMAGINATION. MUST HE ALWAYS TALK OF HIS FRIENDS THAT NO ONE EVER SEES?

The date of this letter was December 9. Beth replaced the letter and once again moved on. This time the envelope's contents were different, newspaper clippings. The first was from a local newspaper with the heading: PLANTATION OWNER DIES IN YPRES OFFENSIVE. THE WAR IN FRANCE HAS CLAIMED THE LIFE OF A PROMINENT LANDOWNER. CAPTAIN WILIAM REMINGTON, 32, OF THE BRITISH ROYAL ENGINEERS AND THE LATE OWNER OF REMINGTON HALL, WAS KILLED

ON THE FIRST DAY OF THE LATEST OFFENSIVE.
CAPTAIN REMINGTON IS SURVNED BY HIS WIFE
SARA REMINGTON, 32, AND SON JONATHON, AGE
6.

This was dated August 6. Beth froze to the spot when she
realized it was William. She quickly looked at the next cutting:
LOCAL BOY DIES IN FREAK ACCIDENT. TRAGEDY
STRIKES REMINGTON FAMILY FOR SECOND
TIME. YOUNG JONATHON REMINGTON, AGED
6, DIED MONDAY IN WHAT SEEMS LIKE A FREAK
ACCIDENT. HIS BODY WAS FOUND BY ONE OF THE
PLANTATION WORKERS FACE DOWN IN A DITCH.
POLICE BELIEVE HE DROWNED, ALTHOUGH THE
DITCH HAD ONLY l0 INCHES OF WATER.

What shocked Beth the most, and took her breath away,
were the dates of the reports. The first, August 6, the second,
August 30, 1917…before Sara's letters. The next clip had an
even greater effect on Beth. This one was dated December 31,
1917, New Year's Eve. This time the article made front-page
headlines: TRAGEDY STRIKES LAND OWNERS FOR
THE THIRD TIME. TRAGEDY CALLED AGAIN NEW
YEAR'S EVE TO THE BELEAGUERED REMINGTON
FAMILY. SARA JANE REMINGTON WAS FOUND
EARLY TODAY DEAD ON THE STUDY FLOOR. SHE
HAD SHOT HERSELF WITH A REVOLVER. SUICIDE
WAS THOUGHT TO BE THE MOTIVE, ALTHOUGH
NO NOTE WAS FOUND. IT IS STRONGLY BELIEVED
THAT HER MIND WAS DISTURBED AFTER RECENT
TRAGIC LOSSES.

Beth dropped the letters. How could one family suffer so
much? What happened stopped Beth dead in her tracks, her
heart missed several beats. As she looked up there standing
in front of her was a young boy maybe 6 or 7. He was dressed
in boots, long socks that came up to his knees and short pants
that that reached his socks. He wore a jacket that tied at the

neck with a bow ribbon, and a large peaked cap of the sort they wore in the early part of the century. It was what Beth saw next that made her nearly faint: the boy stood in a small pool of water. She tried to scream but no sound would leave her lips, in fact, there was no air left in her lungs. The icicles of fear slowly coursed through her veins and arteries, making her body stiffen with horror. In a moment of panic and sheer terror she mustered her last remnants of energy and strength, and ran for the hatch and ladder.

Beth didn't remember if she climbed or fell to the landing below. All she could remember was slamming the hatch and bolting for the study and Nat below. She ran into the room, and Nat turned and walked towards her. He had never seen her so upset. "Beth, please tell me what's wrong? You look like have seen a ghost!"

Breathlessly, Beth said, "Nat, you are dead right, I have just seen a ghost!"

"Babe, you could never comprehend what I saw in the attic. I just saw a child that died in 1917. Please, Nat, you must tell me what you know about this house!"

"But Beth, you didn't want to know."

As he comforted her in his arms, she said, "That has all changed now, this is something I need to know. Nat, I saw things that don't exist, tell me about that, and don't give me any more shit! I just saw a child that drowned!"

"Honey, tell me what you saw?"

"He was a young boy, dressed in the turn of the century clothes and I really need to know what is going on. I need you to tell me the full story of this place."

Nat took in a deep breath. "OK, sit down," he said. After she sat, he began slowly pacing as he explained things to her. "The foundations, as it were, were laid in 1727. A British sea Captain Niles Remington retired his commission in the British Navy. He chose to end his stint in Jamaica. He was Captain of HMS *Plymouth,* a British ship of the line. He purchased this land and started a plantation. He bought slaves, at that time they were quite cheap. Niles brought his family over from England, and they settled. The plantation grew and grew. The family became quite a social event in the area. It is said that they had the biggest cotton plantation in the whole of the South. Niles' wife was of Latin descent, her name was Marietta and she was from Cuban Royals."

"Oh come on, Nat, you got all this from paper and a CD Rom?"

"No, Honey, from good old fashioned hard work."

Beth folded her arms. "You never told me any of this."

"Beth, you didn't want to know, you had no interest, you wanted to come and I was happy with that. So please don't blame me if this doesn't sit very well, because you asked."

She did not reply, so he continued. "Anyway, Niles never really owned all this, his family in England held the purse strings. And how is this for an oxymoron, in 1777 his grandson James fought the British at Featherstone and died. Though the family moved on, you must understand that this family is large and they have some kind of trust. Aristocracy."

Beth's face was still creased with worry. "Nat, I understand I only came along for the ride, but things change."

"Well, Honey, let's continue with the story. The plantation was built, they thrived, then along came the Revolution, the Tea Party and all of that. James's took with the British and died at Valley Forge. The War of Independence had started and there must have been a rift in the family. Anyway, all that passed and time heals all wounds. We must move on. The family stayed on the land. In 1812 another war with England, this time the family lost one of its children on the American side, at Lake Champlain. Major George Remington was killed by a mortar shell."

Now Beth's fear was being replaced by frustration. "Nat, you're telling me the history of the family, but not the haunting."

"Well, Honey, the first documented occurrence came in 1795; you must remember that at this time people were very superstitious. A child was seen in the garden in a basket chair, he was thought to be the son of Niles Remington who died from polio. Several of the servants ran away. Then we move on and there was a local newspaper story that covered a wedding at Remington Manor in 1825. Sir Arlington Remington married Emily Ann Jackson, quite a society event at the time. But unfortunately the day was marred by a strange event. A basket case! A child in a basket wheelchair was seen by many guests to run his chair directly into the lake and drown. On investigation it was found or rather not found, that there was no one there. Many passed it of as a prank as Sir Arlington was prone to do.

Beth seemed a bit more at ease now. "Please continue," she said.

"OK, back to where I left off originally, the twins. It would seem that they are the main brunt of the hauntings. Jonathan and Clair were born around 1830, sickly children with a rare blood disease. Jonathan had an accident when he was 12, he fell off his cart and cut his leg badly. The doctors couldn't stop the bleeding and unfortunately he died that night. His sister Clair never recovered from his death. Four mouths later Clair was found in her bedroom dead with her wrists cut."

"Oh, Nat, that's so tragic!"

"Yes, Honey, but that's where the story starts. Beth, you asked me about this house, and now you know!"

"But what I saw today, tell me about that?"

"The boy you saw was Jonathan Remington, he died from drowning in a ditch."

"But Nat, it was so clear. I saw him as I see you, standing in front of me"

Nat had a playful grin. "Now do you believe the house is haunted?"

The following morning Nat made breakfast, pancakes and scrambled eggs with coffee. "Oh, come on, Nat, since when did eggs go with pancakes?"

"Well, Honey, I'm not a cook, you get what you get. Be grateful."

Nat spent the day in the study on his computer. Beth wrote to family and friends. They had dinner at about 6.00. Chicken and salad. Nat went back to the study; Beth washed up and dried the dishes. They sat in the kitchen with a glass of wine until 7.30. She knew Nat was busy doing his work and she didn't want to disturb him. Beth poured another glass of red wine and walked across the flagstones and into the conservatory, and that cold feeling went with her. At the end of the conservatory she passed through a door and walked down to the lake. The night was still very warm and quite humid. She felt the grass under her feet soft and wet. Beth sat at the dock on the north side of the lake and just took in the atmosphere. Man, what a good time to be alive. The lake gave off a small mist like a fog. The night was balmy and warm. Everything seemed so serene and calm. Beth thought how beautiful this moment was. She took a drink from her wine, such a feeling of calm and contentment.

"DER--DE--DUR--DER--DE--DUR--DER--DE--DUR..." Children playing! Beth went cold. She looked to her right and her soul stopped in its tracks. On the lawn she saw two children playing with a skipping rope. "ONE--WILLY--TWO--WILLY--THREE--WILLY." A boy and a girl maybe 10 or 12 years old. *Why are ghosts always dressed in white?* Beth was frightened but not afraid, she felt an attachment to these children, not fear. At that moment the girl turned her gaze and looked directly into her eyes. Beth felt the gaze burn deeply into her soul and unlock a part of her life she had hidden away in a deep dark cellar. She then proceeded to piss herself. "Wow, I haven't done that since I was 10 years old."

Beth was afraid to look but had no choice. She felt the warm water run down her inner thighs, and she did the only thing she knew how, she screamed at the top of her lungs like a banshee. The apparition dissolved. "WHY ME!" Beth cried. "Pull yourself together, girl!" Beth said out loud. *I sure hope no one heard me,* she thought. *What is it with this place?* Beth looked around sheepishly not knowing what she might see. There was nothing there to see, and for that she was eternally grateful. Beth rose and walked back towards the conservatory with very mixed emotions. Had she really seen a drowned boy and two children skipping or was she going out of her head? She ran into the house but stopped before she got to the study. Instead, Beth ran up the stairs to the bedroom. She sat down on the bed, her mind racing. She started to remember things she thought she had lost forever. She took off her clothes and got into the shower, the last thing she needed was Nat to know she had peed herself.

After the shower she toweled and got into dry clothes. Boy, I really need to think things out. A shadow came over her memory. Things best left forgotten. She saw a lake in cold wintertime, not yet ice but a frosting. The trees where covered with a beautiful crystal sugar topping. Doctor Brig Thomson had taken his daughters to Lake Norman each Christmas for the last five years. Brig was very much a family man and extremely close to his children. After a messy divorce, he lived for his girls. This Christmas Beth saw a difference in her father. He somehow didn't seem the same. It was something she couldn't quite touch, but she felt it deep inside. "Daddy, are you alright?" Beth asked her father.

"Yes pumpkin, I'm fine. You and Francis go and clean up for dinner."

Brig never got over his divorce from Chantal, it was always painful when he thought of the betrayal. How could his friend Lucas have been so deceptive? They had been colleagues for so many years, working at St James Hospital in Chicago. Brig and Lucas had met at St James five years earlier when Brig was an intern. Lucas was an anesthetist, and both became great friends. Chantal changed everything. She had taken all they had, their love and friendship. After the divorce she left him with their children. Brig was happy with this. He knew Chantal had no love for any human. She was completely selfish and only lived for herself. Brig felt sorry for Lucas but could never forgive him. Chantal had emptied the bank account, and left him with nothing but his beloved children.

Beth had been six at the time; Francis had been four and a half. Doctor Thomson had kept the apartment they had shared, but Chantal had taken everything else. She had not challenged custody, as bad as she was she knew that the girls would become too much trouble for her to handle. Chantal settled instead for visitation rights, although she barely managed even that chore. That Christmas they had taken the same log cabin, as Brig had become a creature of habit. Beth remembered very well how cold it became that Christmas, it had snowed early, but she recalled the log fire in the cabin, how warm and cozy it was. How she and Francis were so happy to be with Dad, in that warm and cozy environment. She found it hard and painful to remember that so distant night in 1973...

"Beth, Beth, where are you?"

She snapped out of her torturous coma. "Yes, Nat, I'm in the bedroom taking a shower."

He walked into the room. "Are you OK, Honey?"

"No, Nat, I don't think I will ever be the same again."

"What is it, Beth?"

"This house has opened up memories I thought gone forever, or at least, I hoped so! I guess, Nat, no one ever really forgets, just lock it in some dark basement safe and hopes no one finds the key."

Nathaniel looked at Beth's pain with compassion. He knew only too well that tortured look in her eyes. "Beth, there are things that we haven't talked about in our relationship. Things that we both thought best left alone, but it seems this house won't let them be."

"Nat, do you believe this house to be haunted?

"Well, Honey, I have always hypothesized that we each haunt ourself but as I said this is only a hypothesis, deep in my own mind I don't think I am really sure. There are things on and around this earth that none of us can be sure of. That is really why I chose this place, the story intrigued me."

He waited for a response, but she reminded quiet. He said, "Honey, I'm not blind I have seen the change in you since we first came here, and I know it's not like you."

"Nat, there are things I haven't told you and up till now I didn't think them relevant."

"Stop right there, Beth. I have done the same. Maybe at this point in our relationship we both feel the need to come clean as it were."

"I need to tell you something that I have kept buried for 29 years," Beth said.

"Go ahead, Honey if you feel right about it."

"You proposed to me, Nat, when we got here and I think that sparked things off, 1 now feel the need to tell you about my past. In 1973 my father, sister Francis and I, went to Lake Norman in North Carolina for Christmas. We had been to the same cabin for the last 5 years, since my parents' divorce. Dad always said the snow at Christmas in North Carolina was the whitest in the world, and that Santa Claus had his toy factories there. Well, Francis and 1 loved it, we had presents, a Christmas Tree with lights and no child could ask for more. But as you so eloquently put it life just waits its time to put in the body blow. That year we had arrived earlier than usual, December 20th. Dad said he wanted to spend more time with us. We all went shopping as usual, bought a tree, and decorated it. But Dad didn't seem the same; something was bothering him. Oh, we made the same moves, went to Church, slay rides, and choral singing. But it just wasn't the same."

Nathaniel was listening intently as she continued recounting the story.

"Christmas Eve, about 8.30, Dad packed us off to bed as he always had for the last five years. This time 1 saw a deep sadness in his eyes, something only a child might see. Francis was as happy as usual, that was the way she was. We went to bed and finally to sleep. At 2:45 in the morning, that was the precise time the police told us."

At this point Beth broke into tears.

"Stop, Beth, this is too painful, save it till later."

"No, Nat, it comes out now or never. Francis and I talked for what seemed like hours, about our childhood, Mommy and Christmas. I told Francis to go to sleep or Santa wouldn't come. But she laughed, and said, 'Daddy is Santa.' I think it was then that I knew that we had both grown up, even in our early years. Eventually we both drifted off into blissful serenity. I awoke to the smell off smoke. 'Francis, where are you?' I called. I knew something was wrong. Smoke was thick in the room. That acrid smell is unmistakable; it chokes the life right out of you. I knew from TV and films to go low and crawl along the floor. I got out of bed and dropped to the floor and crawled to Francis. Oh my God, Nat, she wasn't breathing! I was only 11 but 1 knew that much. I held Francis in my arms for what seemed like hours, but that didn't help. I knew she was gone. Oh God! I loved her so much!"

"Calm down, Beth. Slow down, not too fast."

"You have had a tragedy, Nat, so I know you understand," Beth managed to say in between sobs. "Please let me finish. I laid Francis down and moved into the lounge to look for Dad. With a heavy heart and a feeling of foreboding, 1 crawled along the smoke filled floor. I went through to the lounge, where 1 thought the fire would be, but that was not its ignition. The smoke was overpowering, 1 couldn't breathe…"

Beth was physically shaken and Nat was worried. "Honey, don't go on."

"I must, Nat, it must come out. I crawled into my Dad's room, and right away the stench caught my senses. Burning Flesh! The room was illuminated by colorful icicles of fire."

Her eyes were filled with tears as she recalled every detail of the tragedy. "I remember pulling at my skin like ammonia had been poured over my eyes and nose. I gagged for breath. 'Daddy, where are you?' I called, but I couldn't see through the smoke. At that moment, I passed out. I awoke in the paramedics' truck with an oxygen mask covering my face. 'Where is my Daddy and my sister?' I asked frantically. A young fresh-faced female nurse, I will never forget her face, it was so sad, just looked at me, unable to find the right words. I knew right away, from the look on her face that they where both dead. She tried so hard to console me. I have often wondered since who was the most upset. I was totally lost and empty. But she seemed totally devastated. I will never forget her name, Susan."

"What happened, Beth? Where did the fire come from? You told me your father built the fire up high, but that wouldn't explain the fire in his bedroom."

"That's what I never understood. The official verdict was accidental death, but to this day I have never believed that, I always knew in my heart it was no accident. I loved my dad, but to this day I have never visited his grave. I could never forgive him for Francis."

A horrified look washed over Nathaniel's face. "You mean it wasn't suicide?"

"The fire started in my dad's bedroom, it was thought to be an electric fault. The autopsy revealed my father was drunk. Nat, he was teatotal. A bottle of Jack Daniels was found at the bedside. He had earphones on listening to a radio cassette, something he never did. I was told that an electric surge had killed him instantly, and caused the fire."

Now Nathaniel looked confused. "But then, Honey, it was an accident after all."

"No, Nat, there was no tape in the recorder. Officially, it ends there. A domestic problem. Case closed."

"But Beth, it has all the hallmarks of an accident."

"I have always known in my heart, Nat, that Dad committed suicide and he killed Francis; that's why I have never visited his grave."

"Beth, you must let go."

Her crying over for now. Beth said, "In order for me to let go, I must apportion the blame, did Dad kill Francis?"

"Beth, if he did, does it really matter? I mean, I don't think it was murder, do you?"

"My dad has always been to me a foreign soldier. A man that seemed distanced but we loved him, Francis and I."

"How did your dad die?"

"Nat, he pissed himself on an electric blanket, he had for years."

"What a way to die."

"No, Nat, he didn't kill Francis, but he caused her death, the smoke and the fumes, that's what killed her."

"Where is your dad buried?" Nathaniel asked.

"He's not buried, they cremated him at Lake Norman. I just never collected the urn. That's why I never visited his grave. He was never really buried. They just kept his urn for collection; I just never got around to collecting. Does that make me a bad person, Nat?"

"No, Beth, that just makes you human. I hate to ask this question, but where is Francis now?"

"Francis was cremated at the same time as Daddy. God help me, she's still there! How can I ever forgive myself for that, for cutting myself off for so many years? They are both still in the Lake Norman Crematorium."

The morning light slowly crept in through the two kitchen windows, it was 7.30 a.m. Nat was making breakfast, bacon, eggs and pancakes. "Honey, the coffee's hot, get your ass downstairs, before this goes cold."

"Nat, forgive me, I am so embarrassed about last night," Beth said as she walked into the kitchen. "Honey, I think you might have been right about this house. Something in it brings out the honesty in us."

"Sit down, I got breakfast, what would you like?"

"How can you take all that has happened so lightly?" Beth asked.

Nat walked over to Beth and took her in his arms. "Beth, I love you so much, I can't imagine what you must have gone through."

"The time we have spent here has bought out more of me than I could have imagined," she said

"Beth, have breakfast, then let's take the day off." At 9:00 they got into the car and headed to the beach, leaving the old house and their problems behind them. They pulled into a municipal car park, and Nat put $2 in the machine. The park was right down on the beach. Nat got the towels and Beth got the cooler. They picked a spot just below the beach guard's station. Beth laid out a large towel while Nat ran down to the ocean. She covered her self with coco butter sunscreen. Nat took his mask, snorkel and flippers and went down to the sea and dived in. God, that water felt good. The ocean was warm that day. He dived down 10 feet, came back to the surface, then dove down another 15 feet. Man, that felt so good, he thought. He was on a roll. He hadn't felt this good in years. The water made him feel so alive. Today he was born again.

"Beth, we really have become close, haven't we?"

"This time we have spent together has made me realize how much you mean to me."

Nat lay down beside her and kissed her full on the lips. They held each other for what seemed like an eternity. "Honey, let's eat in."

"I'm not dressed, Nat."

He smiled. "There's a Tiki bar at the beach, look!"

They held hands and walked off the sand onto the tarmac. On the car park it was very hot, 90 degrees. Beth laughed at Nat as he jumped on the hot ground. Nat hadn't put his sandals on, Beth had them in her beach bag. She threw them down for him to put on. In the center of the car park was a small Tiki bar and restaurant chairs and tables under umbrellas draped around a bar. They crossed the car park and walked up the three steps onto the deck. The air immediately seemed cooler. They both felt a relief from that sun. Nat pulled two stools from the bar and they sat down and felt a 20% drop in temperature and immediately began getting comfortable. A blond in her early 30s with an ample bosom and more than a friendly smile, said, "What can I get you guys?"

Beth said to Jenny (as she had seen her name on her Tee Shirt), "Can we get two burgers and fries with ketchup, two Diet Cokes, and hold the chips!"

"I haven't seen you guys around here before," the girl said to them.

"No, we are just tourists."

"Where are you from?"

"UCLA."

She gave them their Cokes and went back to the kitchen. "We should do this more often," Nat said.

"What's that, act a bit more like human beings?"

"Beth, hold that thought," he said as Jenny arrived with their burgers, and said, "Enjoy, guys."

They ate like it was a feast, then returned home in Nat's dark blue Kia SUV. As they crunched up the drive, Nat said, "You know, Beth, I thought this house would be frightening but it now has quite a warm feeling. Like, home."

Beth looked up at the front of the house and said, "Nat, it's lit up like a Roman candle."

Something about the three-story building left Beth with a feeling of foreboding. They walked onto the front porch where the moths and mosquitoes fought to be the lucky ones to be consumed by the bright lights. Beth wondered why they spent so much time in competition to see who's the first to fry. This house has more light than the Empire State Building, she thought. "Whoever built it must have had a terrible fear of the dark," said Beth. "Whoever constructed this mausoleum with all these windows and lights must have had a paranoia for a three-story building."

"No, Beth, this is only two stories."

"What about the attic?" she asked. "I'll never forget that floor."

"I guess you could count the attic as a floor," he conceded.

"It seemed like a pretty big floor to me," Beth said. "Nat, it's only four in the afternoon and all the lights are on."

"I know, Honey, as long as we don't have to pay the bills, I don't care."

They walked through the front door down the hallway and into the kitchen. "Why is it we always, no matter what size the house, retire to the same room?"

He didn't answer, he just said, "I'll put the coffee on, Honey."

"Please, Nat, no more coffee, I need a drink."

"That's unlike you, Beth."

"Give me a break," she snapped, "this house is no holiday camp!"

"Don't over react, Babe, I know that what you experienced must have been traumatic."

"Cut the crap, Nat. I just want a drink."

Without another word he went to the fridge and pulled out a bottle of Brandy. "Just saving it for a rainy day," he said.

"I think you mean medicinal purposes."

They both went quiet and looked into each other's eyes. Then Beth said, "Nat, do you smell that?"

"Dear Lord, is that from the laundry?"

"More like the sewer," she said.

Suddenly, they heard the car alarm, WI-IOOER--- WOORER--- WOORER EY ARE---ERARE! They both ran out to the driveway. The alarm stopped as soon as they got outside the front door.

"What's going on, Beth?"

"I'm not sure, but I think we are about to find out."

Nat turned off his car alarm. Then they both ran back into the house. The smell was unbearable. "Nat, what is that smell?"

"I think it's the smell of death," he said. A vibration moved slowly over their minds and into their souls. They heard a loud crash, like breaking glass.

"Quick Beth!--- it must be the conservatory."

They ran into the conservatory. There was no damage; everything was as it should be.

"What's going on? I think something is about to start."

At that moment everything stopped. No smell. No vibration. No noise. Beth quietly asked, "Has it gone?"

Nat looked perplexed. "I don't know if it was really here."

They held each other like there was no tomorrow. That is when the temperature changed. It must have gone down to 20 degrees. The air as they spoke came out like frozen fog. "Something is certainly not right, Beth."

"You must be kidding me, this is really fucked up."

A sound touched their ears, smooth at first, like ahumm! "That sounds like bees," Beth said.

"No chance. That only happens in the movies."

"Is it really this cold or are we imagining this."

A light bulb exploded, showering both of them with shards of glass. Without saying a word they ran back into the kitchen and the protection of light. "My God, what just happened?" Beth said.

The smell came back, this time with the pungent odor of rotting seaweed. "A pipe must have broke, Beth."

"You have got to be kidding me, that's no broken pipe and this is no Hollywood Movie. This is the real thing."

"Don't let your imagination get the best of you, Beth, there's always an explanation."

"Bullshit, I can smell rotten fish and seaweed. You want to tell me where that's coming from?"

The light in the kitchen started to dim and then came back on. The temperature came back to normal. "Why do I get the feeling that this is only just the beginning," Beth said.

"Wait, be quiet! Listen, what's that sound?"

They listened, and at first the sound was faint, as though it were on the breeze. "What is that sound?" Nat pleaded.

"It's children, and they are crying," she replied.

"Are you sure, it seems so far away?"

"That sound, I have heard it before in my dreams and nightmares."

Nat threw his arms around her. The sound slowly grew louder. It was a young boy and girl crying. Nat went to the cupboard and got a flashlight. "There must be a simple answer to this, Beth, let's look in the conservatory."

They held each other and walked back into the room. As they walked through the kitchen door into the darkness, the crying became more profound. "It's the twins, Nat, I just know it is!"

"Calm down, Beth, there's a simple answer to all of this."

Beth shivered as they inched their way forward. "I don't feel threatened, but I am frightened. There's a sadness to this house that goes right down to its foundations."

A moment later a high-pitched scream destroyed the fabric off their thoughts. Beth felt ice-cold fingers walk down every vertebrae in her spine. Nat's brain stopped functioning. He had never been this frightened in all his life. Beth said, "Nat, you're shaking."

They both smelled fear. "What the hell was that," they said in unison. The cry came from the garden by the lake.

"There's no way I am going out there, Beth, not right now. Let's go to bed and face this in daylight."

"We can't walk away now," Beth insisted. "We must find what's going on."

"Beth, I brought you here to research the paranormal, but I never expected this."

"We are here together, Nat, so let's do it."

They held hands and ran through the conservatory and into the garden. The garden and lake seemed quiet and serene, not a soul around. Their eyes came to rest on the lake. The water had a calming effect as though nothing was ever out of the ordinary, totally sublime and calm. At this point they both relaxed a little.

"This can't be happening, Nat, it must be a nightmare and we are going to wake any minute."

Nat agreed. "Tomorrow everything will seem so normal and this will be a bad dream."

They suddenly noticed a mist, or more like a fog, arising from the lake. The cloud of mist came towards them.

"Wow, what's that smell?" she said.

"It's sulfur, Babe, coming from the lake."

"No, Nat, I know that smell, it's Black Powder, my Dad used to shoot ducks with an old Percussion Gun. He was a black powder enthusiast. Dad would go down to Lake Okeechobee in Florida duck hunting. Now and then he would take Francis and I to a muzzle-loading club he belonged to. That smell, I don't think I would forget it, the odor of rotten eggs."

"You want to tell me what gunpowder smoke is doing in the garden," Nat said. "There haven't been any explosions."

Beth's only reply was, "I think we are about to find out why this house has never sold."

A strange noise slowly drifted from the weeds at the east side of the lake. "What's that noise?"

"Quiet, Beth! I think it's children crying."

"Oh, this just gets better," Beth said.

Then something happened that froze their souls to the ground. A scene that seemed like it came from some surreal nightmare unfolded in front of them. Two young children, a boy and girl who Beth knew as the twins, appeared. They seemed to swim right before their eyes. The children walked or floated just above the ground. "Am I really seeing this or is it some illusion?" Nat said.

"Now you know what I saw." The twins' heads turned and looked directly at Nat and Beth. Their eyes pierced into their very being. "HELP US," Beth heard them say.

"I never saw anything like this in any investigation, I ever did," Nat said.

Beth was staring at the children. "I think they are trying to tell us something!"

"Honey, the only way I want to communicate with this apparition is through an exorcist."

"Nat, please, I feel they are trying to tell us something in some way."

"For God's sake, Beth, they are ghosts."

"Is that what you believe?"

"Don't you think they may just be spirits trapped on the earth? Maybe they need help!"

The apparition floated on across the grass and into the night. "They spoke to me, Nat"

"What did they say?"

"HELP US."

"God, don't you know that's in every movie."

"Please, Nat, this is not a game or a dream. These children need help!"

"Are you sure it's not us that needs help?"

"I believe we have a job to do here," she said resolutely, "and I don't think it's going to be easy."

"I came here to write, not save the spirits of long lost children."

"Don't you see, Nat, it's not just the children, there is a lot more here than the children. There is some kind of memory in this building."

"What do you mean?"

"Do hauntings go on this long and this diversified?"

"I really don't see what your getting at, Beth."

"It's simple, there are just too many ghosts!"

"Let's get back inside, we really need to talk."

They walked back inside happy to be away from so many horrific apparitions. They went back through the conservatory into the kitchen.

"Let's go to bed, Beth, and talk about this in the morning!"

They hardly slept a wink, drifting in and out innumerable times throughout the night.

In the morning they awoke with what seemed like a hangover. "I've felt better after two bottles of Jack Daniels," Nat said.

"What the hell happened last night?" asked Beth as she put on her robe. "I think that we are about to get into more than you expected,'"

"Honey, we really need to talk."

"What about, Nat, you came here to study the paranormal, I just came along for the ride".

Nat didn't seem amused. "That may have been the way things started out but you know a lot has changed since then."

"I don't know where this is going, but I do know I am going to follow it through to the end," Beth declared.

"Honey, this has become a joint project."

"Can you live with that, Nat?"

"You better believe it," he replied.

"I know that I am not a university professor, but on this trip I am all you've got."

"Honey, a man could never wish for more. I believe that two spirits belong together. It may be that you and I may be two such spirits."

Beth frowned. "Forgive me for repeating myself, but I still think that is bull shit."

"Wait, Beth, give it time! After what we saw last night what else can we think?"

"I tell you what I think, this place has its own spirits. Now tell me again, why are we here?"

""You and I have a relationship, I think we both know that, Beth. I never expected this to happen and you were never meant to be part of this. My only dream for you was a holiday, not part of this. But it happened."

"So where do we go from here?"

"I have only one thing to ask you, please be my wife?"

"In our world or theirs, Nat?"

Beth then broke down and cried. In fact, she didn't just cry she sobbed.

"Beth, what's wrong, this is so out of character for you?"

"What do you think, I am a machine?"

"No, Beth, this just makes you human!"

"Is that what you think, more human? Nat, I'm a woman and I have just seen two ghosts, who where children and they were asking for help. I don't believe this is a paranormal investigation anymore, it seems to me it's more like a rescue mission."

"You mustn't get personally involved, Beth."

She didn't seem to be listening. "Have you ever encountered this kind of a haunting before?"

"No. Never! Not this plain and open."

"You mean you have never seen a true haunting before?"

"I guess not!"

"Don't you understand, Nat, this is the real thing. It's not just those children, what about all the other apparitions? The boy in the attic, the noise, the smell, the gunpowder, all the windows in the place, all the light..."

"I know, Beth, it's kind of scary, but you know there's enough material here for a whole book."

"Is that all you are thinking about, a book, what about those children?"

"Don't you see, Beth, they are dead, we don't even know if they ever existed."

"So let's find out," she said. "Wouldn't that make an even better book?"

"OK, Honey, let's start at the library, the one in town should tell us all we need to know."

They finished their coffee, got into Nat's SUV and headed to the library. They arrived at Calhoun Street just off Washington Street at 11.a.m. The Colonial style building stood out from its more modern counterparts. They walked to the front desk. A woman in her late 50s met them with a sweet smile. "Hi! What can I do for you folks?"

"Ma'am, we need some background information on a family that has lived in this town for 300 years."

"Well, that should be easy," replied the librarian. "Who were they?"

"The family's name is Remington. The house is on Bush Grove Lane."

"You mean Remington Manor?" she said, with not quite so much of a smile.

"Yes, that's right, do you know it?"

"I know of it."

"What we really need is any information on haunting and strange happenings that have taken place over the years?"

The woman looked at them suspiciously over her half glasses that she wore on a chain. "What did you say your name was?"

"Nathaniel James."

"Well, Mr. James..."

"Nat, please."

Her tone of voice was not as pleasant as before. "Well, Nat, you picked the right house to chase haunting, Remington Manor must be the most haunted house in the South, possibly the North as well. I suggest you contact all the local newspapers, check their records, I'm sure you'll find what you need. Try the Internet, there must be a world of information on that house. I would imagine it must be a well documented family."

"Thank you for your help. I never got your name?"

"Jane. If I can be of any more assistance please don't hesitate."

They left the library and went straight back to Remington Manor. Arriving back on the gravel driveway at 1.30 p.m. Nat said, "Home sweet home."

"This may be home right now, Nat, but there's nothing sweet about it."

"Well, I need to get to work," he said.

"Nat, you go to the computer, I will be glad to see what you come up with. In the meantime I'm going to take a good look around while it's still light."

Nat went into the study to work on his computer. Beth walked through the kitchen into the conservatory. She had walked halfway through the conservatory when she suddenly stopped. She froze on the spot. "Oh no, not again, not in the daylight!"

She felt her stomach tighten. A noise reached Beth's ear's, the sound of scraping. She held her breath as long as she could.

Just as she thought she was about to pass out, a vision saved her life. A man in his late seventies stood to her far left. Beth walked over to the man. "Are you the gardener?"

"Yes, ma'am."

He had an accent, Beth thought, must be Spanish. "Hello! My name is Beth, have you been working here long?"

The first impression Beth gleaned was that the man was very shy or maybe illegal. "What is your name?"

"My name is Charles, ma'am."

Beth thought, *More like Chavez.*

"I have worked here for 22 years."

"In that time have you see anything strange?"

Beth watched his expression as she said, "GHOSTS."

Charles became agitated. "I don't know what you mean, ma'am."

He turned and stooped to fill two pots with soil and whatever his secret mix was.

"Charles, my partner and I," Beth thought, how's that for diplomacy, "we are here to make a log or try to document the strange things that happen in this house."

He looked nervous. "There is not much I can tell you, ma'am, I don't see anything."

"So, Charles, you have never seen the twins?"

Charles face crumbled inside itself. His eyes gave away his soul. Beth could see right away that he was very uncomfortable with her question.

"Charles, have you seen the twins?" She knew that he knew what she meant

"I have seen many things while I have been here, ma'am."

"Please, it's Beth," she said, hoping to make things a little more informal.

"Ma'am, it's just an empty house. When you're on your own in an empty house your imagination can sometimes get the best of you."

"Where are you from, Charles?"

"Cuba, Ma'am."

"Please, Charles, help me out here. You're telling me you've worked here 22 years and you've never seen the twins?"

At this his attitude changed. "Ma'am, over the years I have seen many things, but this is an old house and you would expect that. But the twins that you talk of, who are they?"

She could see that he wasn't telling the truth. His eyes held the specter of fear.

"Charles. I know that you have seen them. Please tell me."

"Beth, is that your name? I have seen many things, sometimes alone a man let's his imagination get the best of him."

"You have seen them, haven't you?"

"Once, maybe twice, but they don't really exist, do they?"

"You tell me, Charles, do they?"

"Please, Ma'am, I only work here. When I first came to work here I was told that I might see things that I wouldn't understand… it is not easy for people like me."

"I totally understand," Beth said with reverence.

"When I first came to your country I had nothing, just the clothes on my back. I was lucky to get this job. In my country there are many superstitions, that is the way we live. My wife and I are paid well to look after this house, and we have done a good job. We clean, look after the garden and take care of things. We don't ask questions."

Beth smiled. "I am not from the INS," she said. "But we really need your help."

Charles looked into Beth's eyes. "If I can help, I will."

"Tell me about the twins."

"There is more than the twins. In my country this house is called El Frecuentar. In your country you call it haunted. There are many things that we don't understand about this world and never will. Things happen here that defy comprehension, and maybe we shouldn't try."

She wasn't about to settle for such an abstract answer. "What have you seen, Charles?"

"Mostly children," he replied, and then he seemed to turn off. Beth thought it best not to pursue it, so she left Charles and walked into the garden.

This must have been some place way back when, she thought. Beth exited the conservatory and walked down to the lake. This time she walked past the seat and around the west side of the lake. She kept going south, the air was warm and she felt good. As Beth came to the south side of the lake she noticed at the far side of the lawn a structure, like a small building. Excitedly she walked on to investigate. "OH MY GOD!" she said to herself, "This must be the family tomb." At that moment a fear like she had never known before spilled into her system. There's no way I'm going in there, Beth thought.

She turned and walked back to the house. As she walked through the conservatory she noticed Charles had gone. Beth made her way to the study where Nat was working. As she opened the door, he turned and said, "Babe, you won't believe what I've found."

"Thrill me, Nat."

"This place has such a rich history, I can't believe it!"

"Tell me about it," Beth said. "You have found things that people can't explain, right."

"You have no idea."

"Yes, Nat, I think I do."

There was excitement in Nat's voice as he spoke. "There are documented hauntings that go back 250 years. There are so many it's hard to catalogue them all."

Beth said, "Tell me one thing, are they all children?"

"How did you know that?"

"Come with me, Nat, right now!"

Beth led him through the kitchen and to where she met Charles in the garden. "Where are you taking me?"

"Just follow me."

It was mid afternoon and the sun was high and insects buzzed in the breeze. "Where are we going Honey?"

"Trust me, Nat, just follow me."

They walked around the lake and down to the tomb. "The answer we are looking for, I believe, is here." The concrete sarcophagus lay before them. It was a foreboding place. Time had taken its toll.

"Beth, this must be where the family rests!"

The front of the concrete grave had a door that looked like it would take TNT to open. "This must be the family grave?"

"I think in there we'll find the answer to most of our questions," Beth said.

"How do we get in without a key?"

"Let's try the door!"

They tried the door but it held fast, no movement. "Now what, Nat?"

They both noticed an inscription on the door. TO ALL THAT ENTER LIFE IS ONLY A DREAM.

"What do you make of that?" Beth asked.

"I guess that's just someone's joke from the 18th century."

"I hope it doesn't mean what I think it might."

"What's that, Beth?"

"When we enter we leave the dream of life behind and enter a nightmare!"

"Well, you proved one thing," Nat said.

"What's that?"

"You called the house a mausoleum and now you've found the real thing."

"You think all of this is funny?"

"No, Beth, but you must admit it does have a certain irony."

"Listen," Beth said, "it's three in the afternoon. I don't intend to enter this place in the dark."

"Then let me make a suggestion."

"And that would be?"

"Let's start first thing in the morning, then we have all day."

"O.K. it's a date, let's leave this crypt and go home. I tell you one thing, Nat, I won't stay up all night looking forward to it."

They went back to the kitchen, their chosen room. "Honey, I have something we should both look at. It came of the computer, the Internet. It seems you were right, this house does have a history. I contacted all local newspapers as far back as I could go. This house has a history of haunting that goes back forever but it seems they all have one thing in common."

"Let me guess," Beth said. "They are all children!"

"Correct, with the exception of just one. Take a look at this, I found it by accident." Nat handed Beth a piece of paper. At the top, she read: *Greenville Gazette, 1751, August 10th. On the night of Tuesday, August 9th, on the property of Judge Niles Remington, a devilish and Godless incident occurred. It was reported by several black workers who at that time where involved in digging and constructing a family crypt, for the good Judge and his God fearing Family.*

At that point Beth stopped reading and looked at Nat.

"I suppose by black workers they mean slaves?"

"Remember, Honey, this plantation was built by slaves."

"Yes, I know," she said, but it still makes me so mad that people were treated so badly."

"But, Hon, Remington was known to be a good owner."

"How can you even use that word, owner?"

Nat said, "Because that was then and this is now, it's just the way things were. It's just like the Roman games, it happened even though we didn't like it."

"Yes, Nat, but we must never get complacent; remember, it's not so long ago."

"Honey, thanks for the history lesson, now can we get back to the article."

Beth started to read again. *The workers, as distressed as they were, spoke of terrible abominations that came out of the bowels of the earth, like a fire breathing dragon.*

"You've got to be kidding me, a fire breathing dragon?"

"Beth, you know how people reacted back then. Everything out of the ordinary was the Devil."

"Yea, but a fire breathing dragon?"

"Remember the Salem witch trials of 1692? It was all out of nothing, yet they hung 19 people, 4 died in prison and one was tortured to death by stones being placed on his chest. Can you believe it took him two days to die! That's what your dealing with, Beth, religious hysteria. Everything to these people, at that time, came out of the earth and belonged to the Devil."

Beth went back to the paper. *The terrible thing these poor workers described is hard to imagine. First came a flash of fire, then a noise like thunder and the awful smell of brimstone.*

"Nat, they just described an explosion."

"Yes, that's what I thought, except for the next passage, read on."

The workers from the plantation were settled down, those that would not settle experienced the lash."

"How barbaric!"

"No, just a sign of the times!"

"OK, Nat, tell me the significance of all this."

"Don't you see? Think of what have we experienced, mostly sounds and smells. Go on, read the last part."

All that witness this abomination said that they also saw a headless phantom and a fire-breathing dragon.

Beth was incredulous. "Come on, Nat!"

"Beth, that's the only report that I can find that refers to an incident other than children! I know it's very old, but there is truth hidden in this old script. Anyway, enough off all this; today, remember, we still have a life of our own. Let's eat."

"I agree, she said. "Let's leave the demons till tomorrow".

They called Dominos and ordered the biggest pizza they had and two six packs of beer. It arrived thirty minuets later. "Let's eat in bed, Nat." They took the food and drink to bed and locked the world and the outside away. They eat the pizza and drank the beer, held each other and went to sleep.

The Crypt

The next morning they didn't speak much, they just did what they had to do. Went to the bathroom, took a shower, and brushed their teeth. "So, how do we do this, you are in charge," Beth said.

"Oh no you don't, you are now in this as deep as I am. I suggest we put together a tool chest and just go for it."

Beth said, "Do you think we should take a picnic and a bottle of wine?"

"No need for sarcasm. "Let's drink our coffee and get the show on the road."

They walked from the kitchen through the conservatory into the garden with a very unsettled feeling. "Are you really sure you still want to do this, Beth?"

"It's not what I came here for, but it's what I want to do." As late as it was there was still a fog on the ground, more a mist really. They walked down through the grass and southwest of the lake. They walked through long grass and trees down to where the stone burial chamber stood.

"OK, Einstein, where do we begin?"

"We have to open this door."

"First look at the inscription, it must give us a clue." ALL THAT ENTER LIFE IS ONLY A DREAM. "Beth, use your logic, tell me how to get in?"

The vault was 18 feet wide, 15 feet long and 9 ft. high. "You know, it seems strangely disproportionate, it seems wider than it is long."

"Never mind that for now, let's concentrate on getting in."

The front was stone, but the doors seemed like they were made from granite. Beth turned to Nat. "You got tools."

"Yes, a hammer, flat bar and small pry bar."

Beth leaned on the doors, and the one on the right opened. For such a large and heavy door it seemed to open very smoothly. The first thing to hit them was the smell, heavy pungent odor of mold and age and old cloth mixed with things that had been rotting for a very long time. Things that had been dead for a very long time. They tuned on their flashlights and were surprised to find steps leading down.

"Take it easy, Beth!" Nat said as he shone his flashlight around the chamber. Now Beth could see why the vaults shape was so disproportionate, it ran at an angle down into the ground. Before they walked down the steps Nat said, "Hold it right there. Don't go any farther until we take stock of our situation."

Nat looked to the right of the door and caught sight of a light switch. There were three steps down into the crypt, but they took none. "Beth, I have seen too many films to make this mistake, we don't move another muscle, until we lock open that door!"

Nat put all the tools he had in the doorway and jammed the door. Then they felt free to investigate the tomb. Nat threw the switch and the lights came on. The illumination hurt their eyes at first, then they saw the inside for the first time. It was dark, dank and foreboding like the grave with light.

"Nat, this is a place I don't want to be!"

"Hold it, Beth, we have to investigate?"

"I don't like this place!" Beth said, her voice rising.

"Babe, remember, this is what we are here for."

They slowly moved down the steps and looked around. The floor was a stone slab, which gave a feeling of cold and things long time past. The air around them felt oppressive. There was an odor of times before. Beth felt an urge to scream, but she suppressed it and she almost gagged. "Nat, this is not a good place."

"Honey, don't let your fears get the best of you."

"You must be kidding, you know where we are?"

"We are in a God damned burial chamber for Christ sake! This place is full of corpses."

At that moment a chill ran through Beth's very soul, she felt like her soul had been put in a freezer. "The children are here!" she said.

"What do you mean?"

"The three children are here, I know they are."

"What children?"

"The ones that I have seen."

"Honey, take control, this is only a crypt."

"No, Nat, its far more than that, it's where they are."

"Please, Beth, help me understand."

"Don't you see," she said, "this is where they are, this is where they exist. This is their world. If ever there was a place I don't want to be, this is all of them."

"Let's look around," Nat said, determined not to allow Beth's fear to stop him.

They moved to the bottom of the steps and looked around. The chamber was deep and long, it sloped at angle and seemed to go subterranean. The air was cold and clinging. "Wow! Who needs this? Let's get out of here."

"Not yet, Beth, let's look around."

They moved forward into the chamber. "Can you feel the cold?" Beth asked.

"Yes, Honey, but remember we are underground."

"This is different, Nat, this is like a fridge."

"Out there it's 70 degrees, down here it's below freezing."

"Hold on, don't let your mind run away. Take control, this is the 21st century."

Beth said, "This is not Star Wars, this is now."

They moved forward through the tomb. Their eyes had now adjusted to the light, and as they got to the bottom steps they noticed that to their left and right were stone squares burial tombs with no names. From the walkway they were stacked two high on both sides. They walked past ten graves, before the first inscription. Beth stopped in her tracks and turned a whiter shade of pale. "Oh my God! Nat, look at this."

On the slab an inscription read. "HERE LIES THE SMALL BODY OF A CHILD OF GOD. HIS NAME ON THIS EARTH WAS JONATHAN REMINGTON, AGE 6. HE DEPARTED THIS EARTH AUGUST 30th, 1917. MAY HIS SOUL REST IN PEACE.

"Nat, that's the boy in the attic! Don't you see I can't take much more of this bull shit?"

"Get a hold of yourself, girl, I don't see any ghosts, do you?"

Beth started to hyperventilate.

"Calm down, Honey there's no reason to get carried away, so far I don't see any spooks or gremlins, just a room full of dead history."

Beth regained her composure and they moved on down the aisle; on both sides, the story was the same. IN LOVING MEMORY, I WILL MISS YOU ALWAYS, NEVER TO BE FORGOTTEN. Row after row of dead memories. As they came to the end of the walkway they noticed another set of stairs at a right angle, this time six steps. With trepidation they walked down to the next level. The cold now became almost unbearable. After traversing the short stairwell they entered the next level. More square sepulchers adorned the walls. Each one had on its own testament of life lost. Beth looked at each one and read each sad story, she felt each one touch her heart. "So many lives, Nat, so much history. The whole family lies here. I feel like an intruder, in their world"

"No, Beth, that is not our mission here, let's see it all!"

At the end of the second level, Nat called Beth over to the left wall. "Look at this!"

Beth read their names and wept. On the top layer side by side were the names of two children, JONATHON AND CLARE REMINGTON.

Beth stopped and her eyes began slowly to transverse from one side of the aisle to the other. She felt her brain slowly shut down. At first she thought she felt fear, then she felt another emotion, an overwhelming tide of sadness and despair. Instead of the horror she had expected, she had a feeling of love, and a strange kind of warmth. "Nat, this is the twins!"

"I know, Beth. Let's move on.

"They tuned the comer and moved down to the next level. "Do you feel that temperature change?" she asked. "WOW! Look at these inscriptions! They are dated back to the 18th century. Look at this one, JONAS REMINGTON, 1780. HERE LIES THE BODY OF A MAN WHO LOVED HIS BROTHERS, BUT DIED AT THE HANDS OF OTHERS. MAY JONAS REST IN PEACE. HE GAVE HIS LIFE IN THE SLAVE UPRISING OF 1780. GOD WILL TEST US ALL.

They moved on. At the bottom of the vault they came to a grave they knew well. The grave of CAPTAIN NILES REMINGTON. "Beth, this is where it all began." He began reading the inscription. LORD CHIEF JUSTICE OF THE PROVINCE OF SOUTH CAROLINA, MAY HIS SOUL FOREVER PRESIDE OVER ALL THAT COMES BEFORE, IN THE YEAR OF OUR LORD, 1769.

"OK, Nat, I'm out of here!"

With that, Beth turned and made her way back to the surface, with Nat on her heals. They broke the surface at the same time. "I don't need any more of that," Beth said.

Nat put his arms around her and they walked home. As they walked around the lake Nat said, "Well, Honey, what do you think of that?"

"That scared me to death!"

"But Honey, nothing happened!"

"Is that what you think, Nat, that nothing happened? All those times that I told you about."

"No, Beth, of course I believe you, why shouldn't I?"

She looked him straight in the eyes. "If you don't, you must tell me now," she said.

"Beth, I really believe you but I must go back in there"

"No chance, Nat, wild horses wouldn't get me back in there."

"Let's go home," he said, "take a shower have dinner and talk about it."

"Nat, you really are an asshole!"

"Thanks, Babe, I really love you too."

By the time they got back to the house it was lunch time. "Beth, let's talk."

"Oh no! Not again."

"Please, Beth, give me a break, you know I need to research this place, and you did agree to help."

"Don't you hold me to ransom, Nathaniel."

Nat 's expression changed. "Wow, that's the first time in I don't know how long you called me by my formal name, this must be serious!"

"Nat, I came here with you to enjoy time together, to be with you while you worked, to take time out from my world. The last thing in the world I expected was to be caught up in it."

"Honey, that's the way the cookie crumbles. It seems to me you have become a channel, a link to this world. Like it or not you better learn to live with it. To change the subject to a lighter note, what would you like for dinner?"

"You know, you really are an asshole!" she said.

"Take's one to know one, Babe."

"Don't you Babe me," Beth joked. "How about you barbecue two rare steaks full blooded loaded with bad cholesterol, and if that doesn't give me a heart attack, this place sure will."

Nat had brought one of those cheap barbecues. It was called a hibachi or some other Japanese name. He put the barbecue just outside the door of the conservatory. "Now this is the way to live," Beth said as she put the glass of red wine to her lips.

Nat turned to the steaks. "Would you like yours rare, Ma'am?"

"I'll take it any way I can," she said with a laugh.

"You should be so lucky. Anyway, it's your turn to get the salad."

With that they both turned and walked back inside. Beth made the salad, while Nat poured the wine. "Nat, will life always be like this when we are married?"

"Who knows, Honey, I guess that's up to us."

They ate the steak and the salad and drank the wine. "What did you say?"

"What's that, Honey?"

"What did you say, Nat?"

At that moment Nat felt or rather sensed a change in the air.

"Do you feel that?" Beth asked.

"Yes I do and I don't have a good feeling about it."

The chairs they were sitting on seemed to move and shake. "This can't be happening, please tell me this is my imagination."

"If it is it's mine as well, Babe!"

A light bulb blew. There was a set of three over the dining table. One made a pinging sound and went out. "Just a bulb, Babe, no need to get shook up."

"Did you here that?"

"Yes I did, it sounded like it came from the stairwell."

They both rose and walked to the door. Neither wanted to admit any fear, only an interest in something odd. Beth was the first to open the door and walked into the hall. What met her shook her nerves ragged. Halfway up the first staircase stood the twins. Nat was right behind her. "Dear God!" he said, as he sucked in his breath.

"He won't help you, not this time, Nat. They are there for real!"

As they watched, the surreal apparition seemed to fade in and out of sight, moving like a dreamscape. "Please tell me this isn't happening, I don't think I can take any more."

"Hold it, Beth, this time we both saw it."

"You saw them?" she asked, surprised.

"As clear as I really wished I didn't!"

The apparition seemed to dissolve and fade. A wisp moved like a fading shadow from the stairs, down the hallway and into the conservatory. This time the form was more like a cloud moving in and out of reality. Both Nat and Beth saw them quite clearly. "Can this really be happening?"

"Yes, Nat, this time you see them!"

Nat took Beth by the hand, and as they made their way to the conservatory the mist seemed to float over the orchids and dissolve through the doorway. "We must follow them," Beth said.

They moved though the conservatory onto the lawn, and then a third specter appeared. Nat almost died. He shouted, "It's the kid in the chair, Beth."

In front of them they saw a child in a basket chair. Beth froze, trapped in time. Nat tried to shake her out of her trance. "Honey, snap out of it, let's follow them."

"Don't you see, Nat, that's what they want!"

"So what, if that's what they want, let's give it to them!"

Beth shook her head. "Don't you see, they're leading us to the crypt!"

"Beth, this is a chance in a lifetime, we must take it."

"That's all right for you to say, but I'm scared shitless."

They continued to pursue the faint mist across the lawn and around the lake. "Nat. I wished you weren't so enthusiastic about this."

"Come on," he insisted, "we must follow it up."

"At what cost, Nat?"

They followed across the lawn as close as they dared, slowly circling the lake careful not to get too close. "Tell me, Nat, what do we do when we get to the crypt?"

"I'm dammed if I know, but I know we can't stop now.""

"So much for caution," Beth said. Then she stopped dead in her tracks just on the west side of the lake. When Nat realized she had come to a halt he too stopped. Beth bent at the waist, her hands went to her knees and she gasped for breath. Nat also stopped for breath; they were only 10 yards apart.

"Nat, this is crazy, do you know what we are chasing?"

"Yes, something I have dreamed about for many years."

"For what, Nat? To settle an old score and to lay shadows to rest?"

"What do you mean?"

"You know what I mean," she snapped. "This is to prove that something beyond life exists, is this really that important?"

"Yes, it is to me, Beth!"

"Is it? Will it really lay a ghost to rest?"

"Don't, Beth, please don't go there!"

"I have to, Nat we depend on it."

"You mean you're holding me to ransom?"

"No, I'm asking you to please consider me now, like you said you did."

"Right now on the lawn?"

"Yes, please! I can't go back in there, not now, not today, not like this."

"For Christ sake, Beth, not now!"

"I have to, Nat, there's no way I can go back in that place!"

Darkness seemed to envelope them, and they both felt as if night had fallen prematurely.

"They are trying to take over our world," Beth said.

"Why, Beth, for what reason?"

"I really wish I knew. Somehow the children have tuned in to me for whatever reason, but I need a break today, I just can't go back into that place!"

He walked over to her and said, "Come on, Honey, let's call it a day."

As they started to walk home, Beth turned to Nat and said, "I am really sorry.

"What for, Honey?"

"For letting you down."

"No way, Beth, the truth is I didn't want to go back into that place any more than you. I think we should go home and discus this tomorrow."

"That's a deal," she said. "Thank you for understanding."

As they walked back across the lawn, Beth said, "Have you ever witnessed a haunting like this before?".

"No. I've investigated many strange happenings and paranormal behaviors. Most turned out to be either fakes, pranks or just plain trickery. Some were publicity stunts to promote hotels and stately homes. In fact, in two years I could count on one hand the amount that had any plausibility at all. One that does jump to mind took place in England at a stately home right in the center of the country. Although that case differed in as much as it was more poltergeist mischief than a straight out haunting."

"How did you come to be involved in England, Nat?"

"Before I answer that, Hon, please answer me a question."

"And that would be?"

"When you saw these apparitions did they speak; please, Beth, this is very important.".

"No, they never spoke."

"There were no communications at all?"

"No, that's not what I said. I said there was never a spoken word."

"Then how do you describe the communication?"

"No spoken words."

"You mean, Beth, a suggestion?"

"No, not at all. Nat, there was no little green men from Mars here."

"Post hypnotic thoughts!" he said.

"No, Nat , you're reaching!"

"Then please explain, Beth. They never spoke a word? Then how did you communicate?"

"We didn't."

"I don't understand, what do you mean they never spoke?"

"They just instilled in me a feeling."

"Can you explain this feeling?"

"No, Nat, the only explanation I have, it was as if they needed help."

"Did they tell you that?"

"No, Nat! I told you it was a feeling, more like a sense, I don't think I can really explain it. There were no words, it was like I always knew it. There was no sound, no words were spoken, I just knew, I understood."

"They never spoke, Beth?"

"What would you have me say, Nat?"

"Please, Beth, please tell me."

"They are ghosts, for Christ sake!"

"But they must have communicated in some way?"

"What do you think, I am some kind of fucking Medium?"

"Calm down, Honey, I didn't mean it like that."

"Nat, let's get some kind of angle on this, I have a suggestion. Please come with me, let me take you to my first sighting in the attic."

They walked back into the kitchen through the conservatory and into the house. From there into the hallway. "Beth, do you really want to do this?"

"No...but let's do it anyway!"

They started to ascend the stairs. As they reached the second floor, Beth turned to Nat and said, "OK. Baby, you are in my world now!" She pulled the stairwell down. As they stood inside, she said, "Well, how does it feel to be in my world?"

"There you go again, your world. You see, Beth, I think you have more contact than you are willing to admit."

"Please don't go there," she replied.

"Come on, Beth, you know you're more involved than you will admit."

"Why don't we just check out the attic?" she said.

They left the ladder and moved into the attic. Beth walked towards the chest she had opened when she had seen the boy who had drowned. Nat said, "Is this where you saw him?

"Yes, right there." She pointed to an area about six feet to their right. The floor was dark but Beth could see that there were no longer any water stains. She felt a cold shudder run down her spine. The feeling, unfortunately, had become all too familiar.

"How do you feel being here again?" Nat asked.

"I could live without it," she said. At that moment something stirred to their far left. "What was that?" said Beth

"Don't get upset, it's only the wind."

"Nat, first, there's no wind, second, we are behind walls in the fucking attic!"

"Please, Beth, there's no need for that language!"

Beth shook her head. "Sometimes I wonder which side of life you think you're on."

"Really? Please tell me, then, how many sides are there?"

"I guess you know the answer to that, Nat. I would think there must be two, our world, and their world."

"Please explain how you see that, Beth?"

"It's very hard to explain, but I don't believe they live on our plane, they live on some ethereal plane in between."

"Coming from you, Beth, I find that fascinating."

Beth sighed. "But it's so hard to understand."

"No, not at all, Honey. Frankly, it just frightens me."

"What, that I can see them and you can't?

"No, Beth, that you can see them at all!"

She arched her eyebrows. And why is that so strange?"

"What really worries me, Beth, is the fact you take it -so lightly."

"What would you have me do, run home to a mother and father I don't have?"

"You know I didn't mean that!"

Beth said, "OK, then, let's put the chickens in the basket."

"Say again?"

"You know what I mean, Nat, it's not easy for either of us to understand. But we have got to work it out together."

The sound came again from the east corner of the room. At first it was no more than a rustle of dust, then it turned into a scraping sound. "Do you hear that, Nat?"

"You bet your life, let's get out of here, Babe!"

They turned and moved towards the door. But to their exasperation a cloud of what seemed like thick smoke surrounded them. "What can that be, Nat?"

"I have only one answer for this, I saw this once before in England and I don't like it."

"What, Nat? What is it?"

"It's called ectoplasm!"

"You really got to be messing with me now?"

"No, Beth, this is the real thing!"

"You mean this is a ghost?"

"Not quite, this is ghost material."

"Please, Nat, I don't understand."

"Lets get out of here," he said.

The temperature was freezing as they made their way to the door. Beth went down first, Nat followed closely behind. They made their way back to their cozy little room in the kitchen. Both of them felt a need to come down.

"I have a suggestion."

"What's that, Nat?"

"Let's go home!"

"No. I am home. I need a drink and I don't mean wine!"

"There you go again, Beth, I think you need a break from this place."

"You're right about that, let's go get a bottle of Scotch."

"No, Honey, I mean a real break, time out."

"Is that what you would have us do, walk away? You came here to investigate this house and that's what we're going to do!"

"No, Beth, I came here to write an article on haunting and propose to you."

"You mean this was your idea of romance, Nat?"

"Wait Beth. Never in my wildest dreams did I imagine any thing like this."

"So you came here thinking you had a nice, easy assignment?"

"That's the reason I invited you along. If I had known any of this was going to happen I would never have asked you here."

"So from all your investigations you're still a non-believer?".

"That's not strictly true, Beth, I have seen many things but until now nothing really solid. It's very hard to accept all of this, I've witnessed many things but none as conclusive as this."

"Nat, did you witness anything unusual?"

"Like what?"

"Coming around the lake, a feeling, a smell, I had the feeling that something wasn't as it should be!".

"But, Beth, after all that has happened, how can you blame me?"

"Blame you for what?

"You do blame me, don't you?"

"Did you sense anything around the lake?"

"You really mean this, don't you, Beth?"

"Yes, I do. There is much more to this place than you can imagine.".

"How can you know this," Nat asked.

"May be I never will. One thing I do know, I have a connection with these children."

"How can you really know that, Beth?"

"Because I feel it. How else can I tell you?"

"I think we should leave this place."

"Don't you think it would be counter productive? Look, Nat, you brought me here, why should we leave now?"

"Because I believe you are becoming possessed."

"Oh, is that what you think," Beth snapped. "Go on, tell me about it."

"I believe that you have now become involved beyond your control. What frightens me is that they seemed to have chosen you as their medium."

"Is that so bad?"

"The answer to that is I don't honestly know. But I can tell you this, it sure as hell frightens me."

"You say you think I'm possessed. Who do you think I am, Reagan? Is my head going to do a 180-degree turn? Will I spew green slime?"

"Stop it, Beth, stop it right there!"

"What are you worried about? No one that I know of ever died from a haunting!"

"No, but a few turned up in asylums."

"Why be so negative, Nat?"

"Negative? Do you realize what's going one here?"

"Yes, Nat, I think I do, I think that that these spirits need help and honestly I'm not frightened."

"This is not a matter of whether or not you're frightened because if you're not you damn well should be."

"Don't you think we should investigate some more before we turn and run?

"Nobody is running, Beth, it's just that I am worried that you don't know what you are getting in to."

"Don't you mean what we are getting into?"

"Beth, you have never had any experience with haunting, it can play badly with your mind!"

"I think I have been through enough in my life not to be frightened by a few sad ghosts."

"It really isn't that simple. Let's stop right there. Honey, can I make a suggestion, remember I mentioned a time I spent in England?"

"Yes, you never finished that story."

"I followed a haunting in England, it was a house in central England, a manor house to be precise, I spent some time with a group of British psychic investigators."

"And what was the outcome?"

"Well, to be honest I found it quite enlightening. They were very good."

"Nat, where are we going here?"

"Why don't you let me give them a call?"

"Do you really think they would come all the way here from a phone call?"

"Its worth a try."

"Tell me, Nat, what could they do that we can't?"

"I'll tell you, they have equipment and technology we don't?"

"You really came here thinking there was no problem, you thought this was nothing more than a hoax? Nat, you deceived me!"

"No, Beth, I just thought this would be a good time for us to find each other."

"Nat, I want an agreement from you."

"What? Please don't go getting all dramatic on me," Nat said.

"No, Nat hear me out. I'm not asking you to sell your soul, just to give me a bit more consideration."

"That's not fair, Beth, the reason I asked you to come here in the first place was to ask you to marry me."

"I know that, and please believe me, I love you for it. I am so happy to say yes and I am so excited at the thought that you want me to be your wife. That will never change. But something else has come into the picture, these ghosts, apparitions or whatever else you want to call them. To me, Nat, they are children. Children who need help."

"Beth, I have to say that I am sorry, I was wrong. I understand you feel very strongly and I was wrong not to have seen that. Please forgive me?"

"There's no need for that, Nat, let's just move on and work together."

Nat took her into his arms and they kissed gently. They both knew at that moment that they had made a pact in Heaven. "Let's go to bed, Beth. I don't care what time of day it is."

Beth returned the kiss and said, "Leave the world outside, I think it's time to be happy."

The Twins

The night seemed to last forever, the most pleasure she could ever remember. If this was going to be their future she felt that this house and these children must be helped and sanctified. Beth had never been religious, after the loss of her sister Francis, the fire and her father, she knew she would never pray again. Beth also knew that Nat needed help although he would never admit it. She always knew that Nat had a problem coming to terms with his wife Linda's death. But that was his problem, she knew she couldn't help him put that ghost to rest. Beth felt for the first time in her life a feeling of belonging. At last she felt at home.

Stop it Beth, she thought, or else you really will be certifiable. Beth wondered if she really had a hold on the situation. Maybe Nat was right, she had become too involved. No, I must not think like that, I really do have a hold on reality. Wait, girl, isn't that the first thing a nut admits to herself? I tell you what, if I keep having these conversations with myself they really will lock me up!

It was 5.30.a m. Beth was looking in the bathroom mirror and she was happy with the person who looked back. Hey, girl, why don't you just lay back and enjoy this happiness, don't you think you deserve it?

But then Beth heard a noise downstairs. It seemed to come from the kitchen. She no longer felt any fear; she had witnessed too much happiness in this house. It was still dark as Beth walked down the staircase. She didn't wake Nat because she felt no threat, why should she? Close to the bottom of the stairs she noticed a strange glow emanating from the kitchen. At that point Beth begin to regret not having woken Nat. With slow trepidation she moved towards the kitchen door.

As she got closer the light seemed to dim slightly. Now Beth was aware of a growing fear rising in her stomach. She slowly opened the door and peered in. Her stomach went into a nose dive. Just behind the breakfast bar underneath the window stood the twins! They were bathed in a strange kind of surreal light, it was there yet it didn't seem real, a kind of florescent glow.

Beth thought she must be in a nightmare, and she had to pinch herself to make sure she awake. As she looked on she felt more than saw a terrible sadness. Beth knew that she should be frightened but she also knew she should face that fear. She walked through the door and looked directly at these lonely children. All Beth's fears immediately disappeared. The children did not, as she thought they might, evaporate. Beth knew right away that this was where she was meant to be. She looked directly at the figures, as they seemed to move in and out of her line of vision. She slowly moved forward into the kitchen. The children, to Beth's amazement, never disappeared. She now felt a feeling of total elation.

Beth heard a sound behind her and turned to see Nat standing in the doorway, wearing an expression of shock. Beth tuned back to the twins, and to her amazement they were still there. "Nat, please stay back, I believe they are trying to tell us something."

As they looked at the strange sight that met their eyes, Nat began to wonder if Beth was-not right and that she was a part of this strange enigma. As the twins seemed to look directly into Nat's eyes he felt a strange sense of sadness but for the first time in a longtime he felt a feeling he had thought he had forgotten, a feeling of intense love and loss for someone who had passed. In the time it takes for the heart to beat five times Nat lived a lifetime of sadness, and Nat knew sadness. Ever since Linda had gone he had a hole in his heart that you could put an ocean inside. Nat had a hole in his soul a place no one could penetrate. But for the first time since the accident he felt life coming back. Beth had been his savior. He now knew that he must move on. He would never forget Linda but he owed Beth a chance.

Nat shouted out in his mind, forgive me, Linda, and he felt and knew at the same time that she did. Nat felt or more, sensed, their life. He couldn't understand-what they were trying to communicate. He did know one thing they were trying to tell them something. "Beth, please help me. What are they trying to do?"

"They are communicating, Nat!"

"How, Beth?"

"Your mind, open your mind, empty your thoughts!"

"Would you please tell me how to empty my mind?"

"Can't you see, Nat, that they need help?"

"But I don't understand?"

"Nat, let me ask you a question. Please tell me how you felt after they appeared?"

"I still don't understand, Beth, please tell me in what context?"

"Goddamn it, Nat, how do you feel?"

"The truth, like I just got hit by a freight train!"

"Because you did, Nat, you got hit by the biggest train you could ever imagine."

"Please explain?"

"Tell me about the twins."

"Tell you what, Beth?"

"Tell me what you know."

"They died approximately 200 years ago, they had a rare blood disease. They loved each other very much and are trapped here in this house!"

Beth laughed out loud.

"Damn it, Beth, I don't understand."

"Then please tell me, Nat, how you know that the children are trapped?"

Nat looked hard at the floor and then slowly at Beth. "Good God! You're right, they did communicate, but I was too stupid to see. They are somehow trapped in between"

"I don'1 understand?"

"It's simple really, try to imagine two lakes divided by a dyke and you were an eel, what would you do? You would find your way in between. You would cross because you can breathe both water and air. Don't you see, Beth, the significance of what I am saying, they can move between two worlds, they never made it home!"

"Say again, Nat!"

"Don't you see? They never made it home!"

Beth said, "You mean they are trapped in two worlds?"

"No, Beth, just our world and the one in between. The world of shadows or as many people call it, the world of ghosts."

"So you admit there are ghosts?"

"Yes, Beth, but only to you."

"Would you do something for me, Nat?"

"And that would be?"

"Tell me about ghosts."

"What would you have me say?"

"The truth, Nat, only the truth?"

"How could I tell about ghosts? They exist in our imagination, they move through our world and theirs."

"I thought dead people go to heaven?"

"Do you, Beth, is that what you really think?"

"Nat, please forgive me, I didn't mean..."

"I know what you mean, and I do forgive you. Yes, I believe Linda went to heaven, at least I hold on to that thought, but unfortunately it seems there is a place in between."

"Why, Nat? Why unfortunately?"

Nat said, "You asked me, so allow me to tell you."

"I'm sorry, please carry on."

"In between is a flytrap a sticky paper that seems to hold on to souls. For some reason that really escapes me they can't move on, so I do believe in Heaven, I believe that there is something better. One thing in this life we need to hold on to is that there is a better life waiting for us."

"Is life so bad, Nat?"

"You asked me, Beth, but I think you missed the whole point."

"No, I'm sorry! I was out of line."

"No you weren't," Nat said. "You know probably better than me or at least as well the feeling of loss. In our hearts we know we will never see them again. We both know how hard that is to deal with. But these children, that's another story."

"Let it go for now, Nat, let's go back to bed!"

They went back to bed, but had a sleepless night. The next morning they awoke, but neither felt replenished. They both felt a need to find the truth. They sat over coffee and toast, and neither felt the need to talk. Both felt a void that they could not explain. There seemed to be an emptiness that they both felt but couldn't explain.

"Where do we go from here?"

"I have a question for you, Beth, do you love me?"

"You Know I do, Nat!"

"Then let's go to their world, let's meet them on common ground."

"You mean the crypt?"

"Yes, the place where they exist."

After breakfast, they left the kitchen and walked though the conservatory into the garden, then around the lake and down to the crypt. As they walked they looked to the far side of the lake and saw to their amassment a shadow that seemed to float alone the outskirts of the lake, a malignant, out of body shape that seemed to just float along on the breeze. As they reached the tomb they felt trepidation.

"I don't like this, Nat. Not this time. Something feels different."

They opened the door and entered. The chamber was cold, very cold. Nat and Beth moved down very slowly. This time they didn't feel so confident. They walked down the stairs into the grave.

"Nat, this doesn't feel so good!"

"I have to admit, Beth, this time there is a different feeling!"

The stones were cold, ice cold. They walked to the end of the first corridor and saw nothing. As they approached the second landing there seemed to be a mist, a cold mist. Not just cold but clammy. "Do you feel that, Beth?"

"Yes, I feel it. This time there is someone else that we haven't seen or felt before."

At that moment a frigid breeze ran over them. "Nat, this might be a good time to get out of here!"

"No, we came here to find answers!"

"At what expense?"

Suddenly mist appeared at the end of the walkway and started slowly to take shape.

"My God! Beth, it looks like a headless man!"

"This can't be happening?"

"You better believe it."

"Let's get the hell out of here."

"This time it's nasty, there must be something we can't see here, it's deeper than I imagined."

"I think we might need help."

"Is that what you think, Nat?"

"Don't you?"

"Let me tell you what I think, they need help! Not some half assed pseudo-psychic morons."

"You really don't know what you are saying."

"Fuck you, Nat, this is deeper than we could ever imagined."

"Beth, for God sake, you see what I see?"

"Yes I do and I am frightened, is this what we came here for?"

At that moment the headless man started to walk towards them. Nat said, "Oh my God, this is like some Boris Karlof movie!"

"No, this is real life!"

That's when the smell reached them. The foul stench of a dead body rotting in the room. Then they felt a cold that soaked in to their very souls.

"Let's get out off here, Beth."

"Not on your life, Nat. Stand your ground!"

He looked at her, perplexed. "What do you think this is, a battle?"

"Yes, that is exactly what it is! We are not going anywhere!"

Beth started to walk down the stairs.

Nat cried, "What are you doing?"

"I am getting rid of this shit." As she walked down the stairs, the apparition dissolved along with the putrid smell. Beth turned and walked back to Nat. "We need to know more of the history of this place, right back to the beginning," she said. "In my opinion, I think there is a malignant force that holds these children to this place and they can't escape."

Nat seemed dumfounded. "What do you mean Beth?" he asked

"I think sometime in the distant past something happened here that holds these children to this earth plane and they can't escape."

"Like what, Beth?"

"I think it has something to do with this house. Something that happened back when the place was first built!"

Nervousness creased Nat's face as he said, "Can we go back to the house now?"

"Not yet, I think we have missed something. A name, someone who doesn't belong to the family!"

"Like who?"

Beth said, "If I knew that I wouldn't ask!"

"Did we or did we not see a headless man? If we did, he's the one we should ask."

Beth nodded her agreement.

"So can we get out of here and find him?" said Nat.

"With pleasure, let's go."

They made their way back to the main house and left the cold crypt behind. Back in the kitchen Nat made coffee. "When I first asked about this house I came against a brick wall, but when I told them I was a Professor from UCLA, they seemed to warm a little!"

"Money talks, doesn't it?"

"No, Beth, it's not that simple."

"Come on, Nat, tell me it didn't help that Linda's Uncle was the Dean of UCLA?

"Don't go there, Beth, please."

She smiled. "You know I never would. But you must admit that these are different circumstances."

Nat did not return her smile. He said, "You promised that you would never bring Linda into this."

"That's right, she replied, "but you must admit this is different."

"In what way?"

"For God sake, we are living with ghosts, what more of a reason do you need? No one has investigated this house because they didn't have enough clout. On the other hand, you have managed to kick in the front door, I doubt there is another house anywhere in the world as haunted and as little investigated as this place."

"Is that so wrong, Beth?"

"Yes, it is yes, it damn well is!" She was clearly frustrated now. "When you and I first met, it was as equals."

"I don't understand, Beth?"

"Fuck you, Nat. Do you really know what you have done?"

"I don't understand Beth?"

"You have released the Demon from the pit."

"Don't be so melodramatic!"

"You were irresponsible, you did the unforgivable, you brought me, an amateur, into a frightening environment and you didn't even know you were doing it. This place is haunted, Nat! With both good and evil."

"Please give me a break, I never thought things would turn out like this."

"I'm sure you didn't," said Beth. "How could you have known this place really was haunted when you never believed in ghosts from the get go. When Linda died you lost yourself in an investigation that you were convinced from the start would never go anywhere. You hoped to bury yourself literally in an investigation that you never for one moment in the world of Peter Pan thought had any reality. You know where you went wrong? You never banked on finding the real thing that was the last thing on your mind. As for me, I think I was just baggage. Someone to keep things light, I guess I must be good at that. You never thought, did you, that you could be opening Pandora's Box?"

"Don't you think, Beth, that you may be a little over the top?"

"Are you religious, Nat?"

"I don't understand that question."

"Yes you do, just answer me!"

Nat drew in a deep breath. I think that I lost any belief in a God or Gods when Linda died." Nat sighed, put down his coffee turned and walked out of the room back to his computer. He turned it on and started to write. His heart wasn't in to it but he wrote just the same. He looked at the screen and started to document what he and Beth had witnessed that day. This time he found it hard to write. He seemed to have a mental block. The screen seemed to dim and then illuminate. He found it hard to concentrate.

Suddenly, the picture seemed to take on a life or it's own. Before his eyes a message appeared on the screen, LEAVE THIS PLACE!

He stopped dead, he must be dreaming. Then he read the rest of the message:

OR YOU WILL DIE!!!!

Nat composed himself, this is not happening. This must be my imagination. Then the screen turned deep green. Nat had never seen this happen before. He was taken completely aback. You must be joking, he thought. Get your head together, Nathaniel!

Then another message came up --- HELP US.

Without hesitation he turned off the computer and went to bed.

In the morning they both awoke to mixed feelings.

"Beth, last night when I was working at the computer a strange thing happened."

"You mean it showed you things you didn't understand?"

"It threatened me and then would you believe, it asked for help."

"I would believe any thing in this place, Nat."

"But not so long ago I would have said you were out of your tree."

"I have a suggestion to make, Beth."

"Hold it right there. Tel me, do you have a budget on this thing?"

"Do you mean money of my own or from the university?"

"Will you cut the crap, Nat, you know exactly what I mean."

"Then yes I do have a small allowance from the university."

"Just as I thought."

"It's quite normal in these circumstances."

"Man, now I really am waking up and smelling the roses."

"Please, Beth, you knew I was on assignment."

"Yes, but up until now I didn't realize just how important it was."

"Anyway, what is so important about my grant?"

"Oh, so now it's a grant?"

"Yes, Beth, a grant."

"You mean you proposed to me on a grant?"

"It's not like that, Beth."

"Oh yes it damn well is. I knew nothing of all this when I came here with you."

"But Beth, you came along for the ride, remember?"

"How can I forget?"

"Who could have known that things would have turned out like this?"

"Okay, how long do we have and how much do we have?"

"$10,000 and another six weeks."

"What, 10 grand and six weeks?"

"Beth, I didn't intend to use it all."

"Isn't that what money is for, to spend? Especially in a good cause like this?"

"I suggest we put our thoughts together, Beth."

"Nat, please tell me what you suggest, I await with bated breath."

"Stop it, I didn't orchestrate all this. Like you, I didn't know things would turn out like this."

"Maybe not, but I think we should deal with it like grown adults."

"What are you getting at, Beth?"

"I'll tell you what I'm getting at, this place is as haunted as it gets and you've got working money."

"As I see it we've got two choices: one, bring in help, two, do it ourselves."

"Either way I think we should follow it through."

"Is this because it's children in distress or do you have a real feel for ghost hunting?"

"Nat, I lost my sister when I was only eleven and the only thing that stopped me from going insane was the thought she had gone to a better place. These children are trapped here and obviously never had that chance."

"This is no crusade and I am no saint. Fate put us in this place for whatever reason and if there is any chance that I -we can help them, why not?"

"Nat, you have the experience and the means. On top of that you're also here to write an article. Don't you think that's all the reason we need?"

"Put so eloquently, Beth, how could I possibly refuse? So tell me your ideas."

"Okay, I don't think we should get outsiders too involved, that's not to say we don't use them. Let's just not tell them too much, keep the main facts to ourselves."

"I can go along with that."

"Also, Nat, we don't need too much of that fancy electrical equipment to find ghosts. We already know they are here."

"Point taken."

"I think what we need is good old-fashioned detective work. We need history of the place, history of the people, and most of all who is that headless man?"

"Well, Beth, that's plenty for a start. We need the Internet, the archives, and the library. I think also an historical architectural investigator."

"Wow, Nat, now we're cooking."

"My God, Beth, I don't believe the change in you."

"Is that so bad?"

"No, not at all, just strange to see. I have to admit I quite like it. Let's set tomorrow for D Day and what's left of today to relax and enjoy."

"What do you mean, Nathaniel, are you making suggestions?"

"No, Beth, I'm making a pass right out in the open and up front."

At that Beth moved closer and put her arms around Nat's neck. Their lips met tenderly but that didn't last long. Passion soon became their master. He felt her tongue searching the inside of his mouth. Nat felt a force that expanded his very soul. His hands reached under Beth's T-shirt and found the lock to his pleasure. In seconds Beth's bra was open. His hands moved to the front and lifted her T-shirt exposing those wonderful globes of delight. As he cupped them in his hands he felt the nipples swell and harden. He slowly dropped to his knees kissing her belly on the way down, his hands dropped to the buckle on her denim mini skirt. As he unfastened the belt his tongue gently moved around her navel.

Taking advantage, Beth slowly wriggled out of her skirt and let it fall to the floor. Without hesitation, Nat removed Beth's panties. He saw before him that mound of delight. Beth didn't shave. He liked it that way. He wasn't a man of clean-shaven or Mohawk tendencies, he liked to kiss the good old-fashioned bush. Nat moved his face forward and pressed his lips into that oasis nestled in a desert of skin. At that moment his right hand moved up the inside of her thighs, causing Beth to moan in delight. As he reached that soft damp area between her legs he slid his middle finger inside.

At this Beth let out a small cry. "Stop right there, Nat, unless you want it on the kitchen table or on the floor, I suggest we take this to the bedroom."

Nat took Beth's hand and with great haste led her up the stairs and into the bedroom.

Nat awoke to a very pleasant exhaustion and looked at his watch. It was 1:24 p.m. He felt slightly hungry. "Hi honey, what's for dinner?" When Beth didn't reply, he turned and to his chagrin, Beth wasn't there. An immediate coldness entered his stomach. He climbed out of bed and walked into the hallway calling Beth's name. Nat walked down the stairs and into the kitchen. Beth was nowhere to be found.

Nat knew right away where she was. He ran through the conservatory and into the garden, still no Beth. He ran past the Lake and down to the crypt. The door was open so he went inside. At that moment his worst fears where realized. Beth stood with her back to him. She seemed to be rooted to the spot. Nat called out her name but Beth didn't respond. She was in some kind of comatose state. All at once Nat knew this was what Beth meant when she said she was here for a reason.

"Beth, talk to me!" Nat cried out. Beth only made a sound like a horse drinking water. "Please, Beth, talk to me!" Nat smelled as much as he could feel the cold. It moved like a mist, like a fog, like something out of a Charlton Heston movie. Nat heard a sound, a noise coming from below. As he looked down the steps into the crypt, he felt he was looking into the abyss. At the bottom of the steps and halfway along the corridor stood the headless man. Nat began to realize at last what had happened. He must have been mad to bring her here, he should have known from the start. Nat had suspected for some time now that Beth had become too involved. But he never imagined she had gone this far. Beth stood there totally oblivious to Nat's presence.

"Beth, please, Beth, answer me."

Beth slowly turned and seemed to acknowledge Nat. As she did he noticed a strange thing happening. The aspersion slowly dissolved.

"My God," Nat cried, "she seems to be in some kind of trance."

Beth dropped to the floor, just as Nat reached her. He scooped her up in his arms. Nat felt his temperature change again. This time, he almost passed out. He pulled Beth into the fresh air, as much for him as for her.

"Come on, Honey! Pull out of it!"

Beth's eyes were still a little blank, but he could see she was coming around fast. Beth was half sitting, half lying. Nat had his arm around her back, holding her upright. He gently slapped her face.

"Are you all right, Beth?"

"What happened?"

"You tell me, Babe. I woke up, you weren't there, I somehow had a feeling you might be here. Tell me what you remember."

"A sound, a vibration and then things went dim."

"Do you remember walking out of the house?"

"No, only waking up in the crypt with you standing there."

Beth had no answers. Nat half carried half walked Beth back to the house. When inside he made strong black coffee in the kitchen.

"Okay, Lady, I need to know exactly what happened."

"Nat, give me a break! I don't know what to tell you. It's all a blank."

"Beth, we need to get real, this is starting to frighten me."

"You're frightened, how do you think I feel? I'm scared to death."

Nat knew now what he had to do and he had to do it fast. He had to help Beth and solve the riddle of this house.

"Beth, go pack us a bag!"

"Now what are you doing, Nat?"

"We're getting out of this house for a couple of days and move into a motel."

"Is that a good idea?"

"It's the best idea I've got at the moment. We need time to think and put all of this in perspective. You pack a bag and let me have 30 minutes on the Internet."

"Okay, Nat, I guess a break to think wouldn't hurt right now."

They each went to their separate tasks and met back thirty minutes later.

"Okay, Honey, let's get out of here!"

"You know, Nat, I can't help feeling we're deserting."

"Not at all, Honey, I have a couple of ideas but I think we need time to regroup"

"Okay, Captain, lead the way."

"You know, Beth, I sometimes wonder how you keep your sense of humor."

"Me, too, Nat, me too."

They drove away in Nat's Kia SUV.

The Professor

"So, Nat, what did you do?"

"What do you mean?"

"You had 30 minutes while I packed, is that when you keep your diary up to date?"

"No, Sweetheart, that's not what I did."

"Then tell me, what did you do?"

"I pulled the strings, you keep accusing me of."

"Linda's uncle?"

"Yes, Beth, we need help and I need a name."

"Did you get one?"

"Yes, I think I did."

"Then tell me who's the brain surgeon who will solve our conundrum?"

"His name is Doctor John Singleton, a retired Professor of Psychology from Boston University."

"WOW! More strings pulled?"

"Is that so wrong, Beth?"

"Not if this guy knows what he's at."

"Let me call him and then we'll know," said Nat.

They arrived at the motel, and settled into their room.

"Beth, no more tonight, please," Nat said as he shut off the light.

That night was the most sleep they'd had in a while. The next morning Beth felt so much better, relieved from the day before. "OK, Nat, let's call this friend of yours."

"He's not my friend, just someone the University gave me."

Beth smiled and said, "So call him!"

Nat dialed the number.

"Singleton here, can I help you?" said the voice on the other end of the line.

"Yes Doctor, I know this is out of the blue, my name is Nathaniel James."

"Well how can I help you?"

"Doctor, your name was given to me by Dean Wallis of U.C. L. A."

The man did not sound surprised at all. "Yes, he did say you might call. How may I be of assistance to you?"

"Doctor, my girlfriend and I have a real problem."

There was a brief silence on the line as the doctor waited for him to continue. Finally, he said, "And, Nathaniel, that would be..."

"Sir, we have a very serious haunting. We really need help. I realize this is not the sort of thing you would talk about on the phone."

"Let me stop you right there, Nathaniel, I have some knowledge of the situation from Dean Wallis."

Nat's face lit up with hope. "Sir, can you help us?"

"Where are you now, Nathaniel?"

"We are staying at a hotel, sir."

"No, Nathaniel, you must go back to the House!"

Now Nat looked confused. "But why, sir?"

"It's of no importance now, but please go back first thing tomorrow."

Reluctantly, Nat said, "OK. Do you know the address, sir?"

"Yes, I will meet you there at lunch time."

Nat hung up the phone. Beth stood behind him anxiously. "So what did he say?" she asked.

"He's going to meet us there tomorrow."

"Just like that?"

Nat held his hands out. "What would you have me say, Beth?"

That day they took things very easy, as each of them felt a little bruised and battered from their recent experiences. Neither of them wanted to put any pressure on the other.

"Why don't we skip lunch today, Nat, and have a Chinese take away in our room tonight?"

"Good idea. I'll get the meal, you bring the wine. " At that they both let out a little laugh.

"It seems a while since I've heard you laugh like that, Beth."

She kissed him and said, "I think we needed this break to get our breath back."

They awoke the next morning, dressed quickly, then had coffee and pancakes at McDonalds. Nat seemed distant. "What's wrong, Honey?"

"I don't know, just a strange feeling I have."

"Nat, I think 1 feel homesick. Anyway, what do you mean by a bad feeling?"

"I'm not real sure, but I just feel uneasy."

"One question, Beth, what do you feel homesick for?"

"The children, Nat, the children."

"You know this is one of the reasons, I'm afraid to go back."

"But Nat, don't you understand that we're too involved, we can't just move on with our lives"

"Beth, do you realize what happened to you?"

Her voice rose an octave. "Yes, and it frightens the shit out of me."

"Can you remember the headless man?"

"Nat, it's hard for me to explain. I felt more than I saw."

"But I saw him right in front of you and you seemed to be in control," said Nat.

"I don't remember that moment," she said. "But I do remember a feeling of euphoria of being warm and at home."

"Don't you see, Beth, it's not your home!"

"Are you sure, Nat, are you really sure? When you brought me here it was just a house, but for me, it no longer has that definition."

"What do you mean?" he asked.

"This House is my home, I think it always was," she replied.

"Please, Beth, don't do this to me now. What you feel, don't you see it's not natural? Don't lose track of who you are!"

"Me!" Beth shouted. "Is this about me? It was always about you! Just who do you think you are?"

"Stop right there, Beth. Please don't go any farther. This is not the time to drive a wedge between us."

"Nat, don't you see what this house is doing to us, it's pulling us apart!"

At that Nat took Beth in his arms. "I promise you nothing will ever tear us apart," he vowed.

"Do you mean that?"

"With all my heart, Beth, with all my heart."

Nat kissed her firmly on the lips. "Let's not speak any more of problems in our relationship, remember that old saying, united we stand."

"Oh, Nat, I really do love you."

Later that morning they arrived back at the manor house. Beth was beside herself to be home. "What time did you arrange to meet Singleton?" she asked.

Before he could answer, Nat heard the unmistakable sound of a diesel engine, and knew right away it was a cab. Beth opened the door and was surprised at the man who stood before her.

"Good day, young lady, my name is Dr. Jonathan Singleton."

"Dr. Livingston, I presume?"

At that moment both Dr Singleton and Beth began to laugh and a bond was formed that would last a very long time.

"Tell me, Beth, where would I find Nathaniel?"

"Here, sir," said Nat as he walked into the room with his hand outstretched.

"Would you please not call me sir! I'm neither your father nor mentor. My name is Singleton, Jonathon Singleton. You may call me John."

The man before them stood six foot three, every inch a Professor.

"This way, sir," Nat said.

"John, please, call me John."

"Then, John, please call me Nate."

"Are you sure you wouldn't prefer Nat?"

Beth broke into hysterics. "How did you know that?" Nat said in almost disbelief.

Nat's eyes turned to Beth.

"Not me, Nat, I have absolutely nothing to do with this," John interceded.

"Nat forgive me I to have my source."

Ignoring the incident for the moment, Nat asked, "John, will you be staying? Let me show you to your room."

"No need to, my friend," said the doctor. "I have been familiar with this house for many years and have a room all my own."

Nat raised an eyebrow. "You've been here before, Professor?"

"Many times. And, please, call me John."

Beth jumped into the conversation and said, "John, if you know anything about this house can you help us?"

"That's what I'm here for, Beth! But all things in their own time. Please don't be impatient."

John walked through the door, as a man would walk into his own lounge. He put down his bags and said with a sigh, "Home sweet home."

"John, we need to talk," said Nat.

"Why don't you and Beth prepare lunch and I'll put my things in my room, and then we'll talk."

Reluctantly, the couple left and Beth prepared bacon, lettuce and tomato sandwiches with sour cream chips, coffee and soda. Doctor Singleton came downstairs 30 minuets later and sat down at the table. "Thank you, Beth, that looks wonderful! It's a very interesting thing you Americans have managed to do with bacon. I grew up knowing bacon and egg for breakfast. While you, on the other hand, turned it into a salad. Although I must admit I do find it quite enjoyable."

The ice now truly broken, they all broke into laughter. John interceded, "May I at this point turn to a more sobering subject? Beth, I'd like for you to have a look at some pictures for me."

"Of course, Professor, but what are they?"

"I'd like you to tell me, Beth, if you would?"

Professor Singleton then produced from a leather case an object wrapped in what looked like muslin. Singleton unwrapped the object, which turned out to be two miniature portraits in oils, one larger painting and three or four old black and white photos. Then the professor proceeded to lay the pictures out on the table. The look of sheer disbelief and horror on Beth's face frightened Nat, and sent a knifing pain through Jonathon's stomach.

"You recognize them don't you, Beth?" Singleton said.

"I suppose, Professor, there was always the chance that they weren't real and that we were dreaming. Now all of a sudden the nightmare has shown its ugly face and cannot be ignored."

"I'm sorry to have shocked you in this way, Beth, but I had to see your reaction."

"Was it what you expected, John?"

"Yes, it was all that and more." He paused for a moment. "You see, up until this time the sightings have been sporadic and we never knew what was real and what was fake. In fact…"

Before he could finish, Nat jumped in with "Who are 'We,' Professor?"

"Not yet, Nat, I'll come to that in a while. Please be patient." He then turned toward Beth. "I'm sorry," he said to her, "but I had to see if you recognized them."

"That's for sure, Professor, I recognize them as if they were my own family."

"That, Beth, is the very thing I wanted to discus with you."

They both looked at him intensely, waiting for his explanation.

"It would seem that you are some kind of transmitter and that these children are drawn to you."

Nat stood up. "For God's sake, Professor, what is going on here?"

"Please, Nat, I'm getting to that. This house is my family seat. I am a direct descendant of the man who built the house. In 1730 Captain Niles Remington laid the foundations to the house, and the dammed place has been cursed ever since."

Beth seemed confused. "But these are just children, John."

"No, Beth, you saw what no one else ever saw."

"What was that?"

"You saw the man with no head."

Beth swallowed hard and said, "I thought that would be the one thing no one would believe."

"On the contrary that was the one thing that we did believe. That's the one proof we never expected to get."

Nat now joined the conversation. "Professor, I must ask you again who are 'We'?"

"We, Nat, belong to a foundation that was put together just over 200 years ago after, as you put it, the death of the basket case child. The foundation was made up of family members who over the years couldn't live in the house because of the haunting. No one was ever able to make sense of the things that happened so the Trust paid the bills and no one lived here."

"That then, Professor, would answer why no garage was ever built on the property?"

The professor smiled. "Well done, Nat, that was very observant of you!"

"We do try, John, we really do try."

"Please, Nat, I didn't mean to be sarcastic."

Nat smiled. "I know. Professor, just kidding."

While this conversation was going on Beth was paying attention to the pictures. She seemed mesmerized. "What is it, Beth?" John said.

"Take a look at these pictures," she said. "The two small portraits are the twins! The photograph is Jonathon, the child in the ditch. Don't you see, Nat? He is still here, he walks the grounds!"

"Beth, please, you must try to see it the way it is."

"Bullshit! Who do you think you people are, there are children who need help, don't you realize?"

Jonathan Singleton intervened at that point. "Please Nat, Beth, stop right there. I above all others should know the needs of these children. This, after all, is where I belong. Please be patient, give me ten minutes and I'll be back with a bottle of wine."

Singleton walked out of the room towards the stairs. He was slow but positive in his steps. Nat and Beth just looked on, waiting for what was to come next. Three minutes later Singleton reappeared with a large bottle of red wine. "I hope this quenches the pallet, it's not cold but it's the best I can do right now."

"Professor, that will do just fine!" Beth said.

"So, young lady, tell me, who are the children?"

"I'm sorry, doctor, I don't think I understand your question."

"Please, Beth, call me John, just John."

"Who are the children to you?"

"I still don't understand."

"What I really mean is, what do the children mean to you?"

"They are children and I feel an affinity towards them."

"Beth, please understand my reason for asking this question, what I am trying to understand is the bond that you have seemed to have formed."

Beth grimaced. "You have to understand, John, that I really don't have an answer for you."

"I think what John is trying to get at, Beth, is a relationship to children you have never met before," Nat interjected.

"Are we only here for this House? Don't you think that we have seen things that we don't understand? Things I don't think I will ever understand."

"Beth, we need to open this bottle, sit down and take a moment to reflect on this, we need to know what this is all about."

"John, you seem too have us at a disadvantage. You came here knowing all about this house and played with us like fools; I think it's time you came clean, don't you?"

Nat was even more blunt. "John, people need HELP, and it seems to me you are only interested in the property. Who are you? How much do you know about this house?"

John was taken aback with Nat's direct approach. He knew now he had to be straight. He said, "It's time I showed you both a little more interesting evidence. I must apologize for being mysterious and a little deceitful. I believe, Beth, that you were right when you said the children must come first."

At that, Beth sat back and for the first time today relaxed and enjoyed her wine. Later, after they'd finished the wine and sandwiches, she got up to clear the table.

"Please stop," John said. "I have something I would like you both to look at."

John placed a copy of what looked like a very old newspaper on the table. The corners were turned and it was stained brown. "Take a look at that both of you."

The paper was the Charleston Gazette, dated Tuesday, September 11, 1739. *On this day 20 Black Carolinians met at Stono's Bridge with guns and powder taken from Hutcheson's store after killing both store keeper and helper. They did set forth to course Murder and mayhem amongst the populace.*

"John, this is just another account of a slave uprising as bad as it may be, and I know we should be ashamed, it's just one of many..."

"Please Nat, read on."

Nat turned his attention back to the old newspaper. *It was thought to be the work of the devil as a headless man led the band.*

Nat and Beth gasped. "Oh, my God, this must be a coincidence!"

John seemed exasperated. "In my experience, Nat, there is no such thing as a coincidence. You saw the headless man!"

Nat and Beth both sucked in a breath.

"Yes, I thought that might shock you! You saw him--- DIDN'T YOU?"

With sudden consternation and horror, Beth cried, "Yes we did!"

John sat back aghast. "Don't you think it's time, Professor, that you tell us all you know?'

"Yes, it would seem that would be the only honest way to go."

John then seemed to retreat into a world of his own. He said, "When I first saw this house I was only eight years old.

I came from England with my mother and father who at this time were in charge of the trust."

"Why is this house kept empty? Why not at least sell the real estate?"

"Please Beth, let me finish, I'll get to all of that. It was around 1946. I remember my parents were talking about not having made the journey because of the war. My father had indeed served in the Royal Air Force and had been shot down in the Battle of Britain. He had suffered a serious leg wound and was given an honorable discharge and later received the Distinguished Flying Cross. To a small boy this house was old and strange and a lot of fun. I was no stranger to large houses; I was born on an estate in England with, as you Americans say, a silver spoon in my mouth. At such an early age I could never have known what a price I would have to pay for that privilege.

Anyway, I digress! My parents and I stayed in a hotel not too far away. Which at that time I thought quite strange, but as a child, I passed it off. I was never allowed in the house but that didn't matter to me because I had the garden. I was strictly told to keep far away from the lake, although I could swim quite well. Anyway, one day in late August my parents were in the house and I was in the garden…"

As he spoke these words, John's mind went back to that day in 1946. BAM. BAM. YOU'RE SHOT DEAD. I SHOT YOU! John had just killed a war party of Redskins; of course, coming from England he wasn't quite sure which tribe it was. They all looked the same, he said to himself with a giggle. John may have been young but he had an I.Q. of 150. He ran through the trees to the west side of the lake. He was Tom Mix and these Redskins were going to pay, For what Redskins do, that is. On he rode on his white steed, when all of a sudden he heard a sound. It was faint at first, but as he neared the southwest side of the lake it became more pronounced. It sounded like a child crying. John stopped at once and investigated. After all, a friend wouldn't hurt him. He held his breath as all heroes do when confronted by danger.

Then he heard the sound again, stronger this time. It seemed to come from a small clump of trees and long grass to his left. John moved closer, the crying became more prominent. He reached the long grass and the trees, and the crying became sadder. John walked over a grassy knoll and in front of him he saw a boy about his age in a basket chair. The boy seemed so sad.

"What's wrong?" Jonathan said.

The boy looked at him with piercing eyes. "How would you like to live your life in a wheelchair?"

"I suppose I wouldn't really!"

"What's your name?"

"Jonathan, what's yours?"

"Jonathan."

Both children broke into fits of laughter.

John stopped his story at this stage and looked up at the ceiling."

"Oh, did you ever tell your parents?" Beth said.

"No, not until we got back to England. I spent one of the happiest and saddest summers of my life that year."

"You mean you saw him again?"

"Please, Beth, let John tell his story," Nat interjected.

At that, John seemed to sink back into his memory. "Would you like to play a game? I know a game we can play."

"And what game would that be? That a cripple can play?"

"If you're going to continue to feel sorry for yourself I might as well go home!"

"No, no, please don't go."

"All right, let's play a game."

"What sort of game?"

"First we must have a name, we can't keep calling each other Jonathan. Therefore I will be John and you will be Jonathan, what game shall we play?'

"I wish."

"I have never heard of that, John."

"Neither have I, I've just made it up."

At that they both started to laugh again.

"If you made it up you have to tell me the rules."

"It's simple, really, I give you a wish and you tell me what in the world you wish for."

"Anything in the world!"

"Yes anything, pretend that we set a Genie free from a bottle."

"What's a Genie?"

"You don't know what a Genie is?"

"No, John, I don't. Please tell me!"

"I don't think I know how."

"Please try."

"OK, a Genie is an Arab giant with a ponytail and is about 20 feet tall with magic powers. Some bad magician put him in a bottle and if you let him out you get three wishes."

"But you said we only have one?"

"Yes, for our game we only have one."

"You go first, Jonathan, tell me your wish."

"I wish I could see my mother and father again."

"Why, Jonathan? Haven't you seen them in a while?'

"It seems like a long time."

"OK, what if you describe your parents."

"My father is a Sea Captain."

"You mean he's in the Navy? Tell me about your mother."

"I loved my mother, my mother was Spanish. She was from Cuba. Southwest Cuba, Santiago."

"Is she still here?"

"Sometimes."

There was a strange silence between them.

"Now it's your turn, John."

"My wish would be to see your mother and father."

"I don't understand."

John repeated, "I want to see your mother and father."

"You can't."

"Why not!"

"You just can't."

"Why!"

Jonathan began to cry. "They're dead!" he wailed.

"I'm so sorry, Jonathan!"

"Please describe your mother."

"I told you, she came from Santiago."

"Was she pretty?"

"My mother was very pretty, she had golden skin, dark hair, dark eyes, and she loved me very much."

"And your father?"

"He was from England. They loved each other very much. I think they were very happy until I came along."

"No, Jonathan! That can't be true! I'm sure they loved you very much. Please tell me about your father."

"He was a ship's Captain from England, and very strict, sometimes he would shout at me, but I always knew when it was time for bed, after Mother had bathed me. He would take me from my chair and sit me on his lap."

"Was he a kind man, Jonathan?"

"Always to me and my mother. Sometimes he would cry, and say it was his fault for what happened to me. The life he had led, the things he had done. Mother always told him a good man shouldn't say such things. I miss him very much, I miss them both very much."

Jonathan began to cry again."

"Stop it," John said. "Don't you see that was your mother and father in your wish?"

"You mean that was my wish?

"Of course, you wanted to see your mother and Father, didn't you?"

"Yes, I did. Thank you, John, thank you very much."

"Now it's your turn, John, your wish. Tell me about the house."

"Why?"

"I came here from England with my parents to see this house. They said they had to look after it but we are staying in a hotel."

"Is that so bad?"

"If we own this house, then why stay in a hotel?"

"Is your wish then, John, to know about this house?"

"Yes, please tell me."

"My father built this house."

"He did?"

"Yes, a long time ago."

"What happened to him, Jonathan?"

"He died."

"How did he die?"

"They say he had a heart attack."

"What does that mean?"

"I don't really know."

"You mean he just died?"

"I think so, it seems so long ago now."

"And your mother?"

"She died as well."

"How did your mother die?"

"They said from a broken heart."

"That's so sad, you must miss them so much."

Jonathan then began to whimper. "I really miss them so badly. They were fun, they always made me feel so normal."

"What do you mean, Jonathan?"

"I have to live in this thing, how would you like to?"

"Please don't ask me that, how can I answer?"

"You can be honest."

"I don't know how to be honest."

"Are we still playing our game?"

"Yes, it's your turn."

"I wish my dad still loved my mom!"

"Doesn't he?"

"No, they fight all the time."

"Why?"

"I don't know really, I just don't think they like each other. I must go now, it's time for my dinner."

"Shall I see you again, John?"

"Yes, tomorrow if you're here."

"I suppose I will, I always am!"

John walked home a little confused. He couldn't quite understand a lot of what Jonathan had said. First, how could his father have built this house when it was quite obviously so old? Oh well, he thought, maybe I'll ask him tomorrow if he's there.

As he neared closer to the house he heard the all too familiar sound of his mother and father fighting. "Why must we keep paying the bills on this mausoleum when we could use that money in England?

"But, Constance, you know the terms of the trust. This trust has been the bane of your family and in the end will be its downfall."

"Constance, is there anything else but money on your mind?"

"William, the one thing that should really matter is the survival of this family, and throwing money away on this Colonial colossus, this decaying Bella Lugosi, house of horrors is not in my eyes right."

"Constance, we are, after all, quite comfortable."

"Could you imagine, William, just how comfortable would we be if we got rid of this decaying lobster pit."

Constance, you know this house has been in my family for 200 years."

"Yes, and doesn't it show."

As they continued arguing, Jonathan walked into the room. "Mom, Dad, you won't believe who I met!"

"Dracula?" his mother said with a strange sort of glee.

"No, I made a friend!"

"The only sort of friend you'll find around here are zombies."

"Stop it, Constance, stop it right there!"

OK, Jonathan, get ready, let's go back to the hotel and have dinner."

"Do we have to go, Daddy? Can't we stay here tonight?"

"Not in a thousand years, young man," his mother said. "Let's get back to civilization and warm blooded people."

They spent that night in a stuffy hotel, and ate dinner in the restaurant. Jonathan hated these places, even at a young age he knew them to be false. "Are we going back to the house tomorrow, Daddy?"

"Yes," William answered the boy.

"Do we really have to go back?"

"You know we do, Constance, we have two more days, then we can go back to England."

"William, can't we just sell that pile of bricks, bones and memories?"

"I wish we could, Constance, I really wished we could. But you know if I break the rules of the Trust we would lose our inheritance."

"Fuck the inheritance!"

"William, please take me home to where we belong."

"As long as this place stands we are responsible and that won't go away."

"I wish the whole God dammed circus would fall down!"

That night they went back to their suite with very mixed feelings. The next day they went back to the mansion. As usual Jonathan was sent to play in the garden. His parents thought, quite wrongly, that was the safest place for him to be. Jonathan walked to the west side of the lake and down towards the long grass and the trees. It was late morning 11 am. Jonathan approached the hollow where he had last seen the boy in the basket chair. "Hi! John," the boy said with so much glee. "John your here!"

"I told you I would come. Did you doubt me?"

"No, I knew you would come."

"How long can you stay?"

"My parents say we have to stay late tonight. They have to meet someone from the Trust."

"Sometimes I have friends that come and play with me. Would you like to meet them?"

"Yes, of course I would."

"Who are they?"

"Be patient, John, you'll meet them soon enough."

They talked all that afternoon. Time seemed to go so quickly. Neither of the boys noticed the light diminishing and the mist slowly rising. It was early evening when the boys heard the first arrival. He came out of the trees and through the mist. Jonathan noticed that his eyes seemed vacant and kind of lost. His clothes also seemed strange. Then a boy and girl appeared they also wore strange clothes but seemed much happier. "Who are they, Jonathan, who is everybody?"

"They are our friends, John, they have come to play with us."

John talked for a while although he seemed a little unsure. He liked Clare very much. She seemed quite approachable. "Where do you live, Clare?"

"Over there!" she said, pointing.

Jonathan looked, but all he could see were trees and grass. "Where, Clare?"

"There."

Jonathan looked but all he could see was emptiness. "I don't see anything, Clare?"

"Over there, Jonathan."

"Stop it, Clare you're frightening me!"

"Why, Jonathan, why should you be frightened?"

"I don't know but I am. You're telling me you don't live anywhere?"

"We live here, Jonathan!"

As Jonathan looked at Clare she seemed to waver in front of his eyes. "Please, Clare, don't go!"

The night now seemed to Jonathan to be so dark. Clare was the first to disappear. Then they were all gone. Like a lost moonbeam.

Jonathan ran like never before in his life. He never stopped until he reached the conservatory door. Jonathan's heart was beating as if at any minute it would jump from his chest. He pounded on the door. Eventually his mother opened the door. "Darling, what ever is wrong?"

"Mommy, the children vanished; they went away!"

"What do you mean, Sweetheart?"

"They just disappeared."

At that William walked up. "Is everything OK, Darling?"

"Of course, William, there are no problems. It just seems that our son has been introduced to Dracula's Castle, NOW CAN WE GO HOME?"

After the trauma at the house my mother decided to take the quick way back to England. We embarked on Trans World Airways. I never saw the children again. My mother and father died in a car crash when I was 19. That's when I became head of the Trust. Can you imagine, in control of millions of dollars and only 19? Well believe me it wasn't easy. I never saw my friends again. Now do you understand why your story intrigued me so much?"

"John, we could never have imagined!"

"Over the years I always thought that perhaps I would meet them again. But alas that was not to be, until you came here, Beth. For some reason they came back for you! I'm not sure I like that thought."

"No, Nat, please wait before you make any judgment."

"I love Beth, John! And now I'm getting very scared for her safety."

"Before you make any conclusion would you both let me finish my story?"

"Go ahead, Professor, please finish," Beth said. "There was something that Clare had said that haunted me."

"I had asked her that evening where they lived."

"She had answered that they all lived here; when I had asked her where she meant she just answered here."

"When I said that wasn't possible she just replied, 'Yes, only here, you see we can't go any were else!'"

"I remember how frightened this made me, but as a child I didn't fully understand. It wasn't until some years later that I began to understand and as ever this house had me frightened again. After that visit I was never allowed back again. Instead, I was sent off to boarding school; from that moment on my father took complete control of the Trust. As the years went on I don't think my mother ever came back to this house. She would never allow me to speak of the subject again. I guess I almost forgot that fateful day when I was called to the Master's office and told of my parents' death. From now I alone would be in charge of the Trust. Although I did my duty well and diligently I never saw the children again. Each year thereafter I would spend at least two weeks, sometimes at the house sometimes in a hotel. Many hours I spent searching the house to no avail I never saw her again. Oh I heard stories from the staff of things they reported to have seen but none of them rang true. Just when I thought that this house had finally settled down. Dr. Wallis, an old friend of mine called. His request seemed strange at first until he explained your background. Nat I must admit my first reaction was, to say no it is too risky but the Dean told me of your experience with the super natural. He told me of your need to be alone with Beth for a while!"

"I thought why not, nothing had happened here for years. The rest you know believe me nobody was more surprised than I at the out come. I understand that you have many questions and so do I. " Beth and Nat let out a sigh in unison. "My God, Nat," said. "So all of this really is true!" Beth felt herself almost drawn to tears. "So, John. I haven't been dreaming all this time?"

"No, you are not going insane."

"I wonder, John, if that wouldn't be better!"

"What you have seen is as real as the shoes on you feet."

"The way I feel right now, John, if I couldn't feel those shoes I wouldn't think they were real."

"I totally understand how you feel but now more than ever you must understand the importance of working together!"

"What is it you really want, john? To find your friends from so many years ago or to end the curse on this place and release them into peace?"

"I have two questions to ask the both of you. Do you want to continue and find the answers?"

"What's the second question, John?"

"If you do, Nat, will you both stay the full course, you have to remember things might get very unpleasant!"

"You mean things could get worse?"

"A lot worse!"

"An awful lot worse."

"Whatever is in control of this house and I don't believe it's the children has been here from the day the dammed place was built."

"What else do you know, Professor, that you haven't told us?"

"That depends on the answer to my two questions."

"If you don't intend to stay I see no reason to burden you more." Nat looked across at Beth and caught her gaze. "Beth, when we came here I came with a purpose and you came to be with me, I never for one moment thought things would turn out like this!"

"Please Nat!"

"No let me finish. I think the way the circumstances have changed and your obvious involvement I must leave this decision to you."

"That's not fair, Nat."

"Yes, it is, and for my part I would stay but I won't risk any harm to you."

"Nat, you know I could never leave this house with a clear conscience if you are prepared to stay wild horses wouldn't drag me away."

"Then it's settled, we start our investigations in the morning."

"Not so fast, John, you said you know more?"

"When I was 19 and took over the trust, I took some time out; why not, after all, I had plenty of money, so I investigated this house. It was built by my ancestor Captain Niles Remington, in 1730; he was Captain of a Ship of the Line in the British Navy. He brought his wife and children here to settle after his time served. He built this house but it's not his story that brings us here today. It's the loss of his child .Do you believe in inherent evil!"

"Isn't that what they do in the movies?"

"No, not this time, this is the real thing."

"You mean we are dealing with the undead?"

"No, that's not what I mean. What we have here is something far worse than fiction, I warned the two of you if you want to carry on it won't be easy."

"John, we have both committed ourselves!"

"Then I suggest that we all get a good night sleep and start in the morning."

That night, Nat and Beth talked until the early hours of the morning. At 6:30 John awoke them with coffee. "Come on you two, we have work to do." John had cooked bacon and eggs. "Indulge yourselves please."

"Where do we start, John?"

"If you don't mind, Nat, I would like to take Beth to the attic. Is that OK with you, Beth?"

"Yes, of course it is!"

"After breakfast they climbed the stairs. Beth felt a little uneasy but as she climbed the stairs her fears seemed to fade. She was the first to climb the ladder. All she found was dust and old memories.

"Come on, John, this is getting us nowhere!"

"Please Nat, indulge me! We have to start somewhere!"

"We are starting with an empty coffin."

"Beth, why would you use such a metaphor?"

"Don't you see this is not where we're going to find them?"

"Why, Beth?"

"Because they are in the place they love, the only place they feel safe, in the garden. That's right, John, the first place you first met and played with them!"

"How do you know?"

"Don't ask because I don't have any answers, I just know. I do know one thing, this is not the right time of day."

"How can there be a right time of day for ghosts, Beth?"

"There is, trust me."

At that moment John interceded. "The two of you stop right there. Please, let's take this to the conservatory."

"Why, John? Why the conservatory? " Jonathan stopped there for a while and seemed to go back inside himself. "There is something that seems to have stayed in the back of my mind. Something Clare said before she vanished into the night."

"John, your answer will be were the flowers grow."

"I never thought much about it at the time, but over the years I grew to know it must have had some significance."

"What do you think she meant, the garden?"

"No, Nat, it's so obvious."

"Please, Beth, enlighten me."

"Where do the flowers grow?"

"For a hundred years or more orchids have grown in the conservatory."

"The gardener told me that."

"Wasn't the conservatory the original house?"

"Yes you're quite right.

"Believe me I spent years investigating that part of the building, I never found anything."

"May be you weren't looking in the right place"

"Nat, I took that place apart."

"You must have missed something."

"O.K. Beth, let's go there now". They left the attic and went down through the kitchen and into the conservatory. "What could I have missed?"

"Something you're not looking for."

"Like what?"

"What can you see that's not here?"

"Explain what you mean?"

"You must look for what's not here."

"Stop talking in riddles, Beth! The two of you can't see what's in front of you. It's not what you can see it's what you can't see."

"I think I understand, I never thought of it like that."

"John, perhaps you'll let me in on it?"

"Nat, whatever we are looking for is hidden behind the walls." At that they all started to peel the paper from the walls but all they found were wooden panels. "This is not right, we must be in the wrong room."

"No, I don't think so, John."

"Then what do you think Beth?"

She looked up. "Let's face it, we can't go down. That's solid concrete, but what about up?"

"What could Clare all those years ago want me to see?"

"Why don't we find out."

"We need help?"

"No. No, Nat, please no one else, I've waited all these years no longer please."

"OK, let's get some tools then." They started crudely at first; the ceiling was very old and quite solid. They discovered what used to be called wattle and daub screwed to what seemed to be wooden beams. The going was even rougher than they had expected. Nat let out a shout that stopped everybody in their tracks. "What is it, Nat? What have you found?"

"I think I may have found the key to this house! Just take a look at that name and date."

John and Beth looked up and to their total amazement there on the wooden timbers quite clearly burned in was the date 1695 and the name Armando Garcia. Below was the name Angelina. "Do you know what this means, John?"

"I'm not sure that I do, Nat."

"John, this house was built from booty, and it's right here in those timbers."

"Please explain."

"Back when this house was built in the eighteenth century a sea captain would keep for himself a prize taken from the sea. In battle the prize was shared between the crew. But the captain at the end of his commission could keep his last ship."

"I think that's what happened here, your ancestor built this house from his last prize a ship called Angelina. I think we need to find out who Angelina was!"

"You mean this house was built from a ship?"

"Yes -- that is exactly what I mean."

"My family was built on piracy?"

"No, John, not at all. You are missing the point. At the time we are talking about it was common practice. I think your ancestor built this house from his last battle!"

"You mean he brought the ghosts with him?"

"No, not all ghosts come packaged!"

While the conversation between John and Nat flared, Beth felt a chill as cold as an ice cube run the length of her spine. She felt a feeling she had not experienced since the death of her sister Francis. Something so open so empty so vacant she had hoped she would never feel again! "What is it Beth, you've gone pale!"

"I don't know, Nat, it's just that there is something about that wood. It gives me an uneasy feeling. It's just as though I have seen it before. There's something strange and familiar about it!"

"Think hard, Beth," John interrupted. "It's very important that you try and identify your feelings."

"It's hard, John, the best way for me to explain it is DE- JA VU, a feeling that I've been here before, and it's not a pleasant feeling!"

Thunder erupted outside that almost seemed to shake the building, followed by rain that came down so hard it sounded like musket balls bouncing off armor plate. "That's some rain storm."

"You can say that again," Beth said, visibly shaken. Beth walked to the window and looked outside. The sky had turned gray; the whole scene remaindered her of that fateful day at Lake Norman.

"What is it, Beth?" John said.

"Have you seen this before?"

"Yes, a very long time ago."

As she spoke, the rain stopped. "There's a disturbance down around Fort Lauderdale, they say a possible tropical storm, but I don't think its anything for us to worry about."

John turned his attention back to the timbers in the ceiling. "It would seem, Nat that the whole roof is built from the same timber. Could this have come from one ship?"

"Yes, I think it did, I think it may give us the answers we need."

Beth walked back from the window and looked up. "Please stop now, guys. Let's finish this tomorrow with fresh breath."

"Beth, have a good night, I will see you in the morning," John said.

Beth turned out the lights as they went their separate ways. She was filled with so much dread she hardly looked at Nat.

"What's the matter, what is it?" he asked.

"I don't know, Nat I just feel something isn't right."

"Let's get a good night sleep and see what tomorrow brings."

Beth brushed her teeth and went to bed, but sleep seemed to elude her; she drifted in and out of consciousness. But the faces kept coming back. Her sister, Francis, the twins, the boy in the chair and worst of all, the boy in the ditch. How could she feel so responsible? She felt and knew that something was about to happen. That history was about to repeat itself. Beth felt at this moment that the bottom of her world was about to fall out. She couldn't quite identify the feeling but she did know it meant something bad was about to happen.

"What is it, Honey? Can't you sleep?"

"Nat, I can't explain it I feel something is going to happen and I don't think its good!"

"Try and get some sleep, Beth, tomorrow is another day."

"Nat, that storm where is it now?"

"Why?"

"Just tell me, Nat."

"If you really want to know let's catch the Weather Channel."

"If you wouldn't mind."

"Come on, Hon let's do it!"

They put on clothes and went downstairs. As they walked into the kitchen to their surprise and horror the 13-inch TV was already on. "Did you leave this on, Beth?"

"No! Of course I didn't; maybe John did." They were shocked to see that the television was tuned to the Weather Channel. They stood with their mouths wide open. The forecaster was on the air in full color with a chart of Florida. The storm hadn't made landfall as predicted but was moving north and growing in strength. "Nat I think we have a problem coming our way!"

"Why, what makes you think we have a problem?"

"I don't know, Nat, it's a feeling I have."

"One thing I have leaned is to trust in your instinct"

"Please, this is not something I am proud of, but it is something that I am convinced will happen."

"Beth, there's something that I have to tell you!"

"I love you very much, Beth, and I feel responsible for you being here."

Nat put his arms around her.   "I love you very much, Beth!" he repeated.

Nat's eyes welled with tears.   "It's not your fault, Nat, please don't blame yourself!"

"How can you say that when it was me who brought you to this place?"

"You asked me to marry you here, that makes the place magic."

"Beth, please, you know I love you."

"Nat, I don't think I could go on with out you!" At that Nat held Beth so tight that it allowed her feelings to release. "Nat after all this will you still marry me?"

"Please, Beth, things between us are so strong nothing can ever change that. In my life there has never been anyone like you."

"But your wife, Linda!"

"Don't go there."

"But I must!"

"I loved Linda as I loved life itself but she has gone, Beth it's you and me now. That's all we have. We need to give us a chance."

"Nat, I love you!"

"And I love you."

"Let's try and forget the past."

"Can you do that, Nat?"

"How can I ever make you see, Beth, love is a thing that none of us will ever understand."

"That's all we need is a hurricane or a storm, but just may be it will do what they say and clear the air."

"Well, Honey, don't you think it's some hell of a way to do it!"

"I think if you asked John about that he would probably tell you he would accept anything that would unravel the conundrum of this house. Anything that would lift the curse."

Suddenly, a voice in the doorway exclaimed, "There is a lot of truth in that statement, Beth!"

"John! Couldn't you sleep either?"

"No I'm afraid my mind is way too busy for sleep."

"So it must have been you that turned on this television?"

"No! Nat, I only just got up when I heard your voices. Is there something wrong?"

"No John, it's just when Beth and I got up we were going to put on the weather channel to check on that storm down in Florida. But when we came in the kitchen the TV was already on and tuned to the Weather Channel."

"One thing I have learned about this house over the years is never to be surprised, it would seem to have a life of it own. May I make suggestion Nat, Beth!"

"Go ahead, John," Beth said.

"As we are all wide awake why don't we sit down and discuss our next move. As it appears we now may have a storm to throw into the Maelstrom". At that all three sat around the kitchen table. "OK. Professor, you appear to have the seat, why don't you start."

"Thank you, Nat, I will, it is my contention that things are coming to a head and I believe it is because of Beth. Please don't misunderstand me Beth after all these years I welcome it. My question to you must be do you want to go though with it?"

"Most definitely, John, I couldn't walk a way now I would never be able to live with myself."

"Your turn, Nat, how do you feel about Beth and yourself staying?"

"I agree with Beth if she wants to carry on let's do the job!"

"But I do have one reservation."

"And that would be?"

"If at any time Beth feels she can't go on that she or any of us are too threatened then we terminate and run."

"I totally agree and give my full blessing .Now to business, I believe you are both right and that storm is heading our way, I would think we may have about 24 hours to prepare at the moment it's only a tropical storm. If you wouldn't mind, Beth, you need to go to the store and collect emergency supplies. There won't be any in the house because no one has lived here let a alone waited out a hurricane. Nat, if you agree you and I will put up the storm shutters, that's if there are any. I'm sure there must be."

"Who usually does that, John?"

"You know I really don't know.   I must ask the gardener."

"Will he be here tomorrow?"

"He's here most days, he should know."

"Now I suggest we try and sleep what is left of the night."

They then went upstairs to bed. They all awoke the next morning and as no one would admit but all knew they were afraid of what was to come. Beth made bacon, eggs and coffee. Without being aware of it in her old fashioned way she was feeding the inner man to give them strength. "OK, guys, let's make a list of what we need from the store?" The list included things like water, batteries, candles and food items. Beth took Nat's truck and headed for the store leaving John and Nat to start their chores. John first looked for the gardener and found him down by the lake riding his John Deere lawn mover cutting the grass.

"Charles!" John called. In his mind he thought, 'Charles my ass.'

Charles stopped and turned off his John Deere. "Yes Sir!"

"Charles, there's a storm coming."

"Yes Sir."

"What do we do to prepare the house?"

"Nothing Sir, that's my job and I have already taken care of it." John noticed the look of pride and elation in Charles's face and knew right away things where taken care of. "The storm shutters, Charles?"

"Taken care of, Sir, we have a company from Charleston that will be here in 30 minutes I have already called them."

"Thank you, I can see that you have the situation in hand. I think that you and your wife should go home now and see to your own problems."

"Thank you, Sir, I'll put the machine away and then we'll go home."

John made his way back though the conservatory into the kitchen and couldn't find Nat. John moved on into the study where Nat sat in front of his computer looking into space. "Penny for them, Nat!"

Nat tuned around with a jerk. "John."

"Just an old English thing, Nat! What were you thinking?"

"A couple of things, are you superstitious?"

"Didn't think so but now I'm not so sure. Why do ask?"

"Do you believe in threes?"

"You mean third time lucky?"

"Yes, that's just what I mean."

"Explain yourself."

"There have been two sightings recorded of the headless man. One in 1739, when the crypt was built. The second in 1751 at the Black uprising at Stono's Bridge. Then nothing else until now."

"Are you suggesting that we are the 'third time lucky' 'third strike and out?"

"Don't you think it's a possibility?"

"At one time, Nat, I would have thought the idea ludicrous but not so anymore. I think that now I may have reached a crossroads and have the ability to believe in anything."

"I don't think it's a matter of believing in anything, more what you see feel and smell."

"No, Nat, I now believe in another dimension. I think it's called the ethereal!"

"You mean that place in between were ghost's and goblin's exit?"

"Yes Nat, that's the place I believe you yourself have seen it."

"Yes, I guess I did see something in the crypt that defies reason."

"How about in the garden by the lake that night?"

"OK. John! I take your point. Now I have a question for you."

"OK. Ask!"

"This area where the house is built, South Carolina, by the beach."

"Carry on, you have my attention."

"Well, it just seems strange that a place like this that has regular hurricanes don't have a storm shelter?"

"You know, I never thought about it before but you are right."

"Surely, John, when this house was built they must have also built an underground shelter."

"I must admit you would think that a sea captain would have experience of hurricanes."

"The point is I'll bet you won't find another house old or new close to the ocean without some kind of shelter."

"I couldn't agree more but I don't remember ever seeing one."

"If you did build one where would you put it?"

"Not at the front, Nat, it wouldn't look good and certainly not on the back that faces the ocean."

"Then that leaves only two choices east side or west side."

"Does it matter, do you think it has any bearing on the things that have happened in and around this house?"

"I don't know. But I think we should investigate."

"If we could find the shelter we could be sure of riding out the storm."

"Nat, do you think it could be bad?"

"With all the things that have happened here I see no reason to think we'll get a break now."

"You mean if you look on the dark side things can only get better?"

"Exactly, John!"

"I see you have been watching Hollywood after all."

"I have a suggestion to make: the contractors are here now putting up the storm shutters. Why don't we take a look around the house and see if we can't find some sort of anomaly in the soil or the grass on the side of the house?"

"You really do think we have a problem, don't you?"

"Not so much me. Beth thinks we are in trouble and I have found that her feelings are usually right". "I agree with one thing that Beth is more in touch than we are."

"So you agree we should have a look?"

"I don't think it would hurt do you?"

"Lead the way, Nat."

"OK. Let's start on the east side of the house."

Nat and John went through the front door and around to the east side of the house. On the way they passed the contractors putting up the shutters who also seemed a little disturbed. Nat asked one of the guys what he thought of the storm.

"Buddy, I have seen many storms on this coast but this one seemed to come from nowhere, that I don't like," the man said.

This only made Nat feel more uneasy.

"What's wrong Nat?" John asked. "I never like it when the locals gets spooked and that feller didn't seem at all happy about this storm."

Nat was visibly shaken.

"Come on, Nat, let's use the time we have to the best advantage." They continued on around the house to the east side. All they found was grass lawns that seemed to be as old as the house. "There's nothing on this side, John."

"How do you know?"

"John, before we came here I did my share of investigating. One thing I learned about looking for graves there has to be some kind of depression or at least a bump. If there's no unusual disturbance in the earth then that hasn't been touched for years."

"I must admit that makes a lot of sense."

"They walked around the south side of the house and came upon the west side. The west side was different in as much as the lawn didn't continue all the way to the house. As they moved north along the west side of the conservatory

John noticed that the earth wasn't even, but about 15 feet north from the south side. At that spot was a flowerbed and cultivated earth. "What do you think, Nat, could this be the spot?"

At that Beth called out, "Hey guys, what are you doing?"

"Come here, Beth, take a look at this!"

Beth walked down to them. "What Nat? What have you found?"

"We think we may have found the original storm shelter."

"Did you get what we need, Beth?"

"Isn't that one of those stupid statements, like are you alive? Of course I did. For what reason did you find it the storm or to see what's in there?"

"A bit of both really, I thought if the storm gets really wild then we have a safe haven. On the other hand it's a room we haven't checked out."

"Tell me, Nat, does any of this frighten you?"

"Yes, John, it does but remember how long I have been searching for proof, if it's here in this house then I want to find it."

"Be careful, Nat, for what you wish for it may not be what you want to find."

"I think I'll take that chance."

"John, I've got an idea. Do you have any cash on you?"

"About two hundred dollars I would think."

"OK, hand it over!"

"Don't worry, Beth, it's for a good cause." John gave Nat the money he had in his wallet and Nat walked off.

"What do you think he's up to, Beth?"

"I really don't know, but sometimes he frightens me!"

"I do realize what this must take out of you and please understand that I do appreciate it. My family has been cursed with this damn ghost train and believe me it hasn't been a fun ride."

"You know, John, I think we are all here to lay are own demons to rest. I don't believe at this stage any of us are prepared to surrender and walk away."

"I take your point, Beth, but I thank you all the same."

Nat walked around the front of the house and made his way to the contractors who were putting away their tools after putting up the storm shutters. Nat walked over to a big man who seemed to be in charge and giving orders. "Excuse me, are you in charge?"

"You might say that, I own the company that's doing the work."

"Can I ask your name?"

"Greg, Greg Summers."

"Greg, do you have any digging tools in your truck?"

"Yes, we do, there's enough tools in that truck to demolish this house and then rebuild it."

They both lightly chuckled and Nat felt an immediate warmth for this guy. "I have a proposition for you, would you and your guys help us move some top soil. I don't think it should take long and it pays $200 dollars cash."

"You never told me your name?"

"Nat."

"OK. Nat we can give you two hours at the most then we have to get back to our own homes."

"Done deal, Greg, when you're ready we're just around the west side of the house."

They shook hands and Nat walked back around the side of the house. Nat allowed his eyes to look at the sky, what he saw didn't install much confidence. It seemed that the world had come to a stop there was an unnatural quiet. The clouds didn't seem natural either they were dark gray and seemed to be moving too fast. Nat thought to himself how would I know how fast clouds travel. All the same it was an uneasy feeling.

Beth and John saw Nat walking back around the building and down towards them. "Where ever have you been, Nat?"

"To get some help, I hope you don't mind. I have just spent your money."

"Nat, if that gets us any closer to solving this anomaly. Then we have a bottomless pit! Believe me, the Trust is not poor."

Five men armed with picks and shovels soon appeared around the north end of the house and walked towards them. "That's where your money went, John, now lets see what we can find!"

Greg walked up to Nat and said, "OK, where do you want us to start?"

"Right there would be fine." Nat had already marked of a section of ground six feet out from the wall of the house and ten foot long. The men began digging right away; two would dig with picks then the remaining three would move in and clear the loose earth. After thirty minutes they hit something solid. They were down three feet. Nat thought that should be just about right. John jumped into the pit with obvious excitement. He got down on his hands and knees and started to clear the earth with his bare hands. Below the dirt he found flagstones. The stones where about four by four and seemed pretty will embedded. Nat jumped in the pit with John and began helping John clear away the earth. "Hey guys!" Greg said, with amusement in his voice. "Are we after buried treasure?"

"Something far more valuable," John said. "OK, guys we're the professionals, let us do our work!"

They cleared away the loose soil, below was an area of about ten feet by four feet. It seemed that someone had meant this to be sealed. "Guys, can you tell me what you are looking for?"

"Yes Greg, a storm cellar."

"In that case I suggest we pull up the center slabs the entrance would only be probable four by six." Everybody lent a hand moving the slabs. In the center as Greg had predicted was what appeared to be an old steel door. "Wow, guys take a look at that! That's old steel."

"How do you know?" John said.

"Because old steel has a different patina and will last longer in bad conditions."

"Where did you learn that?"

"I used to work in the steel mills of Pennsylvania. That steel looks like it might be a few hundred years old."

"Two hundred and seventy three to be exact.

"Can we get it open, Greg?"

Nat said, "Yes, I think so. Hey, Joey, go get some crowbars and anything else that might lift that door."

Joey and two others left and went back to the truck. A few minutes later they returned with some large bars and two hydraulic jacks. "That should do the trick, Nat!" Greg said. They labored for another thirty minutes with the bars until the lid finally gave. There was a sudden sound like mud sucking down a dead animal. "Oh God," Greg said as he turned his head away from the awful stench.

"What is that foul smell, Nat? I don't think I've ever smelt anything so bad!"

"Well, Greg, I believe it's age."

"Man, nothing can smell that bad least of all nothing I've ever smelt!"

"Thanks, guys, you earned your money. Now go and take care of your families."

At that Greg and his men took their money and left. Greg was the last to leave. He turned to Nat. "I don't know what's in that hole but I wish you luck, I think you may need it." He turned and walked away.

"Did you pay them, Nat?"

"Yes, I gave them $300 dollars."

"But I only gave you two hundred!"

"I put the other hundred. They earned it." They all turned their attention to the steel door. Before Greg's men had left they had placed two by fours under each comer of the steel door. "OK, guys, we now need to lift the door."

Nat and John stood at each comer with Beth in the middle. They all lifted in unison but the door only gave an inch. "One more time. One, two, three." This time the door gave another six inches. "And again, one, two, three." This time the door gave and daylight shined in that cellar for the first time in nearly three hundred years.

"Did you get flashlights, Beth?"

"Yes, they where on the list."

"Can you bring three here now?"

"I'll go get them but promise me you won't go down without me?"

"You have my word, Beth," John said. "We are going to shore up the door." Beth left and almost ran to Nat's SUV. When she got back Nat and John had the doors blocked open with two by fours. Nat, John and Beth each took a flashlight. As they looked into that black, seemingly endless hole the first thing to catch their attention was the smell. "John, do you think this is how King Tut's tomb smelled?"

"I don't know, Beth, but it was no wonder they all died after." They shone their lights into the pit. The first thing they saw was a set of steps leading down. Nat was the first to descend the steps, John followed and Beth came behind. The steps went down about ten feet into a black abyss. As they went lower they were gagging for air. Nat shone his light into the stygian gloom. Slowly his eyes adjusted to the dark. He waited as John and Beth moved down the stairs and stood beside him. They all shone their flashlights around the room. From the bottom of the stairs the room ran off to the left. "It's empty! It's completely empty!"

As they moved their beams around the room the emptiness sunk in, the room gave off aura of loneliness and grief. The walls were built of regular brick the floor was the same four by four flagstones The only thing that could be called constant was two hundred and seventy years of dust. John spoke first. "Let's get out of here, Nat, it's oppressive!"

"I'll second that, Beth, I agree, let's get out of here."

As they reached fresh air each one took in a gasp. "Well, that was a big nothing!"

"No, Beth, it may come in useful!"

"Come on, Nat, this time I think we drew a blank!"

"Indulge me, Beth, I have one more thing I would like to do. Let's run a lead down here, I guess there's no electric, I want to leave a tape."

"You mean you want to record an empty room?"

"Yes, Beth, that's exactly what I want to do."

All three exited the room and went back to the kitchen. "Nat, are you serious?"

"Yes! Do you want to help me?"

"Of course I do."

"Nat, you must have something in mind would you mind letting us all in on it?"

"OK, John, answer a question for me."

"Fire away, Nat!"

"Don't you think it strange to put a steel door, concrete slabs then earth and flowers over an empty room?"

"Yes, of course I do but remember I have witnessed many strange and inexplicable thing happen in this place."

"I understand that in the short time that we have spent here I don't think anyone would believe what has taken place."

"There is something to that room and I don't know what it is!"

"So I'm going to do the only thing that I know and that is to investigate the past with the tools of the present."

Nat went off to get his tape player.

"Hang on, Nat, I'll come with you."

"What's the matter, Beth, you think I'm afraid of the boogie man?"

"If it was only the boogie man I wouldn't bother."

"As they walked out together, John felt a strange kind of loneliness. A feeling he hadn't experienced before. Until this moment John hadn't realized how totally alone he was. He mused over his life and wondered what it all meant. Why after all these years was he so alone? Was it the memory of Clare, could she have made such an impression? He thought, God only knows. John walked up to the bar and poured himself a large Scotch and water. Where did my life go, what did I do?

Nat and Beth came back into the kitchen they laughed and talked. John allowed his mind to go back to that time in the field by the tree when he felt young and alive, he realized until now he had never felt so alive. "Did you do it, Nat, did you put the recorder in there?"

"Yes, John, it's done!"

"What do we do now?"

"Now we wait!"

"What news of the storm, John?"

"It's now moved east and is expected to be a category one hurricane by night. It seems to have slowed down and that's not a good thing. It will intensify."

"How long do we have?"

"It's hard to tell when these thing's slow down over open water that's when they get stronger. This could put hours on landfall. I suggest we all get ready!"

Beth and Nat went upstairs to take a shower and get ready for the coming storm. John couldn't have felt more alone, was it that last meeting fifty-two years ago, or was there some other reason to torture himself. John felt a desire so strong to walk out side he topped his drink up and slowly walked out of the door. The evening was warm and oppressive. John thought what a good time to be alive! He turned right and with out knowing came upon the entrance to the cellar. He looked down and saw Nat had installed a light along with his tape. This made John curious. Why did Nat feel so strongly about this room? He felt an urge to walk down the steps an emotion so strong he couldn't deny. As John walked down the steps his fears seemed to disappear into the night. With each step he took another degree of ease drifted over his mind. His feet left the last step and he seemed to float across the floor. His eyes followed the electric lead and came to rest on the small tape player. A little light in the player told John that it was alive. You really mean business, Nat, he thought. There's something about this room that has your attention. I wonder what it is? What can there be about an empty room that could so hold you? John walked to the center of the room and slowly slipped to the ground and into what could be called a half lotus. That's funny, John thought, I don't remember doing that before. He sat there and just stared at the wall. It started very slowly and quietly at first like a bee buzzing in the distance. The light slowly dimmed, but John just thought that was his imagination. Then a feeling like a mild electric current ran though the length of his body. Slowly at first he started to recognize the voices muffled and mixed together. Mostly the voices of children, but there were adults in the background.

The air in front of John's eyes started to move a new emotion arose from John's stomach. He felt the fear rise to his throat. A haze in front of him slowly took shape; now he really was scared. John knew he was in trouble but was unable to move a muscle. He tried to shout for help, but his mouth wouldn't work. The form in front of him grew clearer and started to take on a shape. At first it was like a blurred television image, slowly the image cleared. My God, he thought, they're all together in this room, he noticed that awful smell was coming back. The smell was like someone had left a body above ground and forgot to bury it. The scene in front of him now turned into a horror story the faces of children contorted in pain and crying for help. John felt so emotional, tears poured down his cheeks, at that moment he would have sold his soul to get out of this room. He thought if he didn't get out now he'd go crazy.

"John, are you down there! John, where are you?"

Nat saw John in the center of the room; he ran down the stairs and took John by the shoulders and pulled him out of the cellar. "John, are you OK?"

John didn't know what planet he was on, he seemed dazed at first then he came around. "Thanks, Nat. I seemed to have got lost in there!"

"What did you see, John?"

"More than I ever want to remember!"

Nat helped John back to the kitchen where Beth met them. "Are you all right, John ?"

"Yes I'm fine, Beth, I just need to sleep then we'll talk in the morning!"

"What happened out there, Nat? John looks really shook up."

"Excuse the pun, Beth, but I think he saw a ghost!"

"Come on, Nat, what happened?"

"I really don't know, Beth, I found him like that he looked like he was glued to the floor."

"You mean he wasn't able to move?"

"That's the way it looked I had to physically pull him out of there."

"What do you think happened?"

"You know I don't have any idea I'm frightened to speculate I know this that room wasn't buried for nothing."

"Did you check the tape?"

"No, not yet, I was too preoccupied pulling John out of there. There's something about that room that frightens me. If you don't mind, will you come with me and stay by the door while I retrieve the tape?"

"Of course, Nat, let's go!"

"Hang on, not so fast. I think I need a drink."

"Of course, Nat, of course. I'm sorry, let me get you a drink. What would you like?"

"A Scotch would work just fine."

"Coming up."

Beth went to the drinks cabinet. There was no wine or beer kept in the house but a cabinet of sprits was kept for infrequent visitors of the Trust. "What a joke," Beth said out loud.

"What was that?"

"Just thinking out loud. I find it sort of funny keeping sprits in the house, you know the stuff in bottles."

"Do you think our lives will ever be the same after this, Beth?"

"No chance, you must be kidding."

Nat took the drink from Beth and swallowed it down in two gulps. He felt the liquid burn its way down into his stomach. "OK, Honey, let's go. By the way, any news of the storm?"

"Only that it's still on the way and packing a punch. It's now gone into open water and stalled, that means it won't come quickly but it will be stronger. "

"How long have we got?"

"Two hours less than the last time you asked me."

"I'm sorry, Hon, with all that's happened I don't think I know which planet I'm on!"

They moved from the kitchen into the conservatory and then outside. They walked along the side of the house up to the entrance to the cellar. "Beth, please do something for me!"

"Sure, Nat, anything."

"Don't come in the cellar, stay up here!"

"You got it, Nat, go and do what you have to do."

At that Nat descended the stone steps. Beth didn't want to admit it but she was terrified because she had seen the look on John's face and it scared her. "Are you OK, Nat?"

"Yes, I'm fine. I've got the tape and I'm coming out."

Beth felt so good to know Nat was on his way out of the hole. Suddenly Beth felt the ground start to vibrate under her feet. "Get out. Nat, get out now!"

To Beth's horror the ground began to ripple. "This is not happening, it's not possible. Nat, for God's sake where are you?"

"Here, Beth, I'm here!" Nat's face appeared at the stairs; he looked ashen gray but he was still moving. "Get the hell out of there, Nat, right now!"

Nat crawled to the top of the stairs and climbed out. "Get me out of this pit, Beth!"

Beth helped and half carried Nat back to the kitchen. "What's in that damn hole?"

"I don't know but I think I may have it on tape."

"OK, let's take a look."

"One minute, Babe. I could use another drink."

"OK. I think you may have earned it." Beth poured Nat another shot of scotch. "Just what is in that dark place?"

"I'm not really sure, it's only a theory."

"First let's take a listen to the tape!" Nat plugged in the tape and switched it on. A little light came on and Nat could hear the little motor start to turn. He stood there for about 30 seconds and then began to turn up the volume; nothing happened. "What is it?"

"I don't know there don't seem to be anything recorded."

"Do you think John saw anything?"

"Yes. I'm sure he witnessed something pretty terrible, that look on his face was haunted."

"You said you may have a theory?"

"Yes but that's all it is."

"OK. Let's have it as far out as it might be nothing can be as crazy as reality."

"OK. Here goes. The cellar has been shut up tight for many years. That would seem to indicate that the family who lived here at that time was afraid of it. They certainly took a lot of trouble to cover it over."

"With what John experienced and what I went though there is definitely some kind of evil force down there."

"What do you think it might be?"

"With danger of sounding insane."

"Come on, Nat, spit it out!"

"I believe the walls in that cellar hold a memory or a recording of some kind, all the things that took place in the house!"

"But that's not enough; that cellar has been closed up for the best part of two hundred and seventy years!"

"No Beth! I think the cellar was closed during the first years of the house."

"Then explain to me how it can have memories of the years after?"

"I don't know but it does."

"So you are saying that a family built this house two hundred and seventy years ago, built that cellar and then covered it over."

"Yes, that's exactly what I am saying!"

"Why else would that most useful cellar be barred?"

"Non of this story makes any sense!"

"Nat, thank you for pulling me out of there!" John stood in the doorway. He seemed a little shaky. "I know I may have been a bit of an encumbrance. But I have to know what happened in that place?"

"I wish we could tell you, John, but we have no idea."

"I heard you mention a theory, what's that about?"

"First tell us what you saw in there?"

"A lot of shapes and shadows nothing solid and sounds again nothing solid."

"But it did frighten you, right?"

"I think the term you Americans use is 'scared shitless'."

"Could you better explain shapes and shadows, John?"

"The best explanation I can give it that it was like a film show and I was a captive audience literally!"

"What do you think it was that held you?"

"I wished I knew, Beth. It was as though I had no control over my body!"

"What about you, Nat? What did you experience?"

"Out of control, that's the best way I can explain it. I had no power over my body."

"I think whatever has happened over the years in this house ultimately stems from that cellar."

"As you have already said my ancestors must have a good reason to close up that room so tight."

"Don't you think we should close it back up again?"

"No not yet!"

"Why do you think that room is so important, Nat?"

"Because of exactly what it is, an evil place that someone has gone to a lot of trouble to hide forever. I think we should respect that, don't you?"

They all nodded to that. Nat thought, you didn't need a lot of convincing did you. "John, I suggest we all get some rest with what is left of the night."

"I agree. After what we just went through and the storm out there we need to be alert."

"Come on, Beth, let's go to bed!" Nat thought, if we can just get two or three hours we'll have a much better chance in the impending nightmare. Nat and Beth awoke about six thirty that morning. "I'll go and make coffee, Nat, see you in the kitchen!" Nat took his turn now in the bathroom as Beth went to make breakfast. As Nat descended the stairs he heard voices in the kitchen. The wonderful aroma of bacon and eggs greeted him. As he walked into the kitchen he saw John and Beth sitting at the table drinking coffee. "Good morning, Nat," John said.

"Wow, John, did we eat yesterday?"

"No I don't believe we did, I think we must have been too busy."

"God, I'm hungry. Beth, did you do toast?"

"Of course I did, jelly as well if you want."

"That works for me. I'm famished; do either of you realize we have been living on bacon and eggs."

"Don't forget the toast and jelly, Nat!" At that they all began to laugh.

"Well," Nat said. "At least our spirits are high, excuse the pun!"

Again they all laughed. "To a more sobering subject, what news of the storm?"

"Well, Nat, it would appear we have a reprieve for the time being, the storm has stalled. That's the good news. The bad news is the dammed thing has intensified. That could mean it could move at any time but when it does it will be a lot stronger."

"Are they predicting its course?"

"Yes, basically right at us."

"Well at least that's given us breathing space. How long would you estimate, John?"

"You remember Andrew in ninety two? Who saw that coming?"

"How far off shore is it now?"

"They are telling us it may be three hundred and fifty miles."

"So we may have gained another 24 hours."

"Yes but at what cost, Nat. What cost!"

"How wide are the bands?"

"They say about one hundred and fifty miles."

"So we should see the first effects in about ten to twelve hours!"

"Yes, so let's make the most of it!"

"Nat, I have a few calls I should make; perhaps we should meet up again at lunch time?"

"Sounds good to me, John, that will give Beth and I time to catch up on each other."

Nat and Beth walked though the conservatory as they had done many times before or at least that's how it felt to Nat. They walked out of the door and into the morning. Beth stopped for a moment. "Listen, Nat!"

"What, I can't hear anything!"

"Exactly. You can't hear anything; the world has stopped."

"I think I see what you mean; there's no sound, no birds."

"They are the first to go?"

"What do you mean?"

"Before a storm the birds leave first."

"Come on, let's walk to the lake."

They walked down to the lake as they had done many times before each with different degrees of horror and sadness. They walked to the wooden seat that Beth had sat on the night she first saw the twins.

"Let's sit down, Nat, and reflect on the things that seem to have changed our lives so!"

Nat again looked up at the sky; the clouds seemed so lonely, he thought. There seemed so little movement. "What are you thinking, Nat?"

"I don't know things have changed so much since we first arrived here, it's hard to know anymore what to think or feel."

They both looked up at that foreboding sky so gray and hollow, it gave a feeling of total emptiness. With that came the first movement of life, the wind slowly picked up. "You know, Nat, I think I can feel rain in the air."

"Yes so do I. It's only fine but I think it's starting." Both of them felt pleased that something was about to happen though neither would admit to the other. They sat there for about twenty minutes while the rain slowly got stronger.

The Storm

"Nat, look across the lake."

"At what, Beth?"

"That tree on the south side."

"I don't see anything."

"Look again, Nat, the tree in the middle on the far shore, look just to the right of it."

Nat strained his eyes through the drizzling rain. He saw the tree and what looked like a small tree along side.

"See the tree and a small tree to the right of it? Nat, the small tree just moved; it wasn't there when I first looked."

Nat looked harder but in this weather at that distance nothing looked clear. "What do you think it was?"

"I don't know but it wasn't there when I first looked, then it seemed to slowly come into view.

"Shall we go and look?"

"Do you think we should, without John?"

"Yes I do, I think he needs to take a rest, remember he's had to live with this place for years!"

"Yes I guess you're right; why don't we take a walk around and look."

"Why not, let's go."

They headed around the west side of the lake. Nat thought, this may not be the cleverest thing you ever did but we did agree to find the answers to this house and find them we will. They walked through the now wet grass and headed south through the trees. Both felt a sense of foreboding because of the closeness of the crypt. Beth squeezed Nat's hand until it almost turned blue.

"The crypt. Nat, don't take me anywhere near the crypt!"

At the south side of the lake they turned east and away from that <u>damned </u>crypt. The rain still came down but not enough to obscure their view. They carried on through the wet grass and to the trees where they had seen whatever it was. Nothing was there, not even a bent blade of grass.

"I don't know about you, Beth, but I think we may have started to see things!"

"You do, Nat, then take a look over there."

Beth pointed to the bottom of the west side of the lake. And there about fifty yards away was an unmistakable figure moving along the south side of the lake. He or she or it was dressed in what seemed to be some kind of monk garb like a black robe with a hood.

"Do you see what I see, Nat?"

"I wished I could say no, but yes I see it!" The figure moved without walking; it seamed to glide over the grass.

"Where's it going, Nat?"

"I don't know but I think I can make a guess!"

"Do you think we should follow it?"

"Isn't that what they do in the movies and get split up?"

"1 don't think so, Beth, not this time, let's get back to the house and tell John. I don't think we should follow that thing whatever it is and get caught again."

The rain now started to fall harder as they made their way back to the house. "What do you think it was, Nat?"

"I have no idea. And quite honestly I don't think I want to know."

"Do you think it went to the crypt?"

"Yes I do; what do you think?"

Beth let out a sigh. "Yes it most definitely went to the crypt!"

"Are you that sure. Beth?"

"Yes I am and there's no way it's going to lure us there today in this bad weather. From now on we act from strength and not get separated as that thing would have us do."

"You called it a thing. Do you think it looked like a person?"

"It may resemble a person but believe me it's not!"

"Then what was it?"

"I don't know for sure I had a feeling from the children that something kept them here, may be it was that."

Nat and Beth walked back to the house through the rain. It was about 9 a.m. when they eventually got back to the house. They went through the conservatory and into the kitchen.

"I wonder where John is. I think we should tell him what we just saw!"

"He said he had some calls to make, maybe he's in the study."

They went through into the study where they found John sitting at a desk with a phone to his ear. "I don't give a damn what you think I want them today. That storm isn't coming yet!" Then he went quiet for a while and listened. "If you value your job I want that equipment here no later than one o'clock!" At that John hung up the phone. "I'm sorry about that tirade but it would seem the only way to get things done."

I'm surprised, John, that such a mild mannered man could show his teeth, Nat thought. *I'm not.*

"I hope it doesn't make you think less of me, Beth?"

"No not at all in fact just the opposite with what lies ahead I believe we need as much strength as we can muster."

"We didn't want to disturb you…"

John cut in. "That's fine, I wanted to talk to you both anyway."

Nat continued. "We need to tell you what we have just witnessed in the garden." John sat back in his chair and gave his full attention. "We were sitting by the lake on a bench just talking when Beth thought she saw something move on the south shore."

"What was it, Nat?"

"We don't know; when we got there it was gone only to appear this time behind us. We followed it but it disappeared."

"I have a question; when it disappeared in what direction was it headed. Toward the crypt?"

"How did you know?"

"While you were out I did a little checking of my own I had suspected because of the sightings some connection between the house and the crypt and I think I have finally found it!"

"We're all ears go ahead."

"I called the architects who handle the trust properties as you can imagine there are more than one. I requested that they check something out for me shortly before you returned they called back." John looked quite smug and pleased with himself.

"Go on, John, don't keep us in suspense."

"They informed me what I had suspected, that the lake is fed from an underground river that runs down from the north under the house and then siphons off into the ocean."

"Wow," Nat said.

"That would explain a lot."

"That conversation you just heard. I was ordering some pieces of equipment that might be of use to us!"

"Like what?"

"Instruments that see and record thermogenesis any variation between hot and cold, also a camera that will shoot if there is a change in temperature no matter how small, also it will shoot from the slightest vibration in the air."

"That certainly could give us the edge that we need. OK, Professor, what do you suggest our next move should be?"

"Beth, I am glad you asked that. Why don't we see what's in the fridge? Maybe today we could have lunch!"

"OK. I take the hint. I'll see what I can find."

"No. No. That's not what I meant. Why don't we all look. If there is nothing usable, why don't we call in a Chinese meal? I'm sure they still deliver, the storm isn't here yet!"

"What about the crypt and what we saw earlier?"

"When the equipment arrives and I'm sure it will we can then install it in the crypt."

"That sounds good to me!"

"I also like the idea of calling in a Chinese meal, after all you were the one complaining that all we have eaten is breakfast!

"OK. I'll order any requests."

"No why don't you just order a selection!"

Nat went off to order the food. Beth went to the kitchen to prepare and left John to finish his calls. Lunch arrived at eleven thirty. Nat paid the guy at the door and took it through to the kitchen where Beth took over. She already had the table laid with plates and condiments. "OK. Guys food is served!" Nat and then John arrived and sat down. Beth had already opened the cartons and set them in the center of the table, so that they could help themselves. After they had finished eating Beth threw the cartons in the trash, then put the plates into the sink; because no one had lived here, there was no dishwasher. Thirty minutes later there was a knock on the door. "That, I hope, is for me," John said, as he walked off to the door.

"What do you think now, Nat?"

"I still have reservations but I must admit that equipment should give us the weapons we need to find what this is all about."

John came back into the kitchen with a big smile on this face. "I take it, John, you got your delivery?"

"Yes indeed. Yes indeed". They walked into the hallway and found four men opening boxes and putting together the equipment. "John, there seems to be quite a lot of equipment there."

"That, Nat, is because I ordered three of everything."

Nat laughed. "Well you did say the trust had a bottomless pit."

"If you can imagine, what it would mean to once and for all get to the bottom of this house." John waited while the men assembled the different camera and sensor equipment. John looked at his watch. "Nat, it's one forty five. I think we still have enough time before dark and before the bad weather comes in, don't you?"

"If we move fast." John thanked the men and gave them something Nat presumed was money. As they left and exited the front door John tuned to Nat. "You know I think I may be a little excited."

"Hold that thought," Beth said. What she felt was a cold hand walk its fingers down the entire length of her spine. "Nat, I suggest we leave the rest of the equipment here and just go straight to the crypt."

"OK. Let's go. I just wish I felt as confident as you. All that place holds for me is horror and fear."

"I understand, I really do but we can't stop now."

"OK. John, let's go!" Nat looked into Beth's eyes and saw the same fear he felt himself. He reached out his hands and took Beth's and squeezed them tenderly. At that Nat picked up two tripods. Beth got the camera and John the sensor equipment. This time each also put on rain gear and rubber boots. They walked through the kitchen into the orchid room, as Beth liked to call it. From there they made their way outside and into the rain and down to the lake; no one spoke, no one felt the need. The sky now was like a shroud. It seemed to linger just above them ready to drop at anytime and smother them. Beth felt the rain on her face not heavy but enough to make it miserable and she certainly felt miserable. How did I get myself into this, she thought. I must be crazy. At that a voice in her head that she knew right away to be that of Francis, said, "You know, Sister, if you don't do this you and I can never rest." Just that sentence installed new courage and vitality to

Beth's steps. That's funny, Beth thought. I know it's Francis, but her voice is so much more grown up!

As they reached the south end of the lake, Nat felt a cold lump in the pit of his stomach. He wasn't afraid for himself he was scared for Beth. They turned south along the west side of the lake. He turned to Beth to try and give reassurance. The look on Beth's face that met him dispelled all his fears. Beth's face told a different story. She beamed a smile he hadn't seen for a long time. He then knew that he had no fears. Nat looked forward and knew from John's gait that he had nothing to worry about. He thought, should I now worry about me? He now felt better for the task ahead. They continued on to the edge of the south side of the lake. From there they had to leave the lake and go through the trees to the crypt. They moved on until the crypt came into sight. All of them felt a dread but they also had a resolve and that kept them going. As they moved down towards the burial chamber Nat noticed something outside the door. "What's that, John?"

"Something else I thought might be of some use."

"As the men unloaded and put together these tools I had two more men place a generator, wires and lights down here. Don't worry they were never in danger I told them to place them here and then leave, all the time we were in radio contact."

"Congratulations, John, you really did get organized. Are there any more surprises?"

"Maybe just one, I had another generator put between the conservatory and the cellar with petrol and leads, lights and stuff. My thoughts were if the storm comes and the power goes out then we'll need an alternative."

"Once again, John, well done. You seem to have thought of everything."

"Not everything, Nat! None of us are that good!" As they got closer to the door Nat saw what John had done.

There was a generator, electric wires, lamps and tools, all they should need.

"OK. Nat, Beth, let's get in this place! Let's hope this door doesn't decide this time to give us trouble. The last time you opened this door I believe you said it just opened from touch?"

"Yes, that's the way it seemed."

"Nat, did the door open in or out?"

"You know I think you're right, it didn't mean anything at the time but I believe the door opened in!"

"Is that important, Nat?"

"Yes, Beth, most doors open out!"

"Well why don't we see what this door is going to do?"

"OK, why don't you give the door a try?" At that Beth moved forward and pushed the door; it opened. "Just like that, Nat?"

"Yes. John, just like that."

"OK. I suggest, Nat, you put the petrol in the generator and I'll start taking the leads into the crypt."

Nat held back a laugh. "Why do Brits insist on calling gas petrol? What would you like me to do?"

"Beth, why don't you just take it easy, your turn will come!"

"I'm not sure I like the sound of that," Beth said.

Nat took the box from around the generator, put in the gas and then began reading the instructions. Simple, he thought, even for me. Move the choke to the left, turn the gas on and pull the starting rope. Nat pulled once, nothing. Then again, nothing. The third time it spluttered to life. Noisy at first and then as if like magic the machine slowed to a rhythmic idle.

"Well done, Nat, now plug in these leads."

Nat plugged in the leads and then he started to pay out the line. Beth watched with fascination and thought, these guys work well together. Nat and John started down the steps hooking the electric leads with metal hooks wherever they could. Although they had wall lights on no one trusted them totally and felt much better with the back up of the generator. Beth, with slow trepidation, moved through the door and followed John and Nat into the tomb. As they moved along the first level Beth looked from side to side and saw those familiar graves that she had witnessed the first time she and Nat had walked the vault. This time, though, she felt no freezing cold as she had before. With an easier feeling in her stomach Beth followed the guys down the walkway into the third level of the tomb. Now the lights were all fitted and working Beth thought, *man this is different.* As she held that thought the cold started to materialize, very subtle at first, just a hint in the joints. Beth began to hang the last row of lights on the third floor. Nat and John had gone back to the surface to check all the bulbs were working and the generator was good. As usual Beth thought the woman is always the one to be left alone with the monster. Why not, she thought, this time it's an anticlimax. The guys reached the top, all the bulbs were lit and the generator purred away. Satisfied they turned to descend again back to Beth. It was then that they noticed the cold for the first time.

"You feel that, John?"

"Yes I do, let's get down to Beth quick!"

Beth felt, smelt, and saw the fog all at the same time. How stupid, she thought, how could I have got separated down here? Shouldn't that only happen in the movies? Beth felt the panic begin to rise from her stomach. You silly cow, how could you have let this happen? As she looked to the bottom of the third layer the fog began to swirl and it seemed that a figure was trying to emerge. That's when the smell started again like rotting seaweed. Beth began to gag; she knew she was in deep trouble and needed to get out. She turned to run but knew instinctively that wasn't going to work she was rooted to the spot. "Beth," she said, "this time you're in deep trouble." The figure now became clearer. "Oh God! He doesn't have a head." Beth felt herself slip into a near faint, and collapse to the floor. It was at this moment that Beth felt a very strange euphoria take over her body as the fear left her. "Beth, Beth, please wake up, are you alright?"

Beth slowly came around to see Nat and John kneeling over her like they had seen a ghost. "What is it, what wrong?"

"Don't you know? Don't you remember what happened?"

"Vaguely, there was a mist and then something came out of the fog like a man with no head."

"Yes, Beth! It was him again but this time you had help."

"I don't understand!"

"Nor do we, even though we saw them."

"Who did you see?" John interceded.

"The twins, Beth, they walked out holding your hands. They saved you from what was down there."

"I saw them but I don't think I will ever believe it not as long as I live."

"Oh, you saw them, Nat?"

"And so did I but like you I don't expect anyone to believe us!"

Beth felt a lump in her throat and tears welling up in here eyes; now she knew for sure what she must do and why she was here!

"Let's get back to the house the next thing we have to worry about is the storm and that must be getting close by now."

With that they turned off the generator and all the lights. Beth noticed one strange thing; the door seemed to have closed on its own. They gathered themselves and moved back up along the side of the lake. The rain and the wind had strengthened in the time they had been in the crypt. Now the rain was coming down in sheets and made it hard to see. They followed each other back to the house and were more than glad to be inside out of the rain and the wind. They made their way through the kitchen after leaving the conservatory, a route they had now become so accustomed to. They had taken off their wet clothes as they came into the house although conversation was at a premium. It wasn't until they sat down and Beth put the coffee on that they began to unwind. John was the first to speak.

"After this, Nat, I will never again doubt the supernatural!"

"Don't be too hasty, John, not all that you see is real!"

"You mean what I just witnessed in that tomb was not real?"

"No not at all. Just don't believe in everything that you see."

"I think after all of this I'll think Mickey Mouse is real." This at last broke the ice and they all laughed. "OK, guys, let's see what the weather channel has in store for us."

Beth turned on the TV and there it was, a red circle on the map, just a red circle with a yellow center but it meant so much. "Well guys if there was ever a doubt, there it is coming right at us and it don't look to me to be a category one!"

"Turn it up, Beth, let's see just how big it is."

While they had been down in the crypt they had missed an evacuation warning that had included them.

"Well, John, it's now the real thing. Do you still think we should stay?"

"More than ever, Nat, after what has just happened more than ever. I realize I can't speak for you so we all must make up our own mind."

Nat looked at Beth but all he got was a smile and that told him a whole story. He looked back at John who had also seen Beth's smile. "Well, John, I guess you know?"

"I suppose I do." They all laughed again. The storm had reached category three status in the time they had been in the crypt. "HOLY MOLEY! That's a big storm and coming right at us!"

"Well, Nat, as they say in England this will sort the men from the boys. Can I make a suggestion again?"

"Fire away, John, you seen to be doing well."

"If you would like to go and get that other generator going!"

"No way, John, I'm not going in that hole on my own!"

"John, I think he's right!"

"Of course you are. I'll come with you, no one should be alone near that cellar."

"Beth, will you be alright here?"

"I don't really feel threatened. After what I have been through the kitchen seems like an oasis."

Nat and John walked around to the generator. Nat, like before, took the machine out of the box. John sorted out the wires and lights. Nat soon had the generator up and running.

"How much petrol did you put in it, Nat?"

"Oh. There was ten gallons in two plastic containers, I put one in." Now the wind was really singing through. The rain was sharp with its intensity and the night was slowly getting darker. "I think we should go inside now, John!"

"Lead the way, let's get back into the warm." They walked back into the house loosing out electric cables as they went. They held their heads low against the rain. As they made their way back into the kitchen they heard as well as felt a sudden gust of wind that seemed to shake the foundations. Nat turned to John. "I guess it's started, John."

"Yes with a blast as they say!" As they walked into the kitchen, Beth was waiting, with a concerned look on her face. "Did you feel that?"

"Yes, Hon! And I think it will get worse."

"One question I have, why do these storms always come at night?" The rain on the roof sounded more like hail. Beth looked at Nat. "I'm scared, Nat."

"So are we, Hon, so are we." John looked at the kitchen table and what he saw wasn't food. The table was a clutter of storm items. Candles, batteries, flashlights, matches, tins of food, bottles of water. "What's this, Beth? Are we in for a siege?"

"I hope not." The wind and the rain now sounded far stronger. "I think, my friends, this may be a night we will all remember for the rest of our lives!" The lights started to get brighter and then dim. "Did you leave the generator running, Nathaniel?"

"Of course I did!"

"Then I think it may be time to run these electric lines."

"Yes I think we should. Let's go."

"So soon, Nat?"

"Yes if we do it now we might just stay that much ahead!"

Nat and John returned to the conservatory. Nat went to check on the generator. John ran the leads they had left just inside. It didn't take long. They had already got everything ready. The bulbs jumped into life. The kitchen and conservatory lit up like a roman candle.

"Guys, don't you think this is a bit overkill?"

"Tell me that when everything goes out!"

And good at his word things started going out. The TV was the first to go then the fridge the time and the light went out in the microwave, last but not least the lights above the table. The lights John and Nat had installed shone, though.

"OK. Beth, you want to run that by me again?"

"No I know when I'm beat!"

"If you wouldn't mind you two we have business to take care of." Nat and Beth both laughed but each had an icy note to it. "What's next, John?"

"Well I did manage to set up a sensor and camera in the doorway of the crypt. I'd now like to put one in the cellar."

"You must be kidding me!"

"No, Beth, not at all, it has to be done. Though I suggest we do it together."

"I second that!"

"OK, let's go."

They all walked into the night together. The rain was still strong, the wind seemed to have shifted a little now the main blast was coming from the southeast, which told them the storm was here. As they made their way to the cellar each had their own feelings and misgivings. Beth heard the generator before she saw it. *Thank God for modem technologies,* she thought. The machine ticked away like a good Swiss watch. John carried the camera and sensor; Nat carried the tripods and other equipment.

"John, these wind gusts are getting pretty strong!"

"I know but this shouldn't take long."

They reached the entrance to the cellar. Lights were already on in and around the doorway.

"Are you really going in that place, John?"

"Yes! I have to; you and Nat stay out here in case anything strange happens again. If it does, get me out of there quick please!" John went down into the cellar with the tripods first and a light.

"How does it look, John?"

"Empty as always and cold as the grave." John set up the lights and the tripods. He got out as quickly as he could. "Right. Nat, you and Beth stay out here. I'll go back set up the rest of the equipment and then we can go home."

Home seemed like a million miles away right now. The rain came down now in torrents and the wind lashed them like a cat of nine tails. John was back in only minutes. But to Nat and Beth it seemed like a lifetime.

"Everything good, John?"

"Yes let's go home!"

They made their way back into the kitchen. Beth put the coffee on. This was going to be a long night. Nat was the first to speak. "What's next, John?"

"I wish I knew!" At that moment there was a loud bang above their head. "Is that thunder?"

"Sounds like a bomb going off."

"Don't get carried away it's only lightning!"

"Some lightning."

As the night progressed they sat around the kitchen table drinking coffee. All the electricity had now gone out. They had only the power from the generator.

"Once again, John, I have to congratulate you for the generator."

"Not yet, Nat. There's a long way to go."

The storm seemed to grow in strength with every thunderclap. Each one was louder than the last. The very foundation seemed to shake. Around the table they sat, each afraid and not showing it.

"We have one more set of tapes, any suggestions?"

Beth was the first to speak. "How about the attic, that's one of the first places we saw them."

"I have another suggestion."

"Go on, John, you seem to be leading the search."

"Why not the kitchen; you also saw the twins in here!"

"Yes, he's right, why not the kitchen?"

"Because we are sitting here damn it. If you were a ghost would you show yourself in the one room that threatened you?"

"Are you saying that we are a threat?"

"No you know what I mean!" At this Nat saw tears in Beth's eyes. "Beth, please, no one could accuse us of being a threat to the children."

"I know, John, I'm just a little shaky. You're right, this would be the best place to set up!"

Nat put up the tripod and John set up his equipment. "OK. Nat, as you say, we are now good to go!"

Outside the storm just gathered in momentum. Nat and Beth knew this was going to be one of the longest nights of their lives. The wind had a sound all of its own just like the torment of lost souls. To Beth it had a quality all of its own. She knew she was only imagining it but somewhere in the distance she heard voices. Low and soft at first, then a little louder. "BETH, HELP US WE NEED YOU!" Get a hold of yourself girl, she thought. Don't you start hearing things now. But the voices persisted. "HELP US, BETH,"

"Are you okay, Honey?" Nat said.

"Yes, of course."

John said, "Beth, what can you hear?"

"I don't know, it seems like there are voices far away."

"Are they the voices of the children?"

"Yes they are."

"I think it has started, Nat, this time for real!"

The doors to the conservatory slammed inwards three doors at once. Glass shattered. Nat, John and Beth held hands around the table as much for comfort as protection. The lights from the generator held. They gave the only comfort they would have this night.

"Nat, did you hear that?"

"Hear what, John?"

"Listen the camera just went off, another click. Now the sensor has just activated."

"What does that mean?"

"It mean's there's now more than us in this room!"

They held each other's hands now like it meant life or death. It was a scene from one of those old movies where the clairvoyant held hands and produced ectoplasm. Only this time the table wasn't dancing on the floor. What happened next wasn't out of some Alfred Hitchcock film, but worse.

This time their lights danced slowly; at first one would go out then another then they would come back on again.

"Hold on, Beth!" Nat called. "Stay together."

The wind now sounded as angry as a lion protecting her cubs. The camera sounded off several times but they saw nothing in the room. It was below zero now; their breath came out like fog. Nat could hear the whirring sound of the motion detector.

"We must have something on that, John."

"Not yet, Nat, give it longer."

The next blast of wind blew in three more windows of the conservatory. All three shattered.

"What next?"

"I fear there is more to come. Beth, just hold on tight."

This time the roof did give a little and they heard wood and shingles come loose and fly across the yard.

"Now I'm getting really scared, John!"

"Hold on, Nat, we have more to come!"

The sound that followed was the gutter coming down and the down pipes falling off the wall.

"Beth, are you okay?"

"Of course; why shouldn't I be?"

The whirring of the camera seemed constant now as it transversed from side to side on its stand. John could see from where he was sitting that the little color screen was capturing some sort of image.

"Nat, something is happening!"

"So let's take a look."

They broke from the table. The camera was the first to take their attention. On the screen all they could see at first was static. John moved to the sensors; they were going wild. Something was in this room and very close.

"What is it, John, what do you see?"

"I don't know. It seems very blurred!"

Beth walked to the camera and looked at the images in front of her. The screen gave off a kind of opalescent mirage.

"What do you see, Beth?" John called out.

"Shapes, just meaningless shapes."

"John, what did you see on the sensor?"

"The same. The thermal imagery shows us movement and shapes but nothing identifiable." The wind continued its relentless attack and it gave no quarter. "There must be more to it than this!"

"Why, John, is that set in stone?"

"What do you feel, Beth?"

"What should I feel?"

"Are the children here?"

"Of course they are, and Clare is waiting for you."

"Is she really? Can I see her?"

"Look into the camera!"

John saw what was a stolen image. One from so many years ago. "Please, this can't be real."

"Of course not, John, they are playing with your emotions. Hold on, don't let go. They are playing with your mind. Don't let them get into your head!"

"Help me, Nat!"

"I don't believe this is the children, this is the work of whatever malignant force abides in this God forsaken place!"

"What's that, Nat, have you started to believe in God?"

"All I can tell you for sure, Beth, is I believe in good and evil and we have both right here. I do believe those images are real."

"I don't understand what you mean."

"John, you yourself admitted that what you saw took place many years ago. Then you are really seeing a memory!"

"You mean what you said about the walls holding memories?"

"Yes. Just that I don't think it's the walls."

"Then what do you think it is?"

"I'm not sure, Beth, but whatever it is I think is in the cellar!"

At that they all sat back at the table. The lights from the generator dimmed again. "John, we must check that generator! It can't have run out of gas yet. Maybe I did something wrong. This time the two of you stay here and I'll go check the generator."

Nat ran this time out of the conservatory and alongside the building. His heart sunk because he couldn't hear the machine. His worst fears were realized, the generator had cut out. Nat shone his flashlight on the damned machine; there was plenty of gas. He checked the on and off switch and that's when he saw it. How could I have been so stupid, he cursed. What he saw was the choke, damn it, he had left it at the half setting; that meant it would run until it finally choked itself and that was exactly what had happened. Nat reset the choke to the off position and started to pull the rope. Nothing first, second and third pull. This can't be happening, he thought. Is this the car that won't start like in all those movies? Fourth pull it spluttered, fifth it ran again. Nat ran back inside the kitchen only to find John and Beth missing; his heart missed several beats. Now what would he do all alone in this damn castle in this storm. He almost cried.

"Nat, come here! Nat, come take a look at this." Beth's voice was like angels singing in his ears.

"Where are you, Beth?" he called out.

"In here, Nat." The voice came from the study. Nat walked through to find John and Beth looking at the floor. As he looked down his blood ran cold in his veins. There was cut into the wooden floor the words HELP US! Nat felt again that cold knife twist in his stomach. The wind was still whipping up a fury and the rain still came down like hail. "How did you find this?"

"I didn't, Beth did!"

"What happened, Beth?"

"I don't know, I just had a feeling as you left for the generator to look inside the study. By the way, what was wrong with the generator?"

"My fault. I'm afraid I left the choke half on. It flooded and cut out."

"Do we have power again?"

"Yes we do."

They walked back into the kitchen and the light. Beth wasn't sure how she felt after all that had happened. She felt she had been on a roller coaster ride. One thing she knew for sure this is not Disney World.

"Can we make coffee, Beth?"

"Yes I'll boil some water on the stove."

"Why don't you plug into one of the leads."

"No thank you! I'm not messing with them again the primas will do fine." Beth walked to the kitchen counter filled a saucepan with water and placed it on the stove. Nat and John took stock. Everything was working. They had full power from the generator. The storm still raged and screamed outside.

"What's the next move, John?"

"I would say sit at the table, have the coffee, relax and look at our position." John and Nat sat at the table and Beth served coffee. "OK. The way I see it our presence along with the storm has brought about a change."

"What kind of change?"

"I think it's you that brought about the major change. Your love for the children and your care for humanity."

"Yes, Beth. I go along with that. It's your innocent presence and this storm that will bring down this evil deck of cards."

"I thank both of you for your vote of confidence, but kind words won't solve this enigma."

"I agree, I think the next move we make is to check the instruments in the cellar and the crypt."

"I agree, but I have to say, and I think this goes for Beth as well, I'm scared to death!"

"Don't think I don't understand that and I also feel the same. I believe that shortly there will be a lull in the storm as the eye passes over."

"John, don't you think that would be the most dangerous time?"

"Yes I agree it would be a very dangerous time. But I think we would have at least one hour to get to the crypt and back."

"I think we are cutting it fine but if Beth's happy, count me in!"

"I don't think that is the way I would put it. But I'm in if it's the only way to go."

"OK. Let's get prepared. I would estimate another two hours before the lull. Nat, in the mean time, why don't we check the cellar?"

"You know, John, I was afraid you were going to say that."

"Come on, Nat, there's not going to be a better time."

"Nat, I agree with John, this is as good a time as any!"

"OK. You win, let's go but I am frightened!"

"So join the club, Honey, join the club."

As they exited the door and into the storm they could barely hear themselves think. The rain was as hard as ever but that wasn't the problem it was the wind. Like a living force all of its own it howled and screamed like a thousand charging Banshees. Nat could see tree limbs down and running before the wind. He knew this was about as bad as things were going to get with the storm. He also knew this was not as bad as things would get for them. As they neared the cellar each in their own way felt pleasure at the sound of the generator. Nat thought, if I ever get out of this, I'll write a letter of thanks to the inventor of the generator. The doorway was well lit even in this subterranean gloom. They stood by the doorway together each feeling their own fear and not wanting to share it.

"NAT!" John shouted above the storm. "You and Beth stay here. I'll go down and get the tapes. If you hear me call, come like the cavalry."

As John disappeared into the hole Nat knew he was just as frightened as they were. John would never have called for the cavalry. Nat and Beth held each other as much for consolation as warmth. Nat started to get panicky and thought John must be in trouble. Beth held him back.

"Give him longer, Nat, give him longer." Three minutes later still no sound from John. "I'm going down. Stay here!"

"Nat, don't look at the walls!"

"I don't understand. Why not look at the walls?"

"Don't ask me now I'll tell you later. Just don't look at the walls."

Nat descended the steps and entered the room. As he disappeared from sight Beth did what she was told not to. She followed. Although terrified, she walked off the steps and entered the cellar. What met her eyes proved that she had been right to be terrified. John was on his knees in the center of the room; he seemed to be babbling like a small child. Nat had a hold on John with his arms curled under his shoulders. When he saw Beth he screamed, "GET OUT, BETH! GET OUT OF THIS DAMNED PLACE!

"Get John out, I'm not leaving without the tapes."

Nat pulled more than carried John out of the cellar. Beth kept her eyes to the floor at all times as she groped around for the tripods. She found the camera first, threw the catch and took the camera. She then felt around for the sensor. Beth felt like a fish out of water feeling around on the ground frightened to take her eyes from the ground. At last she found it - the tripod for the sensor. Reaching up she unclipped it from the stand, held them both real tight and got the hell out. At the top of the steps in the rain and the wind Nat was waiting. John lay on the ground in the mud with a blank look on his face.

"Are you alright, Beth?"

"Yes, I'm fine. Let's get John back inside!"

Nat lifted John over his shoulder in a fireman's hold. They made their way back in what seemed like battlefield conditions. Back to the house away from all the mayhem of the storm, Nat put John down on the floor. Beth got a pillow from the lounge and placed it under John's head.

"Get a blanket. Nat, we must make sure he doesn't go into shock."

Nat ran upstairs to get a blanket and Beth made John as comfortable as she could. John started to shake. "Please, Nat! Hurry up with that blanket."

A minute later, Nat came back in the room carrying two blankets. Beth put them immediately around John. "How is he, Beth?"

"How should I know? I'm no doctor!" Beth quickly realized what she had done. "I'm sorry, Nat, forgive me?"

"Nothing to forgive. We're all under stress. Let's concentrate on John."

At that moment he started to come around. "What happened? Where am I?"

"Take it easy, John, don't try to get up yet." Turning to Beth he said, "Get him a Brandy!"

Beth poured a Brandy from the cabinet then handed it to John. As the drink touched his lips John felt a fire flow through his veins. "What happened in there, Beth?"

"I'm not sure but I think it must have something to do with your family's heritage."

"I don't understand; you mean I'm the weak link?"

"Yes I believe that's exactly it!"

"How do you know this?"

"I don't know I just do!"

John came around slowly at first. "You know I think we should all take Brandy for breakfast instead of tea or coffee! It's a more civilized way to start to day."

"John, tell me what did you see?"

"Take it easy, Beth, let me get my thoughts back."

"I don't think we have time!"

"Beth, what do you know that we don't?"

"I'm not real sure it's like I know but no one told me. I know that doesn't make a lot of sense but it's the best way I can explain it."

"After all I've witnessed it makes as much sense as anything else."

"I agree, Nat, but I think you better let me explain what I think I saw. It was as though the walls came to life, like being in a cinema."

"But what did you see?"

"I didn't just see, Beth, I felt and lived the experience."

"I don't understand."

"No, Nat, I'm sure you don't but I have a feeling Beth does."

"What is it, Beth, what do you know that we don't?"

"I can't say that it's something that I know it's vary hard to explain."

"So try us."

"Have you ever had a dream that you have forgot that came back days or weeks later?"

"You mean like deja-vu?"

"Yes like that but not the same."

"Beth, you're talking in riddles."

"Please, Nat, let her finish, I think I know what she means."

"It's like I lived here before. It's not a strange place to me."

"You know, Nat, the funny part to all this since Linda's death and please forgive me for bringing the subject up. It has been your continued pursuit to find a medium or a channel to reach the other side. You have traveled thousands of miles for the very thing that is right in front of you. Your girlfriend Beth, the woman soon to be your wife. She is the very thing you have been looking for. I'm sorry, Beth, excuse me for referring to you as a thing, but that's the best way for me to explain to Nat."

"Keep going, you're doing fine. Maybe Nat needed to hear this from someone else!"

"I take your point, you are right of course and the funny part is I had already thought as much." At that a huge bang, a noise like an explosion and vibration, reverberated through their souls. "What the hell was that!" Nat cried. John slowly pulled himself from the floor.

"Take it easy, John, don't get up too fast."

"It's alright, Beth, just shaken a little, let me up."

They helped John to his feet and quickly walked to the kitchen door. What they saw froze the blood in their veins. Half of the conservatory roof had fallen in. The ship's beams they had tried so hard to find were as bare as a dinosaur's skeleton.

"Any suggestions, Nat?"

"Honestly I think this house will weather the storm. It's us that I'm worried about." With the storm churning outside each took stock of their own feelings.

"Well, at least the electric is still working."

"As you say, Beth, there's something to be grateful for."

"John, would you mind telling us what you saw in that cellar?"

"I saw it all, the whole history of this house and more."

"Please explain?"

"Well that is hard to do!"

"John, please tell me were the images in or on the walls?"

"Yes, Beth, they were."

"Beth, explain to me what you mean."

"It's simple; the walls as you suspected act like a cinema screen."

"All that has happened to this family is somehow recorded in that room."

"Yes, John, that's exactly what I mean!"

"How? I don't understand! What do you think; what do we do next?"

"John, as you said, this storm is going to give us a break shortly for only one hour."

"It's the eye, Nat, the eye of the storm. We have a window of about one hour."

"You mean then we are thrown back into the maelstrom?"

"Yes! That's exactly what I mean."

"Before we do anything else I suggest we take a look at those tapes; after all, we worked hard enough to get them!"

First John played the tape from the camera. "Nothing! It's blank again!"

"Wait, Nat, look. It's not blank, there's something coming up now." They all stared at the screen as an image started to appear. Blurred at first, it slowly began to clear, like setting the auto tracking on a TV control. What they saw next was disturbing. "What is that, Nat?" What's is happening?"

"It look's like some kind of a ceremony." As the screen slowly cleared, they saw a wooded clearing backing on to cliffs. In the center lay a large gray flat stone. They were horrified to see a young girl naked on her back, tied at the wrists and ankles with what looked like vines. The sheer terror on the girl's face became all too evident. Around her stood ten or twelve native Indians, chanting. In the fore of the picture just at the back of the girl and the stone stood another Indian, who stood out from the rest by what he wore. He was richly adorned with many colored feathers.

"Are you all seeing what I see?"

"Unfortunately, yes, I fear we do," said John.

The Chief or medicine man wore a headdress of feathers as well, but that wasn't the main focus of their attention. In the hands of the feathered man a knife glistened in the sun. The blade was triangular shaped about ten inches long and awe inspiring to look at.

"Can this be real?" Beth asked. "If it recorded then it must have happened sometime."

At that the feathered man lifted the knife above his head. They were glued to the screen. "I don't think I want to see what comes next."

The knife descended in a flash of steel and sunk deep into the girl's flesh, and as he pulled the knife free deep red blood gushed from the wound. Beth let out a scream. Nat reached to turn off the tape but John held him back. "Wait! Nat, not yet."

Beth turned and walked away. As John and Nat looked on, the Priest put the knife to the girl's throat and began to cut backwards and forwards as if cutting a joint of meat, the blood now ran freely. The girl's struggles slowly subsided and then she lay still.

"What have we just witnessed, John?"

"I'm not sure but I feel it happened a long time ago."

The picture slowly began to dissolve. In its place a message came on the screen. GET OUT WHILE YOU STILL CAN!

Beth was retching and coughing in the sink as John and Nat walked though from the study. All of a sudden the storm didn't seem to count so much. Beth turned to them with a towel held to her mouth. "Do you think that could have been real?".

"Yes, Beth, I do. I also think it happened a long time ago!"

"Why, Nat? Why would you think that?"

"I still think that room is some kind of recording device or at least there is something in there that has the capacity to record!"

"That was the most awful thing I ever saw in my life. Real or not I never want to see anything like that again."

"John, what's your take on this?"

"I tend to agree with you, Nat. It would seem the only logical explanation"

"But why has it been trapped in there all these years and who are those Indians?"

"I don't know, Beth, I really don't know."

"What about the censer, John, we haven't checked that yet?"

"I think we should check on the progress of the storm first, don't you?"

"Yes, of course, let's take a look outside."

"Why don't you wait in here, Beth? We won't be long."

"Not on your life, you'll have to tie me up first."

They walked to the kitchen door. Outside the sound of the wind and rain was just as intense as before nothing had changed.

"Well, guys, thankfully it doesn't look as if any more of the roof has come down."

As if in answering her, one more beam broke free and fell almost at their feet. "That will teach me!" Beth said.

"Nat, tell me if I'm wrong but can you see light on the horizon?"

"Yes, John, I do believe I do!"

"I think we should get prepared, don't you?"

"What about the censer?" Beth asked.

"No time," he replied. "If we miss this opportunity we'll not get another chance."

"He's right, Beth, let's get prepared."

They moved back into the house to prepare. "You know, John, if I thought it would help I'd carry a gun."

John smiled. "Do you for one moment think Wyatt Earp could help us now?"

"No, I guess you can't shoot holes in a ghost."

"OK, you two, you want to tell me how we solve this?"

"I believe, Beth, if we keep going something will show itself."

"I wish I had your confidence, John!"

"Come on, Beth, aren't you Americans taught to think positive?"

"Yes, of course we are, but no one mentioned we had to believe in ghosts."

John laughed nervously. "Point taken," he said.

"What do you think we're going to need?"

"Rain clothes, boots, and flashlights in case we have trouble with the generator."

"How about a Crucifix, John, if there is one in this Godless place?"

"You make a good point there, Beth. I can't ever remember seeing one in this house, but if you do find one I think it might work better than Nat's gun."

"OK, guys, I give in, the gun idea was pretty stupid."

"You know, Beth, I don't remember ever seeing a Bible in this house."

"Why should there be, no one lives here!"

As John and Beth were talking Nat had walked to the door to see what was happening with the storm. "Guys, come and take a look at this!"

As they walked over to the door, Nat went outside. "Did you ever see anything like that in your life?"

They joined Nat in what was left of' the conservatory. The sky looked alien. "I don't know how I would categorize that sky, beautiful or scary!"

"With what we have to do I would say scary."

"Scary or not, Beth let's get in gear!"

The storm now was reaching its lowest ebb. The rain and the wind had begun to slow and the light had begun to return. "Let's go, my friends, we won't get a second chance!"

They put on their rain gear and boots, picked up the flashlights and walked out the door. This was the moment they had all waited for, the lull in the storm. As they headed towards the lake, Beth thought, what a surreal scene this is. A clear day in the middle of a storm. That must be an oxymoron, she thought. They walked south past the side of the building towards the lake. This time Beth noticed they had picked up speed considerably. They walked past the lake and into the trees, where they came to a halt. All eyes were on the crypt. Beth thought, I wonder what sweet surprises await us this time. No one spoke as they walked from the trees to the crypt.

Nat moved ahead of the others, feeling he was responsible for the generator. It wasn't running, but that was OK because this time he had turned it off. He arrived at the generator and turned the electric switch to On and pulled the string. The machine started without a splutter and ran like a new car. John walked up and took the initiative and pushed the door. As it had before the door opened and laid bare that dark pit. All the lights were on in the place; it was lit up like a Christmas tree. Beth walked up to the door and said, "OK, let's go."

The sky above was clear with no rain, and there was no wind. All three descended the steps together. John and Nat first, Beth bringing up the rear. They walked to the first floor past the graves that had become all too familiar. "Well, here we are, no point in holding back now."

"Not so fast, Beth, take it easy. Remember, fools rush in."

"Yes, John, but I never looked at myself as an Angel!"

Beth walked past John and made her way along the first floor. "She means it, John, I don't ever remember seeing her so focused."

Beth reached the end of the first corridor and turned the comer.

"Let's stay with her, John. Heaven knows what could be down there."

"If the knowledge is anywhere, Nat, it won't be in Heaven."

Beth felt she was on a roll. She felt after the first tape that this one must contain the proof they needed. The tape and censer were still running when Beth reached them. She thought, something must have got them going. She turned her gaze to the bottom floor. She had by now witnessed many things, and horror and fear were no longer strangers. But she was not prepared for what she saw now. There at the bottom of the third floor stood her sister Francis, all grown up and looking beautiful in a long, flowing white dress. Beth stopped dead in her tracks. All the air in her lungs disappeared and she became rooted to the spot.

Nat and John turned the comer. Nat saw the woman at the bottom of the stairs in the white dress slowly evaporate. "That was not one of the children!"

"No, Nat, that was my sister Francis."

"Hold on, Beth, let's get the tapes and get out of here."

Nat and John half carried, half dragged Beth back to the surface. "We need to get her back to the house before we get any more surprises."

The sky was clear. They headed back to the house along the west side of the lake. "LOOK, NAT! Look at the south side of the lake!"

Nat looked and there by the tree that Beth had first pointed out stood the figure in a brown robe. Before they could focus their eyes it seemed to disappear into the mist. "Come on, John, this place just gets spookier."

As they made their way back to the house, they heard thunder in the distance. "Here we go again!" Nat said. "It's going to be a beautiful day"

They set Beth down on a chair in the kitchen, Nat made coffee. "Must we always drink coffee, Nat, every time things get tough?"

"You know, you're right, I don't think I could drink any more coffee."

"Beth how do you feel?"

"Just great, Nat! How would you feel just seeing your dead sister after thirty years?"

"OK, my friends, I think the storm is on its way back."

"Thanks, Professor, the timing is just perfect."

"Beth, what you saw I don't believe was real, a kind of mirage conjured up somehow by this house."

"You mean the house is alive?"

"No, that's not what I mean."

"There is a presence in the house that none of us can conceive. Why don't you both face up to the fact that this house is haunted."

"Wouldn't that be taking the easy way out?"

"I don't think there's anything easy about this house."

"Shall we look at the tape?"

"I think first we should prepare for the next installment of the storm."

As if on cue, thunder sounded in the distance.

"Well, guys, here we go again. Was that really her, Nat? Was that really Francis? Or was it just some cruel, evil illusion?"

"I don't know, Beth, I honestly don't know. She certainly looked real enough"

"What do you think, John?"

"I can only tell you this, Beth, whoever or whatever, it meant you no harm. Either she was your sister or not, only you can answer that."

"You're right about one thing, I didn't feel she meant me any harm, just the opposite. I felt love!"

Beth turned and walked away, she sniffed and they both knew she had tears in her eyes. Ten minutes later came the all too familiar sound of the rain and the wind. The storm came out of the west this time and appeared to be much stronger. The first part had come from the east but now the eye had passed. Ever thing switched to the west.

"Am I getting paranoid or has this storm gone up a notch?"

"No, Beth, I think you're right, it does seem to have grown in strength. What do you think, Nat?"

"I think you are both right, the storm's coming from the west now the second part of the storm can be stronger than the first."

The next blast of wind seemed to shake the very foundations. "You know, guys, we might just be in trouble from this storm."

"How strong do you think this house is, John?"

"The old part, the conservatory, is not too strong, that's already partially fallen in. The rest of the house was built with more modem materials, and with help from the storm shutters that should hold up better."

"I suggest we move into the northern end of the house, that should give us maximum protection."

They moved out of the kitchen through the hallway that the study ran off into a lounge that Nat hadn't spent time in before.

"This room is cold or am I starting to panic again?"

"No, Beth, it's cold but I don't believe it's supernatural. I think the room just needs warming. In the summer these rooms aren't heated; after all, no one lives here. I'm afraid, though, that without electricity all we can do is light a fire."

"No, John, I'll settle for a jumper."

"No need, Beth."

Nat took off his coat and wrapped it around Beth's shoulders. Again they felt the building shake. "You know, Nat,

I think this main building will stand this kind of punishment but I'm not confident about the orchid room as you call it."

Again as if on cue a thunderous sound emerged from the old house. "I think we may have spoken too soon, John. It sounds as if we have already lost the conservatory. Do you think we should take a look?"

"No, Nat, not at all. Let's hold up here until the worst is over."

"I'll second that," said Beth.

"OK, that's you and me, what about you, John?"

"I'll go along with you two, let's stay safe."

"There's one problem, guys, these flashlights aren't going to last too long."

"Do we have any more cable, Nat?"

"Yes. There're two more just in the kitchen door, but you're going to have to come with me. I don't trust what's left of the roof."

"Beth, will you stay here while I go with Nat to run the cable? I think we would both be happier knowing you're safe in here."

"OK, but please don't be long!"

"A few minutes, that's all."

Beth watched as Nat and John's lights slowly disappeared out of the room. She took this moment to look around the room. She shone the naked beam of her flashlight though the heavily clothed darkness of the room. The beam touched the wall above the fireplace, and she noticed a portrait hanging there. "So that must be the man himself in all his glory."

As the torch beam slowly moved down the picture Beth could see this man belonged in the eighteenth century, the clothes and the wig gave that away. Beth was transfixed and maybe a little hypnotized when a noise brought her out of her trance.

"Are you OK, Beth?" Nat said as he came through with a cable and light. John was right behind with another light.

Now the room really came to life. With all this light Beth could now see that there where portraits all around the walls of the room.

"You know, it's funny, John, as long as I've been in this house I don't think I once came in this room."

"Why should you, it's a big house, there must be rooms that I've never been in either. I don't live here."

Beth's attention went back to the portrait over the fireplace. "That must be Niles Remington?"

"Yes, that's the old Judge himself."

"He must have been quite a character."

"Yes, Beth, I'm sure he was."

"Who were all the others?"

"Just my ancestors. Three generation's of them."

"The good, the bad and the ugly."

"OK, Nat, no need for sarcasm, we all have a skeleton in the cupboard."

Nat looked a bit sheepish. "I'm sorry, John, I mean no disrespect."

"I know, Nat, I never thought you did. I think we are all a little jumpy and scared. This storm has us all on edge. Beth, if you look at each portrait, there's a name and date at the bottom."

Again they felt the house shake.

"What was it like out there, Nat, when you got the cable and the lights?"

"Pretty scary, there's really not much left of the conservatory, just ship's beams and dust. The old house was pretty much gone and the storm doesn't seem to be slowing down anytime soon."

"Do you think we are safe in this room?"

"Yes, Beth I do. Like I said before, this part of the house was built much stronger."

Beth walked around the room looking at the pictures. Nat and John took care placing the lights where they would do the most good. "Tell me, John, why are there no women here?"

"Because that's the way it was in this family, Beth."

"OK, then, tell who is the father of the twins Jonathon and Clare?"

"Right here."

Beth looked up too see a man not so harsh as she had expected. "John, he looks almost human."

John let out a laugh. "Thank you, Beth, I needed that! You are right, of coarse, Sir Arlington was the first of the family to go into Politics. He enjoyed some success in the British Parliament. He was knighted by George IV of England in 1822. It was commonly thought that the family bought his Knighthood. He never excelled in much after that and dissolved into obscurity after the death of the twins."

"Who's he?" Beth pointed to the picture to the right of Arlington.

"That is Major George Remington, he died from a mortar shell fighting the British, would you believe, at Lake Champlain."

"What a contradiction it must have been for your family to have fought on both sides of the War of Independence."

"Not just that, we also fought in the American Civil War. This family would appear to have fought in every War we could find."

"Do you have a portrait of Captain William Remington?"

"Yes, we do. Take a look at this other wall."

John took Beth on a journey past the back wall to the south wall where the door was. Just to the right of the door a portrait hung of a sad man. "John, he look's so sad."

"Yes, Beth, we always think of him as the sad man."

"Why?"

"As you Americans say, he never got a break."

"You mean he had no luck?"

"It would seem that way, bad luck seemed to follow him."

"Some bad life, you die in a war, your son dies in a ditch, then your wife commits suicide. This room is full of sad stories, just pick one."

"I don't think I want any more of this family's history. It's too sad."

"That's right, why do you think we the family want the end of this house?"

"Is there anyone else in this room that you feel needs scrutiny?"

"Just one more, Beth."

John took Beth by the hand and led her to the end of the south wall. "This one may be of interest to you." John pointed to the last picture on the wall.

"It's you, John, younger I must admit, but you nonetheless."

"No, Beth, a likeness I admit, but not me."

"OK then, judging from the clothes he must be your father?"

"Right, he is my father, he's William Jackson Singleton."

"If he's your father, then that would make Captain..."

"John stopped her right there. "That's right, Captain William Singleton Remington, the sad man, was my grandfather and the boy who drowned in the ditch was my uncle."

"I'm sorry, I didn't know."

"How could you until now?"

"But I read the letters and the newspaper reports of the time, and they said young Jonathan was the only child."

"Yes, he was in this country, but not so in England. They were the last family to have spent any real time in this house. After them the Trust didn't want any more. No more bad publicity so the family closed ranks. It would appear that

William had an indiscretion while in England with a young single lady of the name Singleton."

"So that would account for the two names Remington and Singleton?"

"Yes, Beth, you see, the family in its rush to cover scandal and the possibility of the end of the family line, put the two family names together, both being fifthly rich of course. That, my dear, is who you have here in front of you now!"

Beth wasn't sure whether to laugh or cry. "John, every story that comes out of this house is so sad. Who did your family wrong?"

"You see, Beth, now you too believe in the family curse!"

Again the house shook with the ferocity of the wind.

"Beth, leave them damn portraits alone!"

"I can't Nat, isn't this what we are here for, to find the answers? Somewhere among these portraits must be the answers."

"All I see so far, you are both getting a world of hurt!"

"Tell me, John, who is missing from this rogues' gallery?"

"You already know, Beth. It' me, I'm the last in line."

"That's right, John it ends with you, and you knew that."

"Beth, I just want it to end."

"Yes, but not at the cost of your own life."

"I am the end of the line and I would like it to end here!"

"OK, you two, let's cut the crap. There's a hell of a storm out there and we have to live though it. I don't know if you noticed but half of this house is gone."

Beth took John's hand and said, "Don't worry, I think this will all work out."

John's hand was as cold as ice. Beth looked at him and said, "Don't worry, I'm with you!. Whatever happened to this family will end soon!"

The rain sounded like machine gun bullets on the roof. Then there came one more thunderclap and a sound like hell had let out its fury, a sound they had never heard before. This time the kitchen had given way.

"Did you hear that, Beth?"

"Yes, Nat, we have just lost the kitchen. This is going to be a long night."

The wind was like a force all of it own. Nothing could stop it. Slowly but surely the wind crept into the room with the portraits. The walls shook but nothing gave. Then a haze like a fog crept into the room. The room became as cold as the grave. Beth held John's hand.

Nat moved closer. "Who is it, Beth?"

"They're here, Nat"

"Who?"

"You know who, the twins!"

At that moment a mist formed in front of the fireplace. The room took on a glow. John started to shake. Beth looked around the room and saw the mist accumulate around Niles Remington. They held each other like there was no tomorrow.

"Who is it, John?"

Right before the fireplace the fog started to clear in front of their eyes and the twins appeared. Beth broke down in tears. John choked and couldn't speak. Nat asked. "Who are you?"

"You know who we are! We need help."

"How can we help you?"

"The thing we all seek is in the cellar, you must look there. If you seek and find it there, you will set us free!"

Nat said, "Screw this! What do you think you two are into? This is not a Hollywood screen. We aren't watching Rebecca; this is no Daphne DuMaurier novel. This is real life. Do you know what you are looking at? They are ghosts, they don't exist!"

"Yes, they do, in this world and theirs," Beth shouted at Nat.

He turned back and stood beside John with his eyes transfixed on the apparition in front of him. John also stood aghast. Beth was now just behind the two of them. As they all stood in awe, Beth felt the temperature drop again. *Now what?* she thought. Slowly, quietly the voice drifted to her ears. "Elizabeth, Elizabeth."

Beth's whole being froze as if someone had stabbed her in the stomach with a freezing cold icicle. As terrified as she was she could not stop herself from turning around. Again she heard the voice, louder this time. "Elizabeth, Elizabeth." The voice seemed familiar but so did the fear. Beth found it impossible not to face that haunting voice. The cool mist was heavy in the air. Beth couldn't work out if the lights had gone dim or whether the mist was obscuring them. It was at that moment she saw it. She sucked in her breath. "OH. MY GOD!" she muttered as her heart missed two beats. There standing in front of her was her grown up sister Francis. Beth felt her feet had been nailed to the floor; she couldn't move a muscle. There was not a single part of her body that answered a command. She was well and truly stuck to the spot.

"You must find the Evil one, fin and destroy it!"

Beth looked on not knowing if she should scream, cry or run and hold her sister Francis. "Beth, you must fin and destroy the Evil one."

Beth tried to ask who, what, where, but no words would leave her mouth.

"It lives with the dead, you'll find it there!"

Beth muttered, "How do we stop it?"

"The cellar, in the cellar."

Before Beth could tell Francis all the things she had stored for so many years, she vaporized. As Beth slowly came down to earth she turned to John and Nat. "Did you see her, Nat, did you see her?"

Nat and John where turning from the empty fireplace, both had a vacant look in their eyes. "Yes, Beth, we all saw them, the twins."

"No, Nat. Francis. Didn't you feel the cold?"

"Of course we did, the same time as you"

"No, I mean the second cold?"

"I don't understand, Beth. I never saw Francis!" John interceded. What did you see?"

"My sister Francis, she was there by the wall."

Beth pointed to the back wall just below the portrait of a very military looking man. John took Beth by the shoulders and said, "Please, Beth, what did she say? You must tell us what she said."

"France's said we must destroy the Evil one and that it lives with the dead!"

"That doesn't make a lot of sense."

"Yes, Nat, it does. The dammed thing lives in the crypt with my dead family!"

"What do you think it could be, Beth?"

"John, the only thing I can think of would be that thing walking down by the lake in some sort of robe."

"Well, guys, I think it's time we looked at the damage and the storm."

"You're right, of course, Nat!"

"Come on, Beth, first things first."

Nat led the way as they walked into the hallway leaving the picture room behind. Of the three of them Nat was the most relieved to put that room behind. They turned right at the door and started down the hallway. The storm by this stage had slowed down considerably. Though they could still hear the rain, the wind had slackened to a mere breeze. John was the first to speak. "Well, at least the main part of the house would appear intact."

The only damage that the hallway had sustained was a coat of dust and dirt. Nat was the first to reach the kitchen door. He just stood and stared in disbelief. Beth and John reached the door just seconds after Nat and witnessed the same destruction. All that was left of the kitchen and the old house was a mass of wood, dirt, and rubble mixed in with furniture and kitchen implements. "Wow, that storm sure did a number!"

"Let's just be thankful that we got out unscathed."

"Yes, John, but it had history value."

"Not for me, Beth, there's nothing about this place that has any value or sentiment. The day that I can walk away from it will be one of the happiest of my life."

Beth took in the total devastation. She had never been in a war, but this was what she imagined a place would look like after a bomb had struck. She experienced sadness at the loss of the kitchen table, the place they had spent so many hours discussing what to do next and drinking so much coffee. She could only just make out the remnants under the rubble. She turned her attention to what used to be the large window over the sink, now almost unrecognizable. To the right where the cooker used to be was now just an empty space. Everything was gone. Nothing was as before.

"Don't go in there, guys, water and electricity don't mix!"

"Ok, Nat, let's use the side door."

They walked out the door into what seemed an underworld. The sky had a strange look about it. Imposing. Beth thought, *Is this what they call calm after the storm?* They all walked down the west side of the house to see the damage from the outside. Beth thought, *My God, the debris field goes on forever. I have never seen so much wood.*

Although the wind was now negligible, the rain still came down as a drizzle. The whole scene was out of a war film. Everything was down and destroyed.

"What next?" Beth asked, with a tone of desperation in her voice.

"Come on, Beth, where's that positive thought?"

At that moment Beth stopped in her tracks. "Nat, what do you see that we don't? All I see is a destroyed family home and we are no nearer to what we came here for than when we arrived"

"No, Beth, you are quite wrong about that. I think we have seen this house for what it really is."

"No, John, this is still a piece of real estate just like any other. It's just dirt and sand. It can't be any different."

"None of us could have been more wrong, could we? When will this damn rain stop?"

At that, as if on call, it stopped.

"Do you have a mobile phone, Nat?"

"Yes, of course."

"Would you mind if I used it?"

"Knock yourself out, John."

Nat and Beth walked down to the cellar first to turn off the generator, then down to the wall of the house to where the main damage was done. Everything had gone.

"Don't you feel it, Nat? It's so much calmer."

"You mean, Beth, the calm before the storm? Well, time to move on as John said. It's only trash and garbage clean up and rebuild."

"But what about all the things we've seen?"

"As they say, tomorrow is another day. Let's start with the clean up."

As Beth and Nat stood there looking at the carnage, John called, "I've just called the local police and you won't believe what they told me."

"Go on thrill us."

"Beth, the storm wasn't!"

"I don't understand. Run that by me one more time?"

"Okay, the storm or the hurricane blew itself down to a tropical storm not big enough to do real damage."

"John, this is an old house. It didn't need much to blow it down."

"Nat, a tropical storm would not have done this much damage, you know that."

Beth looked at Nat and said, "He's right, you know."

Nat looked down. "Of course he's right. That's what makes it so hard to accept"

"What's next, John?"

"Yellow Pages, I guess. Builders to clean this mess up."

"What about Greg, the guy who dug out the cellar?"

"You're right, Nat. Why don't you call him, you seemed pretty friendly."

John handed the phone to Nat. "Where is that dammed number?" Nat said, as he searched his pockets.

"Right here, Honey," Beth said with a smile, as she handed him the card.

Nat took the card and started punching in the numbers. "Can I speak to Greg Summers?" Then came a pause. "Greg, is that you? This is Nat from…" Nat paused again. "Greg, hey listen, we need some help right now. Well, we seem to have some storm damage. It would appear to be a little extreme. Okay, Greg, see you then."

He punched the phone off. "Well, guys, that's done, he's bringing around a team."

"The good news is the Police Department tells me the electric will be back on within the hour."

"So, Professor, what's the next move?"

"You can cut out the crap, Beth, nothing has changed; it's just another day. As to what we do next I suggest we clean up and then start again."

The Green Room

Two hours later Greg and his team arrived. They quickly reached a price and started the clean up. John had instructed them to take all the ship's beams and lay them out on the grass in the order in which they had been built. Every body was busy doing their own thing when Greg came to Nat. "I think there's something you should see!"

Greg led Nat into the ruin; there seemed so much of it, Nat thought. Greg's men were carrying the timbers and laying them on the grass as instructed. "This way, Nat." Greg led him through the ruined house to where the kitchen used to be. "Take a look at that."

"What should I see? I don't understand."

Greg pointed to the wood on the floor. "That is not from a modern building!"

Nat looked at the wood he had pointed out. "What are you trying to tell me, Greg?"

"Look at it, Nat, that wood is hundreds of years old!"

"You mean, the kitchen is part of the old house?"

"Right, in one."

"Well, that should excite John!"

"There's more."

"Please go on, this house has a twist around every comer."

"Look down there." Greg pointed at a spot. "There's a door down there and at a guess I would say it's the original cellar. Do you want us to open it?"

"No, please tell your men to stay clear and leave it alone."

"OK, you're the boss."

Greg went back to his men, then called out to Nat, "What is it, what have you found?"

"You better call John and then let him take a look at this!"

Nat stood there as if spellbound; something wasn't right but he couldn't quite put his finger on it. Looking at the debris he could see all the old timbers from the kitchen. He could tell that Greg was right but something else wasn't right. "Greg," Nat shouted, "can you spare a minute?"

"Sure, what's the problem?"

"That trench that runs between the kitchen and the conservatory, why would it be there?"

"It's really not unusual, I've seen this sort of thing before on properties as old as this. It looks to me that the conservatory was the original house. It's not unknown for the drain ditch or even sewer ditch to be close to the house. Remember, the front of this house was this west side, not as it is now the north side. Three hundred years ago the road wasn't there, so this house would have been in a meadow."

"So what you are saying is that the kitchen was built on later."

"Yes, but not much later than the original. If you look you'll see the floor was built with large flagstones that also ran across the ditch and if I'm not mistaken they will also be under the kitchen floor. It would seem the storm and the fallen rubble disturbed them and opened up the ditch.

"Thanks, Greg, you've answered a lot of questions for me."

"No trouble, glad to help. There is something that troubles me, though. Why so much damage was caused by such a mild storm?"

"I guess it must have been the age of the property," Greg said, then he went back to work.

Nat continued to stare into the trench until he heard Beth call as she and John came walking over. "What have you found, Nat?"

"It's not what I found, John, it was Greg. He really seemed to know what he is talking about. Take a look at the wreckage from the kitchen."

John looked. "What am I supposed to see?"

"The timber and building materials are all hundreds of years old."

"You mean this was part of the old house?"

"Yes, it would certainly look that way. It seems the kitchen was added later but not much later."

John seemed amazed. "I never knew that," he said in disbelief.

"One more thing, take a look in the bottom of the ditch."

Nat pointed to the door. This time John's mouth really dropped open. "My Lord!" he said. "Could that be another cellar?"

Beth at last spoke as if to herself. "It sure looks like it."

You could have cut the atmosphere between them with a knife. "OK," Beth said. "Will one of you guys tell me what we do next?"

"Yes, Beth, that door could be the answer we have been looking for. That could be the reason that the other cellar we found was a pit of dirt and nothing else."

"I think you're right, John, this could be the cellar we have been told about or warned about depending on which way you look at it," Beth jumped in.

"Well. I suggest we let the guys carry on the clean up and save the cellar until they go home."

"I agree. How about you, Nat?"

"That's fine by me."

John and Beth went back to what ever they were doing before Nat had called them over. Nat walked over to Greg and asked if he could put some men to clean out the trench. Greg agreed and then they both went back to do their own thing. It wasn't until five that afternoon that Greg found Nat and told him they had done what they could for the day and they would be back tomorrow to finish up. Nat thanked him and then the guys went home.

With the kitchen gone and without saying a word the three of them had moved to the study. The study had seemed the obvious choice. No one wanted to go near the picture room again. Earlier that day the electric had comeback on and Greg had brought with him an electrician to make safe any damaged wires. By now the computer was also on line. Nat and John were quite excited at the new turn of events but Beth had learned better and not to take things so easily at face value. "OK, you two, we have to make a decision, do we watch the tape or open the cellar?"

Nat spoke first. "For my part it's the cellar."

"I agree with Nat, John. After all, we have been told we need to check the cellar. Plus I don't think I'm in a rush to see a film like that again."

"I must admit I concur with both of you so let's get organized and open the cellar."

"You know, John, it may be a bit of over reaction but I think I should run the generator to make sure we are well covered and don't get any surprises."

"I second that, Nat, we don't need the electric to go off for whatever reason while we are in that hole."

"Please do it, of course you're right."

Nat went off to start the generator and run the leads. Beth and John collected flashlights and tools to open the door. Like the other cellar door it was metal; this one, however, had a heavy padlock and chain. "Someone didn't want this door open again!"

Earlier that day Greg had loaned a set of metal bolt cutters to Nat for opening the door. Nat came back into the room. "Well, the generator's running. I've fixed up some wires with bulbs for emergency in case the power goes out again, but honestly I don't feel it will for some reason. It was six thirty when they walked out the side door and around to the damaged area. Night was slowly closing in. John had got Greg's electricians to set up floodlights and run cables and bulbs into the ditch to be used when they opened the cellar. Now the whole place looked like the morning mist after the Battle of Waterloo, light but with a surreal feeling to it.

As they climbed through the last of the rubble Beth said with mixed emotions. "Here we go again guys."

They made their way into the ditch and up to the cellar door. This time John was first there, he had the bolt cutters in his hands. Although there was plenty of light Beth still shone her torch on the chain as John cut through the heavy padlock. The lock and chain gave way without a fight. Although old and rusty it was still formidable. Nat had a can of WD 40 and sprayed some on the hinges. John took a large crowbar from Beth that Greg had also loaned them. As with the other cellar door, resistance was strong, slowly giving under Nat and John's relentless pressure. As the door opened a foul odor overcame their sense's not like anything they had smelled before.

"What the hell is that smell?"

"I don't think it's anything to worry about. Like before, Nat, that's just musty damp and age mixed in with air gone bad after hundreds of years!"

"Well done, Beth, I have to agree with you. I don't feel a threat either. I suggest we proceed with light and caution."

With the door open now they shone their flashlights into the subterranean darkness. Beth noticed first that the cellar was not just dirt, but that there was color inside. Even with the foul smell, Beth was the first inside. She walked in with a flashlight. Nat followed close behind. He carried with him a lead and bulb shining light into this forgotten place after centuries. John brought up the rear. As they all stood together at the bottom of the three steps with the ample light they had color and truth strike them. This was nothing like the other cellar; this was no dirt pit. It took only seconds for their eyes to adjust to the bright light. This was undoubtedly the strangest room they had been in throughout the whole experience.

"WOW!" Take a look at that," Beth said.

"The room is like a children's grotto; as if someone had built a shrine and then locked out the outside world."

In this case two hundred years.

The first thing to catch Beth's eyes and cause her immediate sadness was a pair of stirrups for a child that could not walk without assistance. "Why do children have to suffer so much?"

As she allowed her eyes to pan around the room she couldn't help but feel a sad kind of closeness to this place. Pictures painted by children adorned the Wattle and Daub walls. A long stretch from the other picture room, she thought.

"Take a look in the far corner, Beth."

In the far left corner stood a basket chair. There was also a rocking horse and several golliwogs. "You don't see them anymore," John put in.

In the center of the room was a green couch. Beth thought that was an unusual color for a couch. In fact, as she looked around there were several things green, also children clothes. On the right wall two portraits hung side by side. John walked over and commented, "This second part of the house must have been built over in the nineteenth century after the twins died! Take a look at these portraits."

As they each looked on, side by side hung the basket chair boy, Jonathan next to him hung the twins. "I guess the parent's of the twins must have buried this room to try and forget all the heartache."

"You know, Nat, one thing that has me puzzled, why two cellars?"

" I have no idea. I don't think there's anything threatening, do you, Beth?"

"No, not in this room, it's nothing like the other cellar!"

"John, one thing though. Don't you think that these two cellars must be back to back?"

"You mean, they must join up?"

"Exactly. Don't you think at one time they must have been joined?"

"For what purpose?"

"I don't know, the only thing that jumps to mind they must have doubled as a storm shelter and escape tunnel."

"I take your point, but why would they have needed an escape tunnel?"

"That's the thirty thousand dollar question."

"I have one other question, why were they separated?"

"Think about it, Nat, that grim pit, wouldn't you want to separated from it?"

"Yes, Beth, but what made it that way?"

"Nat, what we seem to have here is chalk and cheese."

"That went right over my head, explain it."

"You must admit at one time these cellars were one tunnel, someone separated them. We witnessed the dirt pit but take a look around you. This room couldn't be more different if it tried."

"OK, but what made them this way?"

"That, Beth, I don't know."

"Well, whoever built the separating wall, they must have known something."

"Don't you two notice something missing again?"

"What's that?"

"Look around you, Beth, again no crucifix or Bible!"

"I'm beginning to think this house isn't consecrated."

"That can't be true, Nat, my family has a crypt."

"Yes. But have you ever seen a religious relic of any kind?"

"No you're quite right, I never have and I must admit that has always bothered me."

"I suggest we all call it a day and get some sleep. Let's start again tomorrow."

"Do we lock the door again?"

"What for, Nat, you think someone is going to sneak in the night and steal anything?"

"No, I guess not. Come on let's go to bed. I'm sure all of this will be here tomorrow."

They all retreated back to the house. "Do we have anything to eat, Beth?"

"To be honest, John, I though it might be a better idea to treat ourselves and call a Chinese take-out."

"I'm in to that, how about you, Nat?"

"Sounds good to me, let's have a table full like we did before."

They all went home. Beth thought, he's right tomorrow is another day.

The next morning as they all awoke they began to miss the things that they all bitched about, coffee or the lack of it. Like everything else in the kitchen it was now destroyed. Nat ran down to Mc Donald's and brought back coffee but it just wasn't the same.

By the time they got outside Greg and his men had already resumed the clean up. Nat walked over to Greg and asked, "How's it going, Greg?"

"Good, Nat, we should be out of here after lunch and then all you need to do is rebuild"

Nat joked, "As easy as that."

Nat and John went back to the cellar to see what else they could turn up. Beth had stayed in bed a little longer, she now felt drained by all that had happened over the last few days. She felt as if a weight had been placed on her body and was crushing her. Nat heard before he saw Greg. "Buddy, we have a problem!"

"What is it, can't it wait?"

"Not this time, Nat, we have just found a body!"

Nat and John froze in their tracks. "Come up top, you need to take a look at this."

They ran as much as walked back up to the wreck site. "This way!" Greg said as he turned to the left. At the top of the steps he led them along the ditch to the far left corner. There Greg's men where standing around what looked like a skeleton. "We must call the police," John said.

"Already done, Professor, I've called the local Sheriff."

As Nat looked down at the corpse he could hear the sound of sirens getting closer. He thought to himself, why is it every time we hear that sound we feel guilty? I wonder if they know that and that's why they do it?

"John, how old would you say that body is?"

"At least two hundred years, Nat"

"That's what I thought."

"We have to be careful the police don't damage it too much."

The police arrived and took control. The Sheriff's name was Garner. Bill Garner. Nat thought he handled the scene quite well. It seemed pretty much everyone knew this was no new crime, but something that had happened many years ago. After the Coroner had made his preliminary investigation the Sheriff called Nat and John over. "It would seem that this body is many years old maybe even hundreds. You understand it must go to the Path Lab. After that you may if you wish claim it, Professor Singleton. As there was nothing suspicious about the body."

The police soon left leaving every one scratching their heads. "What do you think, Nat?"

"I tell you, Greg, this house baffles me at every turn, but one thing: that's no recent death!"

"I'm sorry, Greg, but the police want all work stopped for twenty four hours. So forensics can be sure the body is old and not some cover up."

"That's understandable. Nat, give me a call when things get sorted out and we'll be back."

"Thanks, Greg, I appreciate that. I'll call you soon."

After Greg and his men had left Nat and John told Beth what had had happened. She didn't seem surprised. "Well, honey, it seems we are going to have cops around for the next twenty four hours so I see no reason not to take a break, do you?"

"Yes, Nat, I do. Why not use this time to catch up?"

"What do you mean?"

"Simple really, we have two tapes we haven't yet looked at."

"She's right, Nat, we still have things to do."

"I know you're both right, I think I was just looking for a way out."

"No, you're like all of us, you're frightened of what may come."

"Nat, this might be a good time to pull some strings."

"What do you mean?"

"We don't have the luxury of time, do you want to wait till the local law enforcement finds what we already know, that that's no twentieth century body?"

"You got that right, John, it belongs to this house."

"More than that, it belongs to my family."

"Please, John, don't take all of this personally."

"Beth, don't forget, this is my family. I don't know who he is but one thing I am sure of is, whoever that is belongs to me."

"Don't you think this would be a good time to reflect and consolidate?"

"Enough of this, Beth, let's take a look at the tapes."

At that they went back to the study. This time they didn't make coffee. Nat put the tape in the video. All three sat down with trepidation. Beth feared more than John and Nat what might appear on that tape. At first the picture was snowed over then slowly it cleared. Beth's heart was in her mouth waiting for Francis but that was not what she saw. The image before them was hazy then the picture cleared. What they saw was the bottom of the crypt.

"There's nothing there!" Nat said, hoping he was right.

"Hold on, Nat, look in the right corner, that mist."

"I wish you weren't right."

They all saw what they didn't want to see. Slowly but surely a figure appeared. For some reason they all expected to see Francis. The figure before them was not Francis. Beth at first was startled then she realized nothing in this house ever went by the numbers. Slowly but surely a figure appeared. Nat and John were glued to the spot. Slowly the apparition cleared. A large man formed before their eyes. He was black at least six foot six, broad at the shoulders; his hair and beard were gray. Although his stature was strong his demeanor seemed gentle. This was not a man to play with.

"Who the hell is that?" Nat said.

"Do you recognize him, John?"

"No, do you, Beth?"

"Not at all, but I have a feeling we should."

"Who the hell is he, John?"

"I have a bad feeling we might find out soon."

This is all we need, another player in the game."

This is no game, Beth. I know that you know what I mean."

The man stood right in the middle of the screen. He was a big man of African descent in his late fifties. He stood with his hands on his hips. The only clothes that he wore were a pair of torn shorts that at one time must have been trousers. He had more than his share of scars. One more noticeable than the rest was his left shoulder. It looked like he had been shot at some time or struck with some sharp instrument that had left a nasty jagged scar.

"Whoever he is, at some time he's been in a battle or war and judging from what's left of his clothes he's not from this century."

As slowly as he appeared he began to disappear along with the mist.

"Well, that's that," Nat said.

"I don't think so. I've got a feeling that there's more to come."

"Looks like you're right, John." As Beth spoke she felt herself begin to well up inside. Tears slowly formed and began to slide slowly down her cheeks. On the screen in front of her stood Francis, her sister, who had so tragically died all those years ago at Lake Norman. As she cried, John and Nat just sat and stared with their mouths agape. No one spoke for at least a minute, a period of time that passed like an eternity.

Finally, John spoke. "She's a beautiful woman, Beth. You must be proud."

"Yes, I am," Beth said, as she choked back the words. "But you must remember she was only six the last time I saw her."

"Why do you think she's here?"

"I can only think that there is some kind of danger and she is trying to warn us."

The image on the screen began to fade but not before she raised her arms and moved from side to side at the waist as if to say it's here. Right here. Then she was gone and all that remained were the cold gray stones of the cellar.

John turned off the receiver and Nat moved to Beth and put his arms around her.

"I can't imagine how you must feel right now, Beth, but please know that I'm here for you."

"I know, Nat, and you know I love you for it, but I have a feeling we still have a ways to go. One thing that gives me a good feeling is the thought that now more than ever we are stronger thanks to some new friends."

"I second that, Beth, and now I think I should get the trust in gear and pull some strings, starting with the body and local law enforcement."

At that, John walked out the door with an air of authority about him. Nat held Beth in his arms, kissed her gently and spoke in her ear. "I LOVE YOU."

Beth began to feel the strength flow back into her veins, she now felt more than ever that they had a chance to lay all the demons of this house of horrors to rest. "OK, Nat, what do you suggest we do next?"

"While John pulls those strings he talks about why don't you and I take another look in the cellar?"

They moved out of the study down the hall though the side door and down to the wreckage. It all seemed so strange that now a place they had known so well no longer existed all that was left now was about to be shoveled into a dump truck. Nat got a very uneasy feeling as he looked into the ditch knowing that whoever lay dead there had been there for along time. The police had thankfully left now they had no doubt that this was no modem homicide, which was what John feared most. There was no real interest, they hadn't even run tape around the scene; in fact, after they took away the body no one had been back. "Where do we start?"

"Why don't we start with the clothes?"

"Why the clothes, Nat?"

"You asked me where to start and that's the first thing that came to mind."

"You know that's the best way to go, with your feelings and not your head."

They moved down the steps and into the cellar. Nat had already fixed lights. There was no need anymore for the generator with the full electric turned back on. Nat for all that still would have felt more secure with back up. The cellar as before amazed them both, especially the memories of small children. Nat and Beth like many others had seen things in this life that defied logic. The thing that struck them both more than anything was the color of the clothes and the furniture. Everything looked so green. "Who do you think chose the color scheme, Beth?

"You know, I thought of that before and I think it must have been the children! Only children would choose a color so vivid."

"Of course, you know what the color green stands for life fertility and rebirth."

"You know, Beth, there's something wrong about this scenario."

"What do you mean?"

"Think about it, why would you create a shrine and then close it off with a ditch and a dead body? The only answer to that, whoever it was must have something to hide."

They looked at each other. "Are you thinking what I'm thinking?"

"Yes, Nat, there must be something hidden down here!"

"Beth, one question I must ask you."

"Go ahead, ask away."

"Do you really love me?"

"More than you can ever imagine."

"I have seen your sister, someone I could never imagine I would ever see but I did, Beth. From now on I will never doubt you."

"And I will never doubt you."

"Beth, I love you!"

"I know, and that is what will win the this game."

Nat and Beth held each other like there was no tomorrow. "If we have each other that's all we need."

"Are you sure, Beth, are you really sure?"

"Yes, I'm sure."

With their arms around each other that was their world and no one would ever take that away. But as always, things didn't quite turn out as they would have liked. Nat saw something in the comer that he had not noticed before. "Look, Beth, over there!"

"What?"

"Look in the comer over there. What do you see?"

"Green, Nat!"

"Don't you see, Beth, it's the color, it must have something to do with their innocence."

"You mean that they are no part in this madness?"

"They do and I don't know why."

"Do you think there is anything else in this tomb that we have not found yet?"

"Yes, I do, this place is hundreds of years old."

"Then what do you think we have here?"

"I think we have a real haunting, the stuff that Hollywood would love."

"All I want is that the children will be set free."

They looked around the room. Apart from the color, Nat thought, what else is wrong? One thing he noticed on the back wall was a picture of two people, a young girl and an older man. "Look, Beth, that's John."

"Are you sure, how can John be in that picture from so many years ago?"

"You're close, Nat, I admit the names are the same even the look; that, I think, must be what we know today as the gene pool."

The voice had come as a bit of a shock but as they recovered and looked behind them, John stood in the doorway. "John, it's you! You had us frozen there for a moment!"

"Forgive me, I didn't mean to frighten you. The picture you are looking at belongs to Jonathan, the boy we all refer to as the basket case. May be you can understand why we became such good friends in such a short length of time."

"Tell me, please, why is he older and who is the girl?"

"I can't answer your question, Beth, the way asked it but I can tell you this. Jonathan is the boy in the chair although grown, as was your sister Francis, and the girl is Clare. Please don't ask me to explain, as I have no idea. Like so many things that happened around this house, it defies reason.

"The color green, I can explain. Jonathan always wore green whenever I saw him. I didn't know if that was his choice or that of his family; after all, he was dying of an incurable disease, in those days it was anyway."

"Maybe they thought it might help his condition in the mind and all that!"

"A good hypothesis, Nat. Who knows, it does make sense."

"John, I don't know how long you were there and how much you heard?"

"No more than that, Nat."

"Well, we have a theory about the cellar and why it may have been hidden here."

"Please tell me, I would love to know?"

"We believe something else may be hidden here."

"Like what, can there have been anymore surprises or tricks?"

"Yes we believe there's something more we haven't found hidden down here."

"And that would be?"

"If we knew that, John, don't you think we would have found it!"

"You both suspect from all the things we have been told that there is something hidden in this cellar. Then I suggest we tear the place apart."

"Well, I guess that decision is left with you do we tear the place apart or not?"

"Nat, you know how I feel about this place let's get started. But before we do I have some news. The body that we found or

Greg's men found. He was a big man about six three, late fifties and black. The bones, approximately two to three hundred years old. The thing that might interest you the most is that he had, earlier in his life, suffered a large wound to his left shoulder." Nat looked at Beth as she said, "The man in the crypt, it's the man in the crypt!"

"Is there anyway John we can find out who he was?"

"I've been in touch with the Trust's lawyers and told them to get someone to check British Admiralty records to see if the ship, Angelina can be found. It was the last ship taken by Niles Remington, it should be on record somewhere. I know it might be as you call it a long shot but we just might get lucky."

"Well done, John, it seems you have taken care of just about everything."

"Not everything, Beth, we still need to take this cellar apart"

All three proceeded to tear the cellar apart being as careful as possible not to damage anything of Historic value or anything that belonged to Jonathan. All that was of value to the children was carefully taken out and put in the house including pictures and anything else in the room they considered worth saving, starting on the walls which were just Wattle and Daub that came apart easily but the floor was stone slabs and they couldn't move them. "Do you think anything could be bellow the slabs?"

"I doubt it, Nat, they are so big and heavy and they would have been the first thing that was laid; it wouldn't make sense to hide anything there!"

"You're both right; think about it; where is the last place you would think to look?"

Beth did what she had done in the conservatory. She looked up. "Why is it the last place we look is up?"

"I don't know, Nat, but I think Beth is right." The ceiling wasn't very high, about six feet. They attacked it with claw hammers. Beth used a shovel. After thirty minutes they were covered in white dust. Nothing had been found just dirt. "This is hopeless guys; there's nothing here."

Beth gave one more gargantuan effort and hit the ceiling as hard as she could. At this all hell let loose when what was left of the ceiling came down and a whole lot more. Beth dropped to the ground with blood pouring from a wound in her forehead. Nat and John rushed to her side. As they did more of the ceiling came down this time a metal box fell with it. The box missed Nat by inches. It hit the ground with a thump. "Beth, are you Ok?"

"Of cause I am I got hit on the head that's all. I'll survive. What's more important what fell out of the roof!"

"A metal box."

"What was in it?"

"Slow up, Beth, one thing at a time," Beth screamed at Nat.

"What is in that damned box?"

"Take it easy, Beth!" John said. "We need to take care of that cut on your head."

"Fuck the cut on my head; what's in that dammed box?"

The box was a dull metal that hit the floor with a soft thud!. John took a handkerchief from his pocket and started to clean up Beth's wound. After close examination John said to Nat, "It's not as bad as it looks, more blood than damage!"

"Nat the box; what is it?"

"Just take it easy, Beth, one thing at a time. I'll take a look right now". Nat moved to the box, at first look the box was dull with age. Nat picked it up and turned it over in his hands. It was about eighteen inches by twelve and very heavy. "You know?" Nat said excitedly.

"I think this box is lead?"

"Lead. Why would anyone want to make a box with lead?"

"Let's open it, John, and find out." The box although dented from the fall was none the less undamaged. It was held together by a brass lock. "Look's like a job for Greg's bolt cutters. Do we still have them?"

"You should know, Nat, you're the tool man."

"Guys, don't you think we should get cleaned up first; after all it's waited for three hundred years?"

"Why the sudden change, Beth, a few moments ago you couldn't open it fast enough?"

"Simple! Nat, I just thought that there might be something in there we might not want to find. If there is, I would like to be clean enough to run." John laughed. "I'm glad to see that the bump on your head didn't make you lose your sense of humor."

"Ok. Then if we all agree why don't you two take it into the study and as you say I'll go find the tools. One thing I would suggest one of us stays with it at all times."

"I have a better idea! Two of us should stay with the dammed thing at all times."

"I agree with that, John!"

"Nat I don't think one is enough after what we have experienced in this place!"

"Fine by me; you take it in and I'll get the tools."

Nat walked out to where the men had laid the timbers on the lawn; it was starting to get dark now but Nat pretty much knew where he had left the tools. He had left them out in the open by the lumber; that didn't seem a problem as after all they were just metal and the rain had long since gone. He reached the south end of the wood where he had left the cutters. He reached down to where the tools should be and felt around in the grass. He didn't find them at first so he started to feel amongst the logs. Where the hell are they? I hope Greg didn't take them with him.

At that precise moment a hand as cold as ice clasped his. Nat almost jumped out of his skin; he tried to scream but his throat wouldn't work. Nat was down on his knees. He jumped to his feet faster than an Olympic athlete before he could run; his eyes took in a picture of madness right out of a Dracula horror movie. Just in front of him stood a robed figure maybe six foot tall. Before Nat could get a good look at its face the figure turned and slowly evaporated into a foggy mist and then the mist dispersed as if it had never been there. Nat ran like never before in his life he wondered if he should have followed the figure but he knew better, not in the dark. So he ran like the Devil was chasing him. Nat ran back into the side door of the house making sure to close and lock it behind him. Now he walked instead of running down the hall and into the study. "What the Hell happened to you Nat?"

"Remember when we first arrived at this house we wondered why there was so many large windows and lights and then we found they come out at night mostly. Well I just found out the reason why."

"What was it, Nat? What did you see?"

"Not what I just saw but what I saw and felt."

"You know for some reason I thought things might calm down after the storm!"

"No way. John take it from me that was wishful thinking."

"Tell me what did you see?"

"The evil one, Beth. I think that's what they said we should call it!"

"What did it look like?"

"It stood maybe six foot tall in a long robe like a monk, but this was no monk at least no live one. It touched my hand and I have never felt anything so cold in all my life."

"You mean that figure that we saw down by the lake?"

"Yes, Beth, and by the crypt!"

"What do you think it is Nat and forgive me for saying this some kind of ghoul?"

"Like you John I would never thought of using that word but I must admit it does seem to fit the bill"

"Do you think we are in danger in here?"

"Honestly, Beth, no I don't as I said earlier; it looks like the danger time is at night. Although we have seen this figure in the day time it was never close up."

"So you think it's dangerous at night?"

"No, Beth, that's not what I meant; it seems that it don't come in this house. If you think about it there is no history of this creature; no one has documented it before."

"You used the word creature it's the first time I've heard you use that term!"

"I know of no better term to use John for what I witnessed tonight!"

"Nat, John, just tell me are we safe in this house tonight?"

"I think so Beth, but I also think we should stay together; you know in all the books I've read and all the films I've seen the danger always seems to be when people spilt up!"

"I think you're right, John, let's get some blankets and stay in the study for the night. Maybe tomorrow we might get some return from the trust!"

"I think we have reached a stage where we have more questions than answers."

"Don't forget the box, Beth! If it's lead we may be able to cut it open."

"Wait Nat! If you are right and I'm sure you are, don't you think it was put in lead for a reason? And if I may suggest the reason could be like in the Arabian Nights to entrap evil?"

"Come on, John, this is no genie in a bottle; this is the real thing."

"Cut it out both of you don't you understand that what ever evil lives or exists in this house is probably responsible for the deaths of many people in this family and we just might have the way to stop even destroy it!"

"1 don't think we should try to open this box without tools tonight, so why don't you and Beth go and get some blankets and we'll stay in here tonight. One thing that I must ask; please don't leave me too long!"

Nat and Beth left the room and went upstairs to get the blankets. John sat in one of the chairs and looked at the box. What are you, he thought. What evil powers do you contain? Nat and Beth came back with cushions and blankets. "Beth do we have bacon and eggs?"

"Yes we do. Are you hungry?"

"No, but I have a feeling we might need a good breakfast in the morning, I think it might be a long day."

"Nat and Beth laughed and laid out the bedding but both of them had a feeling of foreboding inside. "Would anyone like a night cap?" John asked. Both Nat and Beth said in unison, "Yes we would!" John poured them each a large jigger of brandy, which they took thankfully and drank. They each made their own bed but no one volunteered to turn off the lights. Each one of them had a fitful night with dreams and nightmares. Nat couldn't get away from the thing in the robe it seemed to follow him where ever he went through both night and day. Beth saw Francis and relived their childhood. She also relived that night and the fire. John relived the day in the garden with Jonathan and Clare. He also saw his father shot down by a German fighter, something he had never seen before. All of them saw the thing in the cloak as it walked the garden. But the worst dream they each had was in the crypt. The dream stopped them all from a good nights sleep. That night they all heard on the wind a laugh it seemed to come from far away a place only in their mind. The sound they heard was very distant but also very close. "Do you hear that?"

"Yes we do."

"John we should really try and get some sleep." The night went very slowly and full of bad dreams. The next morning they had breakfast as John had requested, bacon and eggs. Beth also cooked pancakes. It seemed like a last meal. Today was the beginning g of the end. "Ok. Guys, today we end this nightmare once and for all!"

They all walked out of the side door, it was just breaking light. Nat said, "Is this really day time or still night."

"I think, Nat, we are a little early!"

"You got that right, John, but I must ask you is there day or night left for us?"

The mist still lay on the grass and the air had a slight smell of jasmine. They could see the sun fighting to come over the horizon and they all felt things were not right. Each knew this was going to be a hard day. Not one of them wanted to admit that they didn't want to open this box in the dark. If anything they wanted to open it in the day light with others around. They took the box to the green room and waited for Greg's men to arrive. Nat had already called Greg and asked him to resume the clean up. He had agreed and said they would be there at eight 0' clock. They waited in the cellar for what seemed an eternity hardly speaking to each other. Greg's men arrived, the strange part of that was that you could hear them laughing and that was in short supply in this house of horrors. Greg walked down into the cellar with his usual smile. "How long have you guys been down here?"

"Since the beginning of time, Greg!"

"Take it easy, guys; too much is never good for any of us!" At that Greg retreated and left them to their own devices. "Ok. Which one of us opens the box?"

"Silly it must be, John. He has lived with this curse for so long."

"Go ahead, John, this is your right." John took the bolt cutters that he and Nat had retrieved before they came into the cellar. Nat had refused to collect them on his own. John and Beth understood. John cut the bolt and took away the lock, then he opened the lead box. Inside was a gold ring twelve inches in circumference, inside the ring was could only be described as an opposite crescent moon not unlike the Flag of

Turkey. But doubled up. Is it really possible to see a feeling or smell a color then this would be the time. All things are possible. Was this what the search was all about? A simply Golden Relic. "What is it, Beth, you look disappointed?"

"I don't know, John, I guess I expected more!"

"Like a book or a scroll or may be even some thing that glows in the dark?"

"Take it easy, John; she's half right, can this be all that held us all here?"

"I'm sorry, Beth, please forgive me?"

"No, John! It's me who was out of line. I really don't know what I expected!"

"It's gold, Beth or at least I think it is! It's been buried here for centuries that must have some significance."

"Nat, do you really think this relic could have anything to do with what has happened to us?"

"Yes, Beth, I do and more than that I think it has to do with what has happened to John's family."

"You think this small gold circle could have been the bane of my family?"

"Yes, I do but I have no idea why, but someone hid it for a reason."

"What reason would you wall up a piece of gold?"

"I don't know right now but I think if we do a little research into the Indians we saw on that tape we'll just find out."

"I appreciate no one wants to look at that tape again but I think we should."

"You got that right!"

"No, wait, Beth, I know how you feel but Nat has a point, maybe there something on that film we missed!"

"If I missed anything on that tape it can stay missed."

"I understand, why don't you let Nat and I take a look if we find anything we'll give you a call?"

"You got a deal guys this way I can take a shower."

"Be careful, Beth?"

"Don't worry, Hon, remember, they come in the dark usually."

John and Nat walked to the study as Beth walked to the nearest bathroom so as not to be out of earshot. Nat had already rewound the tape so all he had to do was press start. John sat down with the lead box at hand. The screen sprang to life as it had before, as did the Indians along with the feathered man. It was at that moment John saw it. "Look Nat! Look at the cliff to the right of the medicine man!"

"What is it what do you see?"

"Pause the tape." Nat pressed pause then handed the controls to John. He pressed the rewind button and then pressed play. Again the screen came to life. The feathered man appeared again with that awful knife, within seconds John pressed pause. John rose and walked to the screen pointed with his finger and said to Nat. "What do you make of that?" Nat could just make out a yellow object that caught the sun on the cliff wall.

"You got better eyes than me, John, I never noticed that before."

As Nat got up to take a look the phone rang. He picked it up. "It's for you ,John." He handed John the phone and then turned his attention back to the screen. Nat stared very hard at the picture; all he could make out was what appeared to be a shiny ring set into the rock. Although not what he would have liked, it did nonetheless make him quite excited. "Nat, we have news from the British Admiralty."

"That was quick, John, even for you and the Trust."

"No, not really; think about it; most of my ancestors were captains or more in the British Navy, or at least in the Armed Forces. I don't think much arm twisting was needed."

"So, what have we got?"

"Patience, wait for the fax." Within minutes the fax came to life and started to do its work. Several pages came through and then it stopped just as quickly as it started. John walked over and took the pages from the fax. "Hey, guys! Anything turned up?" Beth stood in the doorway. Nat thought, I have never seen her look so good; she stood there dressed in a long towel like gown, the sort of thing that doubles as both a towel and gown, and he was impressed. She had washed her hair and it hung loose around her shoulders still wet. Nat could now see the similarity between Beth and her sister Francis. They were both beautiful women although Francis had been dead thirty years. How cruel, he thought, how could God have parted these wonderful girls. "Beth, I think you may be impressed with what we have turned up!"

"Tell me, John?" she said, as she looked at Nat and melted his heart.

John couldn't help but notice the looks that passed between Nat and Beth. You marry this Lady, he thought, she's your destiny. "First of all why don't you and Nat look at the tape and see what you think, don't worry it's not the bad part."

John watched them sit together and couldn't help but feel a pang of jealousy. He picked up the papers from the fax and sat down to read them. Captain Niles Remington served with out exception. His Commission started under Her Majesty Queen Ann and ended with King George although he never won any accolades. He was a good Captain and loved by his men. The paper went on Captain Remington's last action was off the Americas, the south of the continent known as the Florida Keys. He and his ship, the Plymouth did give chase to a pirate known as Franco; he and his bark, Angelina had sunk several vessels in this part of the Americas. His Majesty's Ship, Plymouth, under the command of Captain Remington had given chase and cornered these ruffians in the island system know as the Keys, a most uncomfortable place. This was one of the places on God's great earth that man could die from so many different maladies. The King's ship cornered this boat gave chase and destroyed it and its crew. All that still lived were taken to Jamaica. Some were hung, others went to jail.

After this the story becomes sparse. John handed the paper to Nat and carried on reading. Nat and Beth sat close together while they read the first paper. As John finished the next part he looked up at Nat and Beth. "There's an interesting part here about the Angelina and her crew. The crew or at least what was left of them where thrown in the brig. The Captain and many of the pirates were killed in the action and get this bit Captain Franco Anais died from a musket ball that took off his head."

This sent a shock and shiver through them all. "Could that be who I think?"

"Do you believe in coincidence, Beth?"

"No I don't!"

"Then I believe he's the headless man!"

"What about you, Nat?"

"He's our man without a doubt."

"One more thing the story goes on to describe their wounds and the fate they suffered. Quite a few were hung on the dock giblet the others were thrown in jail with sentences ranging from seven to fifteen years. It goes on to name names and some of the wounds suffered. There's one here that might sound familiar a large black man with the name La Belle; he had suffered a ball wound to his left shoulder."

"What happened to him?"

"He got ten years, Beth."

"Then what happened to him?"

"There's no mention off that, but I rather think we know!"

"What do you think, Nat?"

"Yes, I'm sure it's our man from the ditch and the crypt but what I don't understand is if he spent ten years in jail in Jamaica then how did he turn up dead in our ditch?"

"Did the police even come up with a cause of death?"

"No, when they found out the age of the body they lost interest in fact the skeleton is ready to be collected if we wont it!"

"Do we?"

"Already taken care of, Beth, I had my people pick it up and take it to a University lab."

"Even now, John, you never cease to amaze me!"

"What else would you have me do? I have the power of the trust at my finger tips, don't you think I should use it?"

"No, John, that's not what I meant."

"Forgive me but Nat and I could never have handled this on our own; I'm sorry, Beth I never meant to jump on you like that!"

"I know, John, after what we have been through anything is possible."

"Ok, you two let's get back to work."

"Nat, one thing I would like to add at this point!"

"That would be, John?"

"If you don't marry this woman you must be out of your mind."

At that, Beth jumped up and threw her arms around John's neck and kissed him. "Thank you, John I love you too."

John was visibly embarrassed. "Ok, back to work." Nat was amused at his embarrassment but thought it better not to say anything. "Anything else on those papers, John?"

"Yes, after Niles unloaded his cargo. He retired his commission. The Navy Law at that time allowed him to take the last prize as his own, so he had the Navy tow his prize back to Charleston and the rest, as they say, is History."

"Wow! So now we know the full story?"

"No, Nat, there's one character missing, tbe thing in the cowl or should we say the evil one."

"You know, Nat, I'm almost embarrassed to say, "the evil one, it sounds like something from one of them fifties movies, you know, in black and white?"

"You mean like the *Creature from the Black Lagoon*?"

"Yes, that's just what I mean. The problem we have is that here there really is a creature from the black lagoon."

"Although I'm in danger of repeating myself again. What do we do next?"

"Well I do have a suggestion."

"Go on, John, let's hear it."

"It's getting close to the end of the day and night isn't far away, I don't think there's anymore we can do today."

"I have a bad feeling about what is coming next!"

"No, Nat, hear me out, I know you don't want to go to the crypt at night and Lord help me neither do I but it wouldn't hurt to put the tape back in the cellar, the old one that is."

"You know, Nat! John's right, but let's do it before dark."

"Ok. Guys, I concede; anyway, I'll lose against you two." At that they all began to laugh, something they all needed. It was before dark and after Greg's men had left after being paid that they ventured outside to the cellar. Nat had given Greg a check for the work carried out with a promise they would call him when ready to start the rebuild. The camera and sensor where still in the cellar were they had been left. They walked north along the wall of the house as they had done before, each had the same feeling of trepidation that cold feeling in the stomach that they had felt so many times in this dammed house. Nat had insisted that they start the generator, he got no argument from John and Beth they were more than happy to have a back up. Nat pulled the string on the starter and as before it jumped into life. Although there was electric in the cellar they all felt that warmth that comes with knowing you have covered all angles. They each set about their tasks. Nat took care of the lights, Beth put a film in the camera and John put one in the sensor. After all, this was done they retreated back to the surface. They walked back along the wall and in the side-door. "Why is it that place gives me the creeps so bad?"

"I think that, Beth, could be said for all of us. What do you say, Nat?"

"You don't need to ask me the sooner we get out of that place the safer I feel."

"Anyone fancy a take away?"

"Count me in, Beth."

"How about you, Nat?"

"I'm in." Beth called in the meal order and they all settled down for another night, not knowing what would come next. The meal arrived forty minuets later. Beth answered the door collected the food and paid the guy. As she walked back to Nat as she walked back to Nat and John she couldn't help but think about Francis and how things had turned out. She thought, *How does that old saying go? There but for the Grace of God. Let it go, Beth, let it go.* She walked into the study and joined John and Nat. The look on their faces told the whole story. "What is it, guys? What's going on?"

"We've been talking, Beth."

"And?"

"We must go back into the crypt."

"Oh, is that all. I thought it might be something I wouldn't like."

"It's the only way, Beth!"

"You think I don't know that, Nat? But please don't expect me to like the idea."

John said, "I suggest tomorrow morning we collect the tapes from the cellar, review them and then depending on what we find take another look at the crypt."

"That sounds like a real fun day."

"You know what I think, Beth, thanks to you two the curse that has held this house is not far from being lifted."

"You're right of course, John; that is, after all, what we are here for."

The Place of Evil

That night was probably the most uneventful night they had spent since arriving in this godforsaken place. After eating, Nat and Beth had gone to bed early, no longer afraid of this house, only what lay outside. John had stayed at the computer and on the phone a while longer to tie up a few loose ends, he had said. Nat and Beth had made love that night, the first time in a while and it made them both feel good.

Beth was the first one to rise the next morning. As usual, she made coffee and toast and called the guys down. Nat came down full of the joys of spring but John never showed. Beth poured coffee and sat down with Nat.

"Nat, will you call John again? It's unlike him to be late for breakfast."

Nat checked the study, then went to the stairs to call him. No reply. Nat shouted, "Beth, I think we have a problem."

Beth felt, as she had many times in this house, a cold chill run down her spine. *Please, John, not you.* She began to panic. The thought of possibly losing John was too much to bear. At that a voice came from the door.

"Do I smell coffee and toast?"

Beth ran to John and threw her arms around him. "Don't you ever do that to me again, you British son of a bitch."

"I think I must take that as a compliment."

"Yes, John, I think you should."

"I'm sorry, Nat, I didn't mean to scare anyone but I went out early to get the tapes from the cellar."

"Anything on them?"

"Well, they run. Why don't we see what we've got?"

John ate his toast and drank his coffee as Nat put the tape in the video. Again as before, nothing at first, then the mist.

This time a different picture. Ships under attack, men dying from gunshot wounds, wooden splinters from the explosions. There was blood everywhere.

"Oh!" said Beth. "Not again."

This time, though, it was different. This time they knew who it was.

"That must be Angelina," said Nat.

"Yes, I think it might just be."

They saw Aggan die then Franco lose his head. Beth turned and walked away but John and Nat kept their eyes on the screen. The one person that held their attention was a large black man who had been shot in the shoulder.

"Is that who I think it is, John?"

"Yes, I rather think it is."

Then again the mist took away the picture. Only this time to come back in what seemed like a different time. In the field there were people working, black people, maybe slaves. A man on horseback rode into the screen. He had a sword at his side and pistol in his belt.

"Judging from his demeanor, John, I would say he was in charge."

The man on the horse drew the pistol from his belt and fired at someone in front of him. As the screen started to dim they could just make out the large figure of a black man falling down.

"Could we have just seen what I think we saw?"

"Yes, Nat, I think we did."

"You mean that big guy was our body in the ditch?"

"Yes, Beth, I rather think it was."

"Just how much horror does this house contain?"

"It would seem that my ancestors hid more than we knew. I would suggest that we put together what we know."

"I agree, John, before we go into that crypt again."

"Don't you two understand that they are trying to warn us to stay away from that crypt?"

"So, Beth, is that what you are saying, stay away from that crypt?"

"No, unfortunately that's the very place we have to go."

"I think we must all face the fact that if there's ever going to be an end to this nightmare it will be in the crypt."

"May I ask you a question?"

"Go ahead, John, ask away."

"Do you believe in God?"

"I told you, John, that isn't fair."

"No, Nat, let me answer. I used to as a child like many others but as I grew older and lost Francis I have to admit that my faith started to slide."

"What's the reason for your question, John?"

"Nat, I believe we will need all the faith we have. If we or rather when we go into that crypt, we'll need all the weapons that we can muster."

"I don't understand, John, what do you mean?"

"It's simple; when we go back into that place as we must we will need all the faith that we have."

"Are you telling us that's all we have?"

"Basically, yes, that's all I think we have!"

"So when we go in tomorrow morning we go on a wing and a prayer?"

"No Nat, not tomorrow morning we must go in tonight!"

"You must be kidding me."

"No, it must be at night."

"John's right, Nat, think about it. It's at night when they come out."

"I'll give you that, it's just that it scares me shitless."

"As it does us, Nat. But I think it's the only way to go."

"Let me get this right, you two are going down into that hole in the ground at night?"

"Yes we have too."

"Do you know what you are suggesting."

"Yes I think I do."

"What do you think, Beth?"

"I agree with John."

Nat laughed inside but he felt a cloud of doubt walk over his mind. "Have you any idea what your saying?"

"Yes, I think we do."

"Are you into this, Beth? I mean really into this?"

"Yes I am."

"Well, I guess this is a time to put up or shut up, I'm in let's do it."

"Nat, you joked about a wing and a prayer. All I have to offer is this James the First Bible and a crucifix that I bought with me in case of trouble."

"Well John you sure got the trouble."

"No, Nat I think he is right we must do this now."

"Beth, we came this far I guess we should go the extra mile."

"Ok, John what time do you suggest?"

"We leave here at ten o'clock that will give us time to set up the camera and the sensor."

"You mean before the witching hour of midnight?"

John lowered his head and said, "Exactly."

Nat looked at Beth. "Is this what you want?"

"Yes it is!"

"Ok, we go at ten o'clock on the dot."

For the few hours they had left, each spoke to their own God and made peace with this life. Nat thought, why not, as they say if all else fails what else have you got to lose. At nine thirty Beth had coffee on the stove, but no one was in the mood to drink it. "Is that all we have John a Bible and that stick?"

"Sorry, Nat it's all I could find at short notice." They walked out of the side door as they had done now for so long, down the west side of the house and south to the lake. Each had a flashlight and a cold feeling inside. The night was not what they would have wished for. It was cold and damp there was a drizzle in the air. A mist was rising over the lake. *Wonderful*, Nat thought, *just what we need*. They kept close to the lake and down its west side. Each, without knowing it they kept close together, very close together. Beth felt that feeling of trepidation. Nat was afraid to look from side to side for what he might see. But John seemed like he was on a mission. He knew were he was going. They reached the bottom of the lake and then they walked over the grass and down to the crypt. When they arrived, Nat started the generator as he had done so many times before. The machine started with out any resistance. The three of them hardly spoke. The atmosphere could be cut with a knife. "I know you're right John and this is when we should be here but I've got to admit that I'm scared!"

"We all are but I would like to say before we go into this place that I wouldn't choose anyone else but you two."

"Thanks for that vote of confidence, John!"

"No, Beth, I really mean it."

"I know you do and I love you for it but that don't make are task any easier."

"Come on you two the generator is running let's do it shall we?"

Beth thought, man I have never been this afraid in the whole of my life. After running the generator, Nat turned to open the door. He froze on the spot. The door was open, blackness was all that emitted from the crypt. For a while Nat was taken aback, then composed himself and plugged in the wires, at that the place lit up.

"Home sweet home!" Beth said.

They entered and descended the steps. Nat noticed that John had lost the confidence and determination he had shown earlier. Beth although, centered, seemed a little frayed at the edges. And myself he thought, I'm scared shitless. As Nat had entered he had switched the lights on, just for back up he thought. Without speaking they walked along the first floor turned the corner and descended to the second floor. Nothing, not a rat, no bumps in the night, and most of all, no ghosts. They made their way alone the second floor turned the corner and started to descend into the next level. Nothing, no one stood in their way. At the end of the tomb stood a brick wall. Is this it Nat thought; the end of life is nothing more than a brick wall. And then he remembered Linda, her smile the way she used to torment him. Stop it, he thought, don't go there.

"Well, guys this seems to have fallen flat."

At that very moment the cold set in. Not much at first, just a draught no more than a whisper, just a hint of cold but each one of them knew this was it. The mist slowly formed. As before, fog was the first to materialize.

"Why does this dammed mist always precede an apparition?"

And as if on cue something or someone started to appear before their eyes.

"Now hold hands," Beth cried. They did," all three held hands. As if a miracle the fog lifted. "Now," Beth said, "walk up the stairs."

Together hand in hand they started to move up the stairs. Moving from the third level to the second, the fog started again.

"Stay together, guys, just keep holding hands!"

"What is it, Beth, what do you know that we don't?"

"Just hold hands, Nat, don't let go."

As the fog started again Beth pulled the two guys right through it. They now reached the top level. Instead of running for the door Beth turned and pulled the two men with her. With the door at her back Beth now stood and faced down the crypt.

"Come on," she shouted, "is that the best you've got?"

This time the mist started to form below them. Nat and John were terrified but they stood their ground. Again the mist started along with it this time came that awful smell. It was the smell of dead fish. Then again the apparitions started to form. Beth held on to Nat and John.

"Let them come, don't give way. OK, you bastards give it your best shot!"

All at once specters started to appear before their eyes. First Nat saw Linda. Dead in that dammed car her face covered in blood. Then John saw Clare sad and dying all alone in her bed. Finally Beth saw Francis sad and dying, choking in that smoked filled room.

"No you don't, you don't have the right. She's all alone and so small!"

"Let it go, Beth, you're just getting wound up."

"That's what they want, Beth, to drive a wedge between us."

"Tell them they don't exist."

"What are they?"

"Your own nightmares!"

"What do you see, John?" The mist cleared and John began to see the boy in the chair, his friend, Jonathan. "Clear your minds," Beth shouted. "This is not what we are really seeing." The visions disappeared as fast as they had materialized. "I think we should get out of here!"

"No, Nat, that's just what it wants."

"Who is it, Beth, who is this thing?"

"I'm not sure but I know we can't give in to it." As they stood there the mist started to clear. "OK, guys I suggest we leave this place right now." Outside the cellar it was dark and rain still drizzled. "What happened in there, Beth?"

"We met face to face with that thing, I know that we didn't see it but it was there."

They made their way back alone the lake and up to the house. As they walked into the side door of the house, Nat stopped and looked at Beth. "Ok. Beth you want to tell me exactly what just happened?"

"We were under attack."

"From what?"

"Your worst nightmare."

"Was it real or just in our heads?"

"Did either of you hear words or a song going though your head when we stood on the steps of the crypt?"

"I did, Beth, but I feel silly and didn't want to say."

"How about you, John?"

"Yes, as silly as it seems I heard an old English song and dance."

"Sing it, John!"

"I feel a bit silly but here goes. Do the Okie-- Cokie do the Okie--Cokie knees bend arms stretch bump, bump, bump, I'm afraid I don't know much more."

"And you, Nat?"

Nat looked at Beth with almost disbelief. "Yes, that's exactly what I heard, it don't seem possible."

"Oh, it's possible, Nat, because I heard the same."

"What can this all mean?"

"I think, guys, the children are trying to tell us something."

"Like what, Beth?"

"Think about the words. It's a song of joy and pleasure. I think the children approve of what we did today; it's the first time anyone has struck back. I think we may have scored today."

"Well, Beth, you may be right but I really don't think I feel like it."

"John, you must know that song better than us. It's from your country."

"I must admit it is heart warming to think we may have help on our side."

Beth turned and looked at both of them. "I'm convinced of it."

Nat looked at his watch. "Well, guys, one good thing, it's eleven thirty, we made it back before midnight. I would really hate to be in that place at the witching hour." Beth turned and looked at John. "What is it, Beth, what are you thinking?"

The Midnight Hour

"Midnight, John, don't you see? That's the time we must go tomorrow." Nat looked at John. "Me and my big mouth."

"Well, I don't know about you two but I'm pooped. If you don't mind I'm going to bed. I suggest we talk in the morning and make our plans!"

"Sounds good to me, John. How about you, Beth?"

"I agree. Let's get a good night's sleep and start again tomorrow!"

They climbed the stairs to bed each with a feeling of satisfaction mixed with a little trepidation. After taking a shower and brushing her teeth she went to bed. Nat was asleep and already snoring. She looked at him and knew sleep was not going to come easy tonight. She allowed her mind to wander back to the crypt and the events that had transpired earlier that night. She couldn't quite understand why they had got away so easily. She also knew the next time wouldn't go so well. The next time she thought we better be more prepared. It was a long night for Beth, her mind racing back and forth first to Lake Norman and her sister Francis, then to the crypt and that faceless thing. What could it be she thought, why has it maligned in these grounds for so many years. Is it a manifestation of pure evil or is there more to it. Somehow she couldn't bring herself to believe that there was such a thing as pure evil. She had always believed that evil was in us all and that it took just a spark to ignite it. The same she thought must be said for the good that we all harbor inside. If she thought all this was true then that thing is here for a reason and not just for malignant deeds, if this is the case then what could its motive be. For evil to exist on this earth it must, she thought, have a purpose. Beth didn't believe in coincidence; she had a lateral mind and was proud of it. One other thing came to mind, cause and effect. She thought for every right there's a wrong, for every up there's a down, the yin yang theory. So if all this were true, what is that thing, and what is it doing here? As her mind raced over and over and the tossing and turning continued, sleep seemed to elude her and back further away at every moment. That dammed Amulet, what was it doing hidden away in the ceiling like that? One thing she was sure of whoever put it there didn't intent for it to be found. Was it good or bad? Then there was the body in the ditch, both had been hidden for nearly three hundred years. So logically whatever this is all about must date back to when this house was first built. And that was when the light of day struck her why hadn't she seen it before now it all seemed so obvious! Beth turned over and tried to clear her mind, she knew if she was to beat this thing then she must get some sleep and keep up her strength. Beth slowly drifted off into a maze of dreams, memories and nightmares.

Nat awoke her with a cup of coffee. "Come on, sleepy head, you want to sleep all day?"

Beth jumped up with a start.

"Where's John?"

"Nat, we must talk."

Beth sat up, put her feet over the bed stood up and walked to the bathroom.

"Hey Honey, what about the coffee I've just made you?"

"Later, Nat. Later." Beth showered, got dressed and then walked down the stairs to join Nat and John. They were both sitting over a pot of coffee in the study.

"Did you have a good night, Beth?"

"Well, John, that depends on which way you look at it."

John looked at Beth questionably.

"Don't worry, what I meant was I didn't get much sleep but I did do a lot of thinking."

"Did you come up with anything?"

"Yes I believe I did.   John, where did you put that amulet?"

"You mean the gold ring in the lead box?"

"There's only one, John."

"It's in my room and I have arranged for the University to collect it tomorrow for investigation."

"Don't you think you should have consulted us first?"

"Why, Beth, it belongs to the trust and I thought we had finished with it."

"Beth, what's wrong. It's unlike you to speak like that."

"I'll tell you what's wrong, Nat, I thought we were all in this together."

"I'm sorry, Beth, I didn't mean to take matters into my own hands."

"That's not the point, John."

"What's the matter, Beth, what is so important about that gold ring?"

"I'll tell you, Nat, it could just be our salvation."

"OK. Tell us what you think?"

"Before I tell what I think, will you fetch it, John?"

"Of course." John got up and left the room. "Beth, I think that's the first time I've seen you so angry with anyone."

"Everyone has their moments, Nat, especially under these circumstances."

At that John came back in the room carrying the lead box. He laid the box in front of them.

"Please, John, would you open the box and take out the amulet?"

He opened the box and took out the gold ring. Beth noticed that he held the ring as though it where on fire. He put it down on top of the lead box just as fast as he could. Beth became slightly amused and loosened up a bit. "John, I'm sorry, I didn't mean to bite like that."

"Forget it, you're right, I had no right to take matters into my own hands. After all as you pointed out we are in this together."

"Ok. Now we got that settled would you mind, Beth, telling us what you have on your mind?"

"Think about it, Nat. We have the ghosts of the children around the house and grounds. Then we have the headless man and that thing in the cowl in the crypt and grounds."

"So what are you saying, that the grounds are neutral?"

"No, don't get ahead of yourself."

"Sorry, Hon, please carry on."

"When we found the amulet we all thought it had something to do with trapping the sprits of the children and holding them to this earth plane."

John nodded and said, "That's right, Beth!"

"I think it must have been that song that we all heard in the crypt that started me thinking. It seemed that the children were happy that we got in and out without being molested in anyway. We came back to the house and felt safe. Why do you think that was?"

"You're right about one thing, Beth, as far as I know there's no history in my family of a visitation in the house other than the children"

"Beth, are you thinking that-this may not be evil after all?"

"Exactly, Nat, maybe we have been looking at this all wrong. Is it possible that it was walled up to keep out evil, not keep it in?"

"You know I think you could be right, maybe we have looked at this from the wrong angle."

"The only thing that worries me about this Beth, if we use the amulet to help us fight this evil and we are wrong."

"Yes John. I take your point but we don't seem to have any weapons."

"Maybe we should keep it in reserve."

"I have to agree with Beth, John!"

"Ok. Then I'll make it unanimous, we take it but keep it in reserve."

"One other thing guys I think we should take another look in the cellar!"

"Which one, Hon?"

"Both."

"What are we looking for?"

"I'll tell you when we find it."

"What do you think John?"

"I'm in Beth! Let's use the day light hours and see what else we can find."

They finished coffee and cookies and then walked around to the green cellar first. "A question John when you took that last cassette from the empty cellar did you replace it?"

"Yes Beth, I did."

"Then may be we are starting at the wrong place. Don't you think we should check out the other cellar and the new tape first?"

"She's right John; I know none or us like that cold place but we have had results on the tape."

"OK. Let's go check in there first." They made their way back to the first cellar and to the generator waiting outside. Nat started the generator as he had done several times before. As usual the machine started without a fuss. As the lights came on they descended into the cellar. The camera and the sensor had run their tapes to the end. "This place doesn't get any prettier, does it?"

"No, Nat, it don't, let's get those tapes and get out of here." Beth could still not get over how this empty dark pit of a room could be so alive to the camera. They took the tapes with them back to the study. "I suggest we look at these later, why don't we take a look at the green room now." With all in agreement they walked back to the green room. It was still a mess from the last time they searched and found the lead box. The room and all that was in it was covered in a layer of dust and pieces of plaster. It looked as if someone had thrown a hand grenade in there. "Well guys where do we start?"

"You go left, Beth, you go right Nat and I'll go in the center." They began the search, as before not knowing what they were looking for. They started by breaking down what was left of the walls. This time luck was with them, ten minuets into the search Nat called out to the others.

"Hey, guys, take a look at this!"

"What have you found, Nat?"

"I'm not sure it looks like some kind of book!"

"Let John take a look after all it's his family."

John made his way past Beth to stand next to Nat. He followed Nat's hand and pointing finger but all he could see was broken plaster. "No, John, take a look there behind the plaster." John saw what looked like a comer of a leather bound book. "What is it, John? What do you see?"

"It looks like a book, Beth, can you get it out, Nat?" Nat got the end of his finger around the corner of the book but it wouldn't give; it was tuck tight as though it had been built as part of the wall. "Take it real easy, Nat" Beth said with a quaver in her voice. "That book just might tell us what we need to know!"

"Don't worry, Hon, I'll treat it with kid gloves."

Nat and John gently broke away the plaster that held the book, taking great care not to damage it. Finally the book surrendered, and Nat pulled it free. The book had a brown leather binding. Nat blew away the years of dirt and dust. The one thing they all noticed was its condition it had weathered the years very well, possibly because of the environment that it had been kept in. THE JOURNAL AND LAST TESTAMENT OF JUDGE NILES REMINGTON. When Nat spoke this out loud they all felt a chill. "I suggest my friends we take this back to the house and study it!" Beth and John nodded in agreement. They left the green room and went back to the house. Nat and John studied the book and Beth made coffee. As the coffee percolated she was too excited to ignore the book. "What is it, Nat? What do you see?"

"It's a diary of sorts, a History of the Family and the house." John was transfixed, a World of his own. "The house was built in 1727 or at least that's when it was started apparently; Niles built the first part of the house from his last prize." At that Beth jumped in. "Angelina".

"Right, Beth, a pirate ship he had engaged in the Florida Keys with his ship, H.M.S. Plymouth. He goes on to say that what was left of the crew and the ship was towed to Jamaica. In Kingston the pirates were dealt with; that's where Niles retired his Commission and had the Angelina towed to Charleston."

"What about the rest of the crew?"

"He had them share whatever cargo the ship held; he doesn't say what that was but it could have been considerable. Then he moves on to say that he and his wife and son, Jonathan, who had joined him from England had made this house a home. There's a kind of sadness to that part as he speaks of his son Jonathan. He suffered from polio, which had saddened them very much."

"How awful," Beth said. "To have a child in those days with such a destabilizing disease. What else does it say?"

"Give me a chance I've only just started, it tells of life from day to day." When the coffee had finished Beth poured the cups. She gave John and Nat one and then went back for her own. As she approached Nat he began to read a passage. Life here is good. The plantation is prospering, the slaves seem content, after all we don't mistreat them. Alas all is not as it should be. Our son Jonathan seems to get worse by the day, it is so heart breaking to see him suffer like this. There are times when I feel so low from guilt that it tears me apart. Sometimes I think that my wife Marietta holds me responsible for Jonathan's condition. "Why would he be held responsible for the condition of his son?"

"Hold it, Beth! I'm getting there." He goes on to say that the disease had been in his family and thought to be hereditary."

"It's not hereditary is it?"

"No, I believe it's highly contagious or at least it was. These days its almost been eradicated except in some third World Countries."

"So what does he mean?"

"I don't know may be there was some death's in the family from the disease and that gave cause to think it was hereditary. Remember back then polio was rife."

"Read on, Nat." Nat went quiet and continued to read to himself. "Let him read on Beth he'll tell us if anything is pertinent."

"OK, I'm sorry I guess I'm just getting too impatient."

"We all are." John and Beth drank their coffee as Nat continued to read on. Thirty minuets past before Nat spoke again. To Beth it had seemed like a lifetime. "Listen to this, guys, 'Dated eighth of September 1731. The days get worse now Jonathan has become really sickly, he slips farther away from us each day. As if all of this were not enough my very own Marietta has gone back to her old ways. It was only two nights past that I found her in the middle of the night in the trees down by the crypt. She was alone in a clearing with a small fire. As I approached I saw that damn amulet. God forgive me for bringing that thing here. I now fear for my wife's sanity. The good Lord help us if anyone should see her like this. Thank God it is only chickens that she sacrifices. I have no stomach for such things, so I left her there with her black arts and retired home to bed.'"

"Wow. Nat, Niles' wife was into black magic?"

"No, Beth, I rather think Nat is talking about Voodoo."

"Isn't that just the same? What about the amulet?"

"Yes, it does seem to keep showing up."

"Is that how you would put it, John?"

"Yes, Beth, I really don't think any of us are sure just what if any power that thing has."

"What about you, Nat, what do you think?"

"I think it's kind of strange that so much store has been set by it, I guess I'm sure it plays a big part in all of this."

"OK. Nat, see what else you can find. Why don't you and I take a look at the tape John?" Nat agreed and continued. John and Beth pushed in the tape. As the picture formed, John sucked in air. "What is it ,John? What can you see?"

On the screen the trees and the clearing took form. "That's the place where I used to meet Jonathan and the children".

The scene that unfolded before them turned out to be nighttime, but it was strange they could see quite clearly as if someone were shining flood lights. In the center of the clearing burned a small fire and all around it objects of art and magic. Sitting in the center by the fire a woman sat with legs crossed."

"Could that be Niles's wife Marietta?"

"Yes, I think it must be." The woman in the picture had her arms held up to the sky and in her hands she held the Golden Ring.

Beth suddenly let out a shout and pointed. "My God. Look!" At the back of the picture just in the trees stood a figure in a long robe with a hood that covered it's face. "It's that dammed thing again has it all ways haunted this place?"

"It would seem that way, Beth."

"We have to find out who that thing is?" Nat called out.

"Hey you guys, come over here and listen to this!" John stopped the tape then he and Beth joined Nat.

"What have you got?"

"Listen to this, Beth." Nat read on. "'December 9th. 1731, my poor son Jonathan passed away last night; he never did get better. God saw fit to take his young suffering life. I can only hope that there is a better place for him in Heaven, than there was on this earth. My only worry now is Marietta; she almost seems insane with grief. She hasn't been to bed all this last night. I can only imagine she has been back to that wretched place in the trees and conversing with those Voodoo Demons from her past. I have been <u>thinking</u> these last few days that maybe it's not all hocus-pocus. For some short time now I have had the feeling of not being alone on the grounds. If it be my imagination then all is well but alas I have a bad feeling.' So that must be when that thing first appeared."

"It certainly looks like it, Beth."

"So that's when the curse on my family first started?"

"Yes, John, it looks like Marietta was the harbinger." It then carried on to say that Marietta in a fit of grief turned on Niles and put a curse on this his whole family." I guess she must have held him responsible."

"Nat, surely there's a hole in that."

"What's that, Beth?"

"If the boys in the family keep dying. How has the line carried on?"

"Think I can explain that, Beth."

"Go ahead, John, I'd like to here it?"

"The plantation as we call it started to fall into disrepair after the death of Niles and Marietta. The family in England couldn't tolerate losing a well paying plantation. Around that time the trust was set up. The terms of the trust allowed for any Singleton descendant to take over the plantation, all bills paid by the trust. You can see how this would appeal to members of the family who were short of funds. This way the plantation didn't revert to the Government and stayed the property of the trust."

"So what we are saying the whole thing was all set up to beat taxes?"

"No! Not just that, Nat! With so many strange happenings and sightings, the family in good conscience didn't want to be seen responsible for whoever followed and purchased the Estate."

"Makes sense, I guess."

"Well, Hon. now you have your answers!"

"Give me a few more minuets and I'll see if anything else surfaces."

"Come on, Beth, let's finish that tape." Nat carried on reading, John and Beth walked back to the tape. John pressed the play button again and the picture came back to life. The same picture reappeared with Marietta in the center by the fire.

"Look, John! It's no longer there." The picture, as it had done before, began to dissolve. "Who is that damned thing in the robe, John?"

"I don't know. I did start to think it may be Marietta, but that can't be, they're together in that picture."

"Perhaps it's some kind of guardian for the ring."

"Yes, that could be possible. It would certainly answer a few questions. Let's see if Nat turned up anything else."

John again turned off the tape and then walked over to Nat, who looked up as they approached.

"Anything else, Nat?"

"Day to day stuff really, John. The only thing that seems relevant was the day of the funeral. It was a very small affair, just the servants and a few close friends and apparently there weren't many of those. It would seem that in the last year of the boy's life they had cut themselves off from everyone around them. There hadn't been a party at the estate for quite some time. They had given their lives over to the care of Jonathan and it had extracted a terrible price. Let me read this part for you:

'December 12, 1731. Today is the worst day of my life. We put poor little Jonathan to rest. I hope with all my heart that he will find some peace at last. I do, however, fear that I now have a problem with Marietta. Her grief knows no bounds. After the curse that she laid upon my family, I have seen very little of her. She no longer sleeps in our bed. She has taken to another room entirely. Many nights I have seen her walking the grounds. Sometimes it seems that a shadow walks behind her, but I'm quite sure that is my imagination. I admit I am at a terrible loss as to what to do.'

Then we move forward to December 17. 'I have not seen Marietta for the last few days. It would now appear that she only leaves her room at night. I can only think that she must sleep all day.'

Let's move on a little farther. 'February 14, 1732. I except now that I have lost my wife though I must admit I cannot blame her. The grief was too much to bear and I fear that it must have unhinged her mind. I have given orders to the servants not to molest Marietta in any way, only to help her if possible. I now find that I can only feel pity in my heart, and I can only hope that one day she will return to me. There are times I will admit that I fear for my own sanity. I cannot, however, shake this feeling that a presence walks the grounds.

I would have sought help were it not for the several occasions that members of my staff had witnessed strange happenings also. Indeed, one gardener refused to work the grass and trees down by the crypt as he insisted that he had seen a figure dressed like a monk in a cowl. Normally I would have had him flogged but this time I could not bring myself to take such action as I did so believe myself.'

After this the journal just carries on with normal life. So I skipped the pages very quickly until two years later. 'March 21, 1734. It is now just over two years since the death of my son Jonathan. I have tried many times to speak to Marietta, to no avail. I now think it to be a hopeless cause and shall try no more. I have given instructions to several of my most trusted men to go out at night and take from her that cursed relic, that monstrous work of the Devil that belongs to another age and time.

June 22. The task was not an easy one but successful nonetheless. My men succeeded in relieving Marietta of that damned ring. Though it pains me I had no choice but to put her in a locked room until I can think of something more appropriate. As for the ring I have told my men to wall it up in the cellar. I have also told them to build a wall to separate the cellar into two halves. With this done I then had them put all of Jonathan's clothes and toys plus furniture into the room. Although it breaks my heart, I see no other way to bring back Marietta from the self-imposed exile that she has made.' He goes on to say that the room was then sealed with the ring and all that belonged to Jonathon. The other portion of the cellar was also sealed over and then forgotten."

"Well, that certainly explains a lot but I still have questions."

"Yes, Beth, you would."

"I'm sorry, John, but there are still a lot of loose ends."

"Just joking, Beth, just joking!"

"Sorry, John, there I go again shooting off my big mouth!"

"Come on, guys, lighten up. It looks to me that we have made a great deal of progress."

"One thing I don't understand, why or how do we keep getting recordings from that dirt pit?"

"It must have something to do with that relic. Somehow it traps and releases things that it witnessed into the ethereal."

"Sounds logical to me, John, what about you, Beth?"

"As you say it does make sense. Guys, it does leave the question is that relic good or bad?"

"Neither!"

"I don't understand, Nat, please explain?"

"In order to explain we must go back to the yin yang theory, up and down, black and white. As the old saying goes beauty is in the eye of the beholder. If we expect this to be true then the same must be said for evil."

"You mean good and evil are the same?"

"Why not, Beth, they can both after all achieve the same result. For years we have accused Hitler of being the most evil man of the twentieth century but you have to admit he did bring his people out of a Depression and made them a world power. Please understand I am not condoning what he did or how he did it but you must admit he achieved the desired result."

"Nat, that's a hell of an answer although I must admit it does have a certain sense to it."

"It's the only way, Beth, how else do you account for the fact that no evil ever entered the house. It must have formed the curse that held the children and kept them safe from the evil one."

"Well there's an oxymoron for you a good evil gold ring."

"No, Beth, the ring doesn't know I would imagine it just does as the strong personally orders."

"Are we getting back to black magic?"

"Yes, Beth, I think we are."

"How old would you say it was, John?"

"I have the feeling it goes back into the thousands."

"What do you think, Beth?"

"Of it's age? I have no idea but if it can help us then more power to it."

"What do you think happened to Niles and Marietta?"

"I know from my Family History that they lived another twenty years or so."

"Is there any records of whether she was cured."

"Before we can answer that we have to accept that she was ill."

"You don't think she was, Nat?"

"No, Beth, honestly I don't; I think she was under the influence of the ring."

"Nat, as good a scenario as that is I find it hard to take in."

"So do I, John, but Nat's come up with the best answer so far."

"Well, I don't know about you two but we have a long day and I'm starving."

"He's right, Beth, we should eat now before the real work starts."

"OK. John, I take the point what do you fancy, the best I can do is toast."

"No thank you! I think as you say I am toasted out."

At that point they all had a much-needed laugh. Nat jumped in. "How about KFC for a change?"

"Sounds good to me, how about you, John?"

"OK. Beth, I'm convinced, would you do the honors."

"No problem, I'm right on it." Beth got out the yellow pages, found the number and called in the order. As Beth called for the food, John showed Nat the tape.

Thirty minutes later there was a knock at the door, this time John got up and went to the door. He came walking back with a smile on his face. "Smells good enough to eat, you know I didn't realize just how hungry I was."

Beth replied, "Time flies when you're having fun." They all eat heartily as if it was their last meal. They had original chicken with sides of salad, mashed potatoes, baked beans, and wedges, and Cokes to drink. "You know, a meal like this can taste better than a ten course meal at the Savoy."

"We wouldn't know, John."

"Don't bother it's overrated." Again they all laughed. "What time is it, Nat?

"Two thirty not long to go now, John."

"Guys, I suggest we take the rest of the day to prepare for what we must do."

"You're right, Beth, I would also like to add that it might be a good idea to get a little rest."

"I second that, John."

After their meal they decided to retire to their rooms and meet back in the study at five o'clock. John awoke with a start; he looked at his watch it was six thirty he had overslept. "Damn," he said, out loud, "I must have been out for the count." He dressed and walked down the stairs. He could smell the coffee. We must get through an awful lot of coffee, he thought. As he neared the bottom of the stairs Nat came around the first stairpost and started to climb. He looked up and John was directly in front of him. "I'm sorry, Nat, I must have been more tired than I thought."

"Don't worry, John, we just got up, Beth put the coffee on and I was on my way to wake you."

John and Nat walked into the study as Beth was pouring coffee. "Do you feel better, John?"

"Yes thank you, a lot better, I think we were all tired out."

"Tired and a little weary."

"Ok you two cut the niceties, we got work to do." They sat at the table and began to plan; John was the first to speak. "Nat, would you take charge of any tools we might need and of course the generator. Beth, I think you should lead us into the crypt so far you seem to be the one they respect the most. I will collect anything that might just give us an edge."

"Like what, John?"

"I'm not really sure, Beth, but let's start with the amulet."

"I have a suggestion to make."

"Go ahead, Nat."

"Well, more of a plan really than a suggestion."

They listened with intensity.

At eleven fifteen they set out for the crypt. They left through the side door; the night air was warm and balmy no hint of wind or rain. Like so many times before they walked alongside the lake and down through the trees and grass. As they walked past the clearing John's mind ran back in time. He allowed himself to remember a place he thought lost forever. Somewhere he had been when he was just a small boy with small boy's thoughts. A part of his life when nothing mattered only joy and happiness. He remembered Clare so well in his mind's eye; he could see her standing in front of him as if it were only yesterday. Stop it, John, he thought. Has it already started or am I just paranoid? Nat looked back at John who was in the rear behind Beth. "Everything all right, John?"

"Yes, just me."

"You ok, Beth?"

"Why, Nat, shouldn't I be?"

They moved on closer to the crypt. Nat could have sworn he heard the sound of children crying in the distance. He knew only too well not to trust anything he heard this close to the tomb he passed it off and walked on. Beth was frightened but she was also determined and was not about to allow anything to sway her. She felt strong but vulnerable. Beth knew what she had to do and hoped that she had the strength to do it. They reached the crypt door at eleven thirty five. Without speaking Nat put down his tools and walked to the generator. John wore a small backpack; he took this off and then held it close to his chest. Beth just stood there and waited. As before the generator started without incident. Nat turned and looked at the others. "Well, guys, this is it, the moment we have all looked forward to."

Nat then moved forward to the door and as in the past it opened without effort. The cables were already connected and the tomb became illuminated. For good measure he also threw the switch inside the door and the main lights came on. Along with everything else Nat also had a carryall; in it he had tools and three flashlights; this time he wasn't leaving anything to chance. Slowly with great caution they entered past the door, the time now eleven forty five. The place as usual gave off its recognizable smell of must and decay.

"Well, here we are again," Beth said.

The time now was eleven fifty. "Well, guys, if we are all ready let's go down." Each one of them felt their own private hell. They walked down the first few steps; nothing moved. Without speaking they walked along the slope of the first floor it was now eleven fifty five. Just before the end, Nat, who was in the lead, stopped. "Nothing so far, do you think it's wise to go down to the third layer? After all, if there is something in here it won't really matter what floor we're on."

"Nat's right, Beth, does it really matter which floor we're on?"

"No, John, I don't suppose it does, it's just that that's were it started each time before."

Nat looked at his watch; the time now eleven fifty eight. Not a sound, the place was as quiet as the grave. As they stood there talking, Nat looked at his watch, it was exactly twelve o'clock. A scream the likes none of them had heard before reverberated through the building. "My God, what was that?"

"I don't know, John, but it sounded like it came from the bottom floor; we better go down and take a look."

"No, Nat, don't you see that's just what it wants."

"She's right, it could be a trap to lure us down farther, and I for one don't want to go down there."

"Yes, of course, you're both right; that's not part of the plan we must make it come to us."

"It knows we're here now, let's move back to the steps."

They retreated back to the steps at the entrance. There was no more sound coming from below. "Do you think it's stopped?"

"No chance, John, its little ruse didn't work but I'm sure it won't give up there."

Slowly the temperature dropped they all felt it but no one spoke right away, instead they just looked at each other. "Well here we go again, I guess this is when it starts."

"I think you're right, Beth, here comes the mist."

In front of them at the bottom of the first floor a cloud of cold vapor slowly formed. From the vapor a figure emerged not very clear at first but it didn't take long for them to recognize it. The figure in the cowl materialized in front of their eyes. Although terrified they stood their ground. "Don't move a muscle, guys."

The hooded thing floated towards them. "Don't anyone move," Beth whispered. It stopped ten feet in front of them, for what seemed an eternity nothing happened. Then it slowly lifted its arm and skeletal fingers pointed towards them. "You have something that belongs to me and I want it back!" The voice sounded like someone speaking with water trickling down their throat. Beth thought maybe it hadn't spoken in hundreds of years. "Nat, John, did I just dream that or did it speak to us?"

"No, Beth, it spoke all right but I'm not sure now if it's dead or alive."

"Maybe John, it's neither, it could be undead."

"You mean part of the curse, Nat?"

"Yes, that's exactly what I mean."

The thing spoke again. "You have trespassed into my domain and for that I will condemn you to an eternity as my slaves."

"Who are you and what do you want?"

"Who I am is unimportant, what I want is your souls."

Beth looked hard at the creature and said, "You have to do better than that, Buster."

"O.K. guys, let's get out of here." All three turned at once and ran through the door. Nat stopped and shut the door tight although in his mind he didn't think it would make much difference.

"Come on, Nat, we need to get out of here." As Beth finished speaking a loud hideous laugh rang through the night air. As they moved into the grass and trees, a breeze began to pick up and a slight drizzle began to fall. "Well, Nat, we got out of there now what?"

"Just keep moving, Beth." There was light from a three quarter moon, which made their escape that much easier. They ran as fast as they humanly could until John stopped and called to the others. "Wait! Please, wait a moment!"

The Revenge

John sat down in the grass at the edge the clearing. "Please give me a moment." Nat heard the crying again this time more pronounced; it was very close by. "Do you hear that ,John?"

"Yes, Nat! The crying"

"Do you, Beth?"

"Yes, of course I do, it's coming from that clearing over there."

"Keep going, ignore it, it's not real it's only in your mind."

"How can you ignore children in distress, Nat?"

"You must just keep walking." Beth wasn't sensing if it was the night that had got cold or it was in her head. The drizzle had become stronger although the breeze remained the same. Under protest they had agreed with Nat to ignore the crying and carry on along the lake and head back to the house. Halfway along the lake Beth looked back and to her horror she saw the hooded thing floating after them but now it had company. The mist had now left the lake and joined them in the grass. The whole scene had a very eerie feeling about it. The abomination and the headless man were still behind them but they didn't seem to be gaining. They made their way along the lake and to the house.

Stopping for a breather, John pointed back. "They don't seem to be trying to gain on us."

"Why should they, John? They know that they can't follow us into the house!" They ran in though the side door and locked it behind them. This time though instead of continuing into the study they turned and headed to the ruins of the kitchen. When they got there they looked out over the bones of Angelina. "You were right Nat, there they are just beyond the ship timbers."

"Yes, John, look hard if I'm not mistaken there are more of them now!"

"Yes, Beth, I see them; it's as though they are just on the edge of my vision."

"Who do you think the others are?"

"Souls, Nat, lost souls who have been kept prisoner here on this earth plain."

"Then who is that thing?"

"The soul keeper, John, and I think it must be very ancient."

"O.K., Beth, any ideas what we do next?"

"Yes, we should go out and confront it."

"I agree, John, it's now or never we've come this far now let's go the final mile."

"O.K, Nat, Beth, I'm with you, let's go."

Instead of going back and using the side door Nat led them through into the wreck of the kitchen, across the ditch where Greg's men had laid boards and into the open. No one could see the eyes of the hooded monstrosity but they could feel them burning deep into their souls. It nor its entourage moved but just stood there and waited. "They look like pirates, John, do you think they could be the crew of the Angelina?"

"Yes, I'm sure of it, that thing must be in control of the gold ring. Somehow Niles Remington took it back and turned it against its Master."

"I wonder if it had anything to do with LaBelle?

"LaBelle must have come here after he'd served out his sentence in Jamaica and joined up with Marietta. That would account for Niles shooting him thinking he may have been part of the curse put on his family by his wife, Marietta."

"You mean he may be innocent?"

"Yes, Beth, you may find him over there with the dammed."

The three walked into the center of the destroyed kitchen then they stopped and faced the hooded one. It moved forward but did not come too close to the house. The whole scene had a surreal feeling about it. The kitchen and conservatory, which were no more now than a series of flag stones. The destroyed wreckage was now long gone. Flood lights kept the area well lit up, as Beth's eyes looked beyond the light she could see the lost souls bathed in the night mist. All just standing there with vacant eyes. No one made a move. Then came that hollow voice again" "'I have come for what is mine!"

"And that would be," Beth said, "your soul."

"Do you think it means it, Nat?"

"Yes, Beth, I do."

"O.K., well, let's not keep it waiting!"

"Before we surrender I have a question. Who are you?"

"I am the keeper of the souls. It is what I have always done for more centenaries than I can remember."

"What for? Why do you do it?"

"Because it is what I do, it is what I exist for." The light from the flood lamps reached beyond the conservatory and tailed off just beyond the minions into endless night. Nat looked at Beth. "Time to go, Hon!"

Beth nodded and turned to John. "Are you ready, John?"

"As I'll ever be, Beth, do it."

Beth turned back to the thing. "I don't believe you came here for our souls. I believe you came for this!" Beth leaned forward and picked up the gold ring that Nat had carefully hidden earlier that day. It was hidden out of sight under an up turned wheelbarrow.

"OK, Nat, here we go let's hope your plan works," John interceded.

"Have faith, Beth."

"I do, John, I do!" Beth held the gold relic at arm's length high above her head. With Nat and John on each side of her.

They moved forward. The hooded thing took a step back but held its ground. Again came that hollow wet voice. "Give it to me, it belongs to me."

"If you want it come and get it." The thing turned and looked behind as if to give orders to its followers and then turned back. Now things changed for the worst, something, Beth, Nat and John had not bargained on. The army of ghouls moved forward with swords and daggers drawn

"Oh, Shit. Now what?"

"Stand your ground, Beth, we can't run now."

At that moment a strange thing happened that shocked every one. Just in between the flag-stones and the wooden bones of Angelina, a tall ship's mast began to take shape. As it formed Beth looked up to see the effigy of a long gone part of history she might never see again. The tall structure of a ship long lost to history the driving force that made it possible to run before the wind. High on the wooden pole crossed a spar that would carry a sail. The giant cross cast a shadow over the dead army and all at once they began to burst into flames, some ran burning in flames screaming and then vanished to hell or were ever else they belonged. The thing now stood alone.

Beth moved forward with the ring still held high. The obscenity now began to back track. "What's wrong, can't you stand a little competition?"

"I still claim the amulet as mine," it uttered.

"Why don't you look behind you and ask them?"

It turned, and standing ten feet back were the children. Jonathan, who no longer sat trapped in his chair but stood on his own feet. Clare and John the twins, who smiled and looked very healthy and at their side the boy from the ditch, Jonathan, who was no longer wet. Last but not least on either side of them stood Francis and Linda. The thing turned back in horror only to find Beth was now within touching distance, standing directly in front of it. As the thing opened its mouth to scream, Beth brought down the ring hard on its bony skull; she felt the crunching of bone and then the thing disappeared leaving only its hooded cowl as evidence that it ever existed. Beth turned to look at Nat and John. They had tears in their eyes and could hardly speak.

"Well, Beth, you did it, the curse has left this house and family forever."

"Not just me, John, we all did it together, and don't forget the other one."

"Who do you mean?"

"Angelina, of course; she finally got her revenge."

That night they had the best sleep in a long time. As usual in the morning they met in the study for coffee. "What next for you, John?"

"Back to the University and get on with my life. Maybe now I can concentrate on doing more good with the funds of the trust."

"What about the house?"

"Well, for now you have a story to write, make it a good one. Stay as long as you wish. I'll clear it with the Dean. When you're done who knows this may once again become a family home."

John then turned to Beth. "Young Lady, I hope I'm not being presumptive but I have a little present for your future and up coming wedding." John handed Beth a scroll of paper; it looked quite old.

"What's this, John?"

"Why don't you open it and see!"

Beth opened it and found an old map of the Florida Keys. "Is this what I think it is, John?"

"Yes, it's Captain Franco's treasure map. You see, it's been in my family for generations but no one thought it to be real. I always kept it as a curiosity; now we know different don't we," John said with a big smile.

"We can't take that John it surly must belong to your family."

"My family, Dear Boy, has more money than we can spend, besides you have to find it first. Although I don't think that should be so hard for you two."

They heard a car pull up the drive and then a knock on the door. "That, I believe, is for me. Goodbye, Nat, Beth it really has been a pleasure."

He shook Nat's hand, then hugged Beth. "You'll be at the wedding won't you, John?"

"Wouldn't miss it for the world."

At that he waved and walked out of the door.

Beth turned to Nat. "Come on, we have a book to write."

About the Author

Carl and Jeanette are originally from England. They have spent many years traveling in search of answers to questions about Life after death and psychic phenomenon. Having spent many many years in the U.S. They felt it only natural to write a Ghost story, that combined a little of both cultures and a lot of their experience.

Charleston, South Carolina seemed a perfect base for such a project.

Printed in the United States
49929LVS00001BA/16-18